A BLANCO COUNTY MYSTERY

© 2018 by Ben Rehder.

Cover art and interior design © 2018 by Bijou Graphics & Design.

All rights reserved.

This novel is a work of fiction. Names, characters, places, and incidents are either the product of the author's imagination, or, if real, used fictitiously. No part of this book may be reproduced or transmitted in any form or by any electronic or mechanical means, including photocopying, recording, or by any information storage and retrieval system, without the express written permission of the author or publisher, except where permitted by law.

This one is for Marsha Moyer,
an excellent editor and even better friend.

ACKNOWLEDGMENTS

Once again, the team comes through big time. Much appreciation to Tommy Blackwell, Jim Lindeman, John Strauss, Becky Rehder, Helen Haught Fanick, Mary Summerall, Marsha Moyer, Jo Virgil, Stacia Miller, Angela Smith, Donny Gray, Liz Ewen, Trey Carpenter, Randall Chancellor, Linda Biel, Leo Bricker, Kathy Carrasco, Naomi West, and Richie West. Any errors are my own.

1

Two hours and twenty-four minutes before he lost control of his vehicle and rolled it four times, Deke Gilbert was cruising south on Highway 281 between Burnet and Marble Falls, testing out the 1973 Ford Galaxie he'd been rebuilding for the past three months. Felt good. Solid as a damn rock. Steering was responsive. Suspension was firm. Big American-made car like this could survive some major damage. It would have to, because in one week, he'd be putting it through hell.

He kept it at a steady sixty-five miles per hour. No reason to test the top end. No need for speed. What he wanted was power. Torque.

It was five minutes before midnight on a Saturday in late September. Open highway. No taillights in front of him, no headlights in the rearview mirror.

He turned west on Ranch Road 1855—what everyone called Fairland Road—planning to follow it out to FM 1431. Then he'd head north through Kingsland and maybe stop at Pardners in Buchanan Dam. Good way to end the night. Celebrate finishing the car with a beer or three. But only if the Galaxie continued to run nice.

Right now, it was growling like a lion.

He'd picked the 1973 Ford Galaxie after carefully considering various pros and cons.

For starters, anything built in 1990 or afterward had crumple zones. He didn't want crumple zones. They were great for safety, but Deke wasn't looking for safety, he was looking for durability. He needed a vehicle that could get hammered from just about every angle and hardly even flinch. Older cars, like the Galaxie, featured body-on-frame construction. Much better for Deke's purposes.

So he wanted a car built before 1990.

Cars built in 1972 and earlier had crappy bumpers that folded easily, but in 1973, the government issued a safety standard saying it was time to fix that. Deke wasn't a fan of the government sticking its nose into the business world, but it was hard to argue with the results. Bumpers became more rugged. A better bumper meant less damage to the chassis.

So he wanted a car built after 1972, but before 1990.

The AC wasn't working, so he had the windows down—windows that would have to be removed later, per the rules. The temperature was only in the mid-seventies, not hot, but the air was thick and muggy. September in central Texas could be that way. The threat of rain hanging in the air almost every night.

He had a pint of whiskey between his thighs, but he was taking it nice and slow. So far. Pacing himself.

On second thought, maybe he'd stop at the Beach Club instead, because he was less likely to see his ex there. Pardners was Tanya's hang-out—where he'd first met her—and nothing would put a damper on this evening faster than watching some sweaty redneck groping her ass on the dance floor. Deke knew he'd lose his temper and—

Damn. Stop thinking about her. Concentrate on the car. Had he made a smart choice? He'd always been a Ford man through and through, but had he let that preference cloud his judgment?

There were a lot of good cars built between 1973 and 1990, but most featured electronic ignition. An old-school ignition system with points would be less susceptible to damage, and that narrowed it down quick—Fords built in 1973 or GMs and Chryslers built in 1973 or 1974.

Advantage Ford.

Why? In most GMs, the distributor was located at the rear of the motor, next to the firewall. Not good. A solid hit to the front of the car could push the motor into the firewall, with the distributor leading the way. Game over. In Chryslers, the distributor was up front, but too far to the side, where it could be damaged by a crumpled fender or hood. But Fords had the distributor in the center of the motor, tucked behind the water pump, somewhat protected.

On top of all that, there was the simple fact that Deke had always wanted a Galaxie—so he'd bought one online and trailered it back from Fort Worth. The paint was dull and one fender had a crease, but those were non-issues. It was, in general, a beast, and it would serve him well. Okay, so he'd made the right choice, and now it was time to seal it with a cold adult beverage.

He didn't see Tanya's truck when he drove past Pardners, but the lot was packed. She was probably in there somewhere. Catching a buzz. Flirting. He kept driving east, just four more miles to the Beach Club.

It was 12:29 when he pulled into the lot and parked. He took a couple of quick pulls on the bottle of whiskey, followed by a couple more. Then he went inside, the air-conditioned air feeling so good as it wrapped around him, and—

Well, shit.

The place was packed, but he spotted Tanya immediately, sitting on a bar stool like she owned the place. Even worse, she was deep in conversation with some pretty boy on the next stool. Who was that guy? Deke couldn't remember if he had seen him before. Looked vaguely familiar. Wearing a black Resistol with a high crown. Tanya kept touching his knee.

Deke figured he should take off before Tanya noticed him. Or should he just ignore her completely and have a beer? Wasn't really interested in driving back to Pardners. Getting too late to go anywhere else. Besides, he saw some friends hanging by the pool table.

Just one quick beer, he decided, then back home. He wasn't getting run out of here by his ex, that was for damn sure.

By one forty-five, he'd had four beers and several shots of tequila. Had to be sly about it, too, saying he was ordering for friends, because the club had strict rules against over-serving, and he'd been known to indulge a bit too much on the premises.

Over the years, the employees here had asked him to tone it down at least a dozen times, and there was one night when they'd made him sleep for a couple of hours on a couch in the supply room before driving home. Wait a sec. That had happened in a different beer joint, not this one. Confused.

Tanya was still over by the bar. She'd made eye contact a couple of times—she obviously knew he was here—but she hadn't even nodded or waved. What a bitch.

So he began to slowly weave his way through the crowd toward her.

Where was the pretty boy with the black Resistol? Deke didn't see the guy anywhere, but he was having trouble making out faces at the moment.

A large group of ten or twelve people was clustered right out in the middle of everything, talking loudly, oblivious to everyone else, so Deke had to pick his way around them.

"Where ya going, man?"

Somebody was talking right in Deke's ear, and he could feel a hand on his elbow.

"What?" Deke said. He turned to see Pretty Boy.

"You should go back and play pool with your buddies," Pretty Boy said, smiling.

Up close, this dude was bigger than Deke expected. Not big, but bigger than Deke. Younger, too. Late twenties.

"Leggo," Deke said, pulling his arm free and stumbling a little in the process.

"She don't wanna see you tonight," Pretty Boy said. "Or any night."

"Who the hell're you?" Deke said.

"Oh, man, you're pretty hammered, huh? You driving?"

"None of your damn business."

"Dude, you're gonna fall over."

"That hat looks stupid on you," Deke said.

Pretty Boy laughed. "Know what? It probably does. But my mother gave it to me and I kind of like it."

Deke had no response. He'd forgotten where he was going.

"Think one of your friends can drive you home?" Pretty Boy asked.

Deke had a critical decision to make. Punch the punk in the face—maybe wind up in jail—or let it slide?

"You ain't worth it," Deke said.

"Can't argue with that," Pretty Boy said, smiling again, with his perfect white teeth.

Another man appeared beside Pretty Boy. Shorter. Older. Uglier. Hair like a Brillo pad. Small, deep-set eyes and a broad, flat nose. But he was a stout little bastard. Big chest and wide shoulders. He stared at Deke intently and held it. Trying to intimidate him.

Then Deke focused and realized he knew the man.

"Oh, shit," Deke said. "Lookee here, it's Eddie Trash—showing up last, as usual."

The man's last name was Trask, but Deke intentionally got it wrong.

"I'd rather be last than be an asshole," Eddie said.

"Hey, you somehow manage to do both!" Deke said, proud of himself for coming up with that zinger in his condition.

"What's the point, Eddie?" Pretty Boy asked. "He's sloshed."

Eddie continued to glare at Deke.

Deke said, "You're right, I must've drank too much, because my vision is all screwed up. Eddie is even uglier than normal."

Eddie moved as if he were going to come after Deke, but Pretty Boy put a hand against his chest. "He's wasted, man. Let it go."

Eddie pointed a short, stubby finger at Deke and said, "I'll see you in a week."

"Better bring a booster chair for your driver's seat," Deke said.

Before Eddie could respond, Pretty Boy grabbed him by the shoulder and turned him around, and they headed back toward the bar.

Deke walked out right at closing time, when a bunch of vehicles would be leaving at the same time. He figured there was less chance of getting pulled over that way—like being in a herd of antelope when a lion comes looking for a meal.

When he stepped outside, the muggy air pressed against his face like a warm washcloth.

He was still worked up from his encounter with Eddie Trask and Pretty Boy. Could've kicked both their asses, but what was the point? Truth was, Deke wouldn't take Tanya back even if she came begging, so what did he care who she was hanging out with?

He was halfway to the Galaxie when he realized he hadn't parked in that direction after all. No, the car was on the west side of the club. He rounded the corner and there she was, hunkered in the shadows.

Deke stood by the driver's door and took a leak. Damn, that felt good. Better than driving home with a full bladder. He heard some people talking nearby, getting into a car, but they couldn't tell what he was doing.

When he was done, he went to slip the key into the door lock—no remote control fob for these old cars—but he dropped the key ring and had to kneel down and grope around in his own piss for it. Found it. Unlocked the door. Climbed inside. Wiped his hands on his jeans. Started the engine. Probably shouldn't be driving, but he'd keep it nice and slow. He'd never had any trouble before. He was a hell of a driver. Everybody knew it. Even the cops.

He dropped the Galaxie into reverse and backed up.

Screw Tanya. Screw Pretty Boy, too, and his stupid hat. Screw Eddie Trask, for sure. Moron couldn't drive.

Deke pulled out of the parking lot and went east, across the river into Burnet County. He didn't really want to go through Burnet because the city cops might be hunting for drunk drivers, but there wasn't a better way to get home. So he played it cool. Five miles under the limit all the way through town. Kept it between the lines. No problem. They couldn't pull him over without a reason.

He went south on Highway 281, and when he hit the city limits, he slowly gained speed. He'd passed exactly four vehicles since leaving the Beach Club ten minutes earlier.

The speedometer showed 68 miles per hour when Deke felt the first wobble. Or maybe that was too strong a word. More like a shimmy. And slight, at that. Deke had to wonder, *Is it really there, or am I imagining it?*

Yeah, it was there. No doubt about it. Subtle, but unmistakable.

He dropped his speed to 60, but the shimmy remained. He crept slowly up to 75 miles per hour, but the shimmy didn't go away. Felt like something in the front end, but that didn't make sense, because he'd replaced everything—tie rod ends, ball joints, sway bar, bushings.

Was it one of the tires? They weren't new, but they still had plenty of tread left.

Maybe he should pull over. But then what? Walk home? Wait for a cop to show up—and realize Deke had been drinking? Spend the night in jail for public intoxication?

So he'd just keep—

It all went to hell in the blink of an eye.

The shimmy became a wobble and then a shudder—

—and the right side of the car lurched downward, steel scraping hard on pavement, sparks flying past the passenger window, and for just a moment, Deke thought he saw a wheel tumbling through the headlight beam—

—and then he was airborne, spinning, everything quiet for one brief moment—

—then the tremendous impact and nothing more.

2

Red O'Brien was seated on the back porch of his trailer, a Keystone Light in one hand and a pellet rifle in the other, when his new iPhone chimed with an incoming photo of his new girlfriend. Well, *parts* of his new girlfriend.

Red had never "sexted" anybody until a week earlier, but he was quickly getting the hang of it. How it worked was, you sent a person—in this case, a blue-eyed blonde-haired hottie named Mandy Hammerschmitt—some naughty words explaining what you might do to them later in bed. Or, if you were feeling even more adventurous, you could send a photo, or even a video. Mandy was big on photos, and Red still couldn't believe his remarkable good fortune to have stumbled across a lady like her.

She was the only reason Red had finally broken down and gotten himself an iPhone. The cheap Korean knockoff he'd owned previously couldn't display the pictures of Mandy's sizable hooters with the clarity they deserved. Most of the time, the photos were all jumbled up or distorted or they wouldn't open at all. Imagine a lady sending you a private photo—on purpose, just for you—and you couldn't even tell what it was. Talk about frustrating. The iPhone had been worth every penny just for the boob shots.

Two or three times a day, out of the blue, Red's phone would ping with an incoming text, and he couldn't check it fast enough.

"You're worse than Pavarotti's dog," Red's best friend and housemate Billy Don Craddock had said at one point.

"Hell, you'd get excited, too, if you was seeing what I'm seeing."

Then Red would flash the phone toward him, but just for an instant, so he couldn't get a good look.

Truth was, many of the photos didn't show any more than you

might see in a lingerie catalog. Mandy said it was better to leave a little something to the imagination. So she might stand in front of a mirror in nothing but a bra and panties, looking sassy, and snap a few selfies.

Or, if she'd had a couple of drinks, she might send him a short video of herself eating a banana with an unusual level of enthusiasm. Now Red couldn't walk through the produce section of the Lowe's Market without grinning like a simpleton.

He'd seen an article recently about this whole sexting thing, and the writer said it objectified the woman involved, which made Red wonder why some egghead was always trying to ruin everything that was enjoyable. Besides, how could it even be true if the woman was sending the photos of her own free will? Checkmate, uptight lady writer.

Red was ogling the new photo from Mandy when he heard Billy Don rumbling down the hallway that ran the length of the trailer. With a man as large as Billy Don—six-four and three hundred pounds, give or take—it was easy to know when he was moving around inside. It was like putting a giant armadillo inside a metal garbage can.

Red could tell from the location of the rumble that Billy Don had bypassed the back door and was going into the kitchen.

"Bring me one!" Red yelled through the wall.

He leaned the pellet rifle against the porch railing for the time being. He'd been sitting out here for an hour with no sign of the squirrel that had been driving him crazy for the past month. Damn thing would jump from a tree onto the trailer roof right at dawn, every damn morning, multiple times. Rushing around, acting all busy. What's a squirrel got to be busy about?

The back door swung open and Billy Don stepped out with a tallboy in each hand, one of which he handed to Red. Then he took a seat in the only porch chair that would support him—an old wrought-iron job somebody had left on the side of a county road. Around here, that meant the item was up for grabs.

Billy Don popped his beer open, took a long drink—about half the can—emitted an enormous belch, and said, "Just found out my brother-in-law died."

This took Red by surprise, because Billy Don rarely spoke about his family, or where he'd been born and raised, or what he'd done with his life prior to meeting Red several years back.

"You had a brother-in-law?" Red said.

"Yep. He was married to my sister about twenty years ago, but the truth is, I'm not sure if they ever actually got married or just said they did."

"You have a sister?" Red said.

"Yep, and a brother."

Red just looked at him for a moment.

Billy Don said, "What—you thought I was an only child?"

"I had no idea, 'cause you never talk about shit like that. I always just figured you was hatched."

"Funny."

"Or I figured you was an orphan, like Gulliver Twist."

"Who?"

"The kid who asks for more porridge in that movie."

Billy Don drank some more beer.

"How old was he?" Red asked.

"Hell, I didn't see the movie," Billy Don said.

"I mean your brother-in-law."

"About the same age as you and me."

"How'd he die?"

"Car wreck."

"Shit, man. That sucks. Sorry."

"Yep."

"You and him close?"

"We used to be, way back when, but then he—"

Red held a hand up to silence Billy Don. He'd just heard a squirrel chattering in the oak trees to the rear of his property. It went on for about ten seconds, then went quiet again.

"Bastard," Red said.

"What'd I do?" Billy Don asked.

"No, the damn squirrel," Red said. "He's been waking me up every morning, jumping on the roof above my room."

"You could cut that cedar elm down," Billy Don said. "Keep him from jumping."

"Or I could shoot him and make some stew."

"That, too. Anyway, I was saying my brother-in-law was—"

Red silenced him again, because the chattering had returned.

"Screw it," Billy Don said. "Never mind."

"Sorry, what was it?"

Billy Don could get sensitive on occasion. Or angry. You were smart to steer clear when he got angry. Couple hundred feet away was good.

"Don't worry about it," he said. "He's dead and that about covers it."

"Where'd it happen?"

"Up north of Marble Falls."

"When?"

"Late last night, but nobody knows what time for sure. All they know is they found his car this morning. He'd flipped a couple of times and went down a hill into some cedars. Looks like he lost a wheel or something. He'd been out at a beer joint earlier."

"Anybody with him?"

"Nope."

"What's his name?" Red said. He knew quite a few people in Burnet County, which was immediately north of Blanco County, and just east of Llano County.

"Deke Gilbert," Billy Don said.

"Yeah, that's funny," Red said.

"Ain't kiddin'," Billy Don said.

"Wait a second. Your brother-in-law was Deke Gilbert?"

"Was, yeah."

"And you never mentioned it?"

"Why would I?"

"That man is like a legend," Red said. "At least around this particular area. Among a small group of people."

Billy Don didn't say anything.

"Weird that he died in a car crash," Red said. "What're the odds of that?"

"Maybe he fell asleep," Billy Don said.

"Or maybe he was drunk," Red said.

Billy Don shrugged again.

"From what I heard, he liked to party pretty hard," Red said.

"Who doesn't?" Billy Don said.

"Kind of a wild man, is what they always said," Red said.

"He was a long time ago," Billy Don said. "Don't know if he still was. We didn't stay in touch."

Red saw the squirrel coming down the trunk of an oak tree. Too far away to shoot him. His tail was twitching back and forth, all cocky.

"You need to put some bird seed out for him," Billy Don said. "They love bird seed. Put it real close and shoot him through an open window."

Obvious, but Red hadn't thought of that yet. He wished he had. "I don't need to use bait to outsmart a squirrel."

"I ain't seeing a lot of proof of that so far," Billy Don said.

The squirrel found something to eat on the ground, and he sat there, just out of rifle range, propped on his hind legs, nibbling on something he held between his front paws.

"Somethin' else I need to tell you," Billy Don said.

"Huh?"

"Deke has a daughter. Had a daughter. Before he died."

"So she's your niece?"

"No, it's not my sister's kid. Deke had this girl with another woman after that."

"Confused? You won't be after this episode of *Soap*."

"Her name is Christie. She's 17 and her mom isn't in the picture. She hightailed it five years ago. And now her dad's gone, too."

"That's rough," Red said.

"Hell, yeah, it is," Billy Don said. "Kinda like what you went through, huh?"

"Kinda," Red said. He didn't like to talk about that much, except sometimes when he'd been drinking.

Now the squirrel scurried over to a different oak tree, climbed about three feet up the trunk, then apparently decided this particular tree wasn't suitable for his needs. He scurried back down to the ground and bounded over to yet another oak tree ten feet away. Went up the trunk and seemed to like that tree much better. What the hell was going on in his squirrel brain?

"What she needs is a place to stay," Billy Don said.

"Who?"

"Really? You got no idea who I'm talking about?"

"Oh, that girl?"

"Yep. That girl. Deke's daughter. Anyway, I'm thinking maybe she could stay here."

Red turned and looked at him. "You lost your mind?"

"How would I know?" Billy Don said.

"Surely she's got kinfolk. Why can't she stay with one of them?"

"Most of 'em live out of state."

"Ain't my problem," Red said.

"What kind of attitude is that?" Billy Don asked.

"The kind that keeps my life simple and hassle-free," Red said. "I don't even want a dog, but you want me to adopt a kid?"

"Adopt, hell. Ain't no adopt about it. She'll be eighteen in November, so you let her stay here for two months and then she's legal to go off on her own. It's two goddamn months."

"No way," Red said. "Forget it. Ain't happenin'."

"Why?" Billy Don asked.

Red couldn't think of a good reason right off the top of his head, so he said, "Because it's my place and I don't need some sulky kid hanging around, cramping my style."

"Suddenly you got style?" Billy Don asked. "When did that happen?"

"Just no," Red said. "That's final."

Billy Don showed up with the girl three hours later.

"For fuck's sake," Red muttered as he stood on the porch and watched them lurching up the long caliche driveway in Billy Don's old Ford Ranchero.

Billy Don had said he had some errands to run. Yeah, some errand. Red absolutely was not going to allow the girl to stay here. Who knew what kind of trouble she might bring into their lives? Red remembered what he himself was like at that age, and he wouldn't wish that on anybody.

As they reached the top of the hill, Billy Don grinned at Red through the windshield and gave him a thumbs-up. Red didn't budge.

Now he got a good look at the girl. She looked small in the passenger seat. Damn, she was 17? She looked even younger. Just a kid. She didn't smile or wave. She looked nervous.

Billy Don parked the Ranchero in its usual spot and after a few seconds, he and the girl got out. She was even tinier than Red had thought—no more than 90 pounds. She wore faded blue jeans, a red hoodie, and tennis shoes. Her long brown hair was twisted into a braid.

"Hey, Red!" Billy Don called out. "This here's Christie."

Red grunted.

"Christie, that's Red O'Brien. He owns this place, and he was generous enough to offer you a room for the next however long. He's got a big heart and might be one of the nicest guys you'll ever meet, which is why he's my best friend."

"Hi," Christie said.

Well, now what the hell was Red supposed to do? Billy Don had totally screwed him.

"Hi," Red said.

Billy Don reached into the bed of the Ranchero for a large black suitcase, but Christie said, "No, I got it." Then she proceeded to wrestle it out of there. Took some effort, but she got the job done.

As she and Billy Don paused near the porch steps, she looked around and said, "This is a nice place."

Red couldn't tell if she was being sincere or not. The trailer admittedly wasn't in great shape, but it was home, and Red didn't need any bratty kid judging it.

"Thanks," Red said. "I've thought about scrapping the trailer and building a house, but that's a lot of work."

"I don't see many neighbors," she said.

"Lots of cedar trees," Red said. "Hey, uh, sorry about your daddy."

Christie nodded and looked at the ground.

"He was a good man," Billy Don said.

"Thanks," she said.

"They got any idea what caused the wreck?" Red asked.

"Jeez, Red, give the girl a break," Billy Don said. "She don't need to talk about that right now."

Nobody said anything for an awkward moment. Red wasn't any good at this sort of thing, which was why he rarely went to funerals or retirement parties.

"How many times did he win the demolition derby?" Red asked, because that was something positive to ask. Billy Don couldn't bitch about that.

"I'm not sure," Christie said. "I never went to any of them."

"Dang. You never went? Why not?"

"It just wasn't my thing."

"That's a shame," Red said. "It was six, by the way. He won it six times."

"Why'd you ask if you knew?" Billy Don said.

"That's as many times as Tom Brady won the Super Bowl," Red said. "Something to be proud of. Ain't nobody won it more times than your daddy."

Christie didn't say anything.

"I went to the very first one, you know," Red said. "There wasn't any more than maybe fifteen drivers, and not that many people watching, but we had a good time. I mean, hell, how could you *not* have a good time watching cars smash into each other? He was a hell of a driver, despite what—"

"Red!" Billy Don said.

"Sorry," Red said. "It's just that my daddy died when I was real young, too, so I know what it's like. Me and Christie got something in common."

Another long pause.

"The derby got postponed because of all that rain we had two weekends ago," Red said.

"That's an interesting observation, Red, but how about we take Christie inside and let her see the place?" Billy Don said.

"Fine by me," Red said. "There's still a lot of junk to clear out of the spare room. You were gonna move all that crap, remember?"

"I don't remember saying—"

"And you was gonna clean the spare bathroom from top to bottom, and then the kitchen. To get it all nice for Christie."

Billy Don glared at him.

"I'll run into town for some cleaning supplies," Red said. "You're gonna need 'em."

He looked at Christie and she was grinning.

3

Gavin McIntosh wasn't sure how it happened, but when he'd woken up three days earlier, a Thursday, his wife had been replaced by an exact duplicate. A phony. An impostor. Oh, sure, she looked like Caroline—the same cute face and thick chestnut hair. The same endearing laugh. She even smelled like Caroline.

But she wasn't Caroline. Gavin was certain of that.

She was too perfect. She was even more like Caroline than Caroline was. But he wasn't fooled.

"Do we need paper towels?" the fake Caroline asked.

Which was exactly the kind of question Caroline would ask whenever they went grocery shopping together at the HEB in Marble Falls, Texas.

"I think we have a couple of rolls," Gavin said.

"But you're not sure?"

Caroline was like that. Always asking follow-up questions. That's why she made a good prosecutor. She had a sharp, quick mind. She considered every issue from multiple angles—including, yes, household supplies. She lived in a totally different professional world compared to Gavin's career as a freelance commercial illustrator.

"Maybe just one roll," Gavin admitted.

Caroline tossed a three-pack into the basket.

Of course, Gavin had challenged the impostor that first morning, and as one might expect, she denied it. Which was exactly what an impostor would do. He'd argued with her for a few minutes, and then he decided he'd better play along. Try to figure out why she was lying. Determine what she was up to. So he pretended he'd been kidding earlier, and that it was part of a freelance project he was working on. Lame excuse, but it had worked. At the time, she'd given him an odd look, but then she'd let it go at that.

"Got any prescriptions waiting?" she asked when they were near the pharmacy. Both of them were in their late thirties and reasonably healthy, although Gavin did suffer from an annoying condition that required treatment.

"No, I'm all set," he said.

The pharmacist behind the counter said, "Hi, guys."

"Hey, Donna," Caroline said. "Coming to book club tonight?"

"Yeah, I'm riding with Brendan, but I haven't finished reading the book yet."

"Kind of slow, isn't it?"

"God, yes, especially when you hit the part when she's traveling in Europe. Do we really need to hear a detailed description of every church in Rome? Just tell me when it was built and who it was named after and move on."

"But the, uh, bedroom scene with Antonio was good, right?" Caroline said. "Tell me you got that far!"

"I've practically memorized it by now!"

It was obvious to Gavin that Donna didn't realize Caroline wasn't Caroline, even though the two women knew each other very well. That meant Gavin was probably the only one who recognized what was going on. Should he come back later and talk to Donna about it? Not a chance. She'd think he was coming unhinged, and he couldn't blame her.

Gavin and Caroline moved on to the next aisle—breakfast foods. The fake Caroline grabbed a box of the store brand of shredded wheat, which meant she had been well briefed, down to the smallest detail. Gavin decided to test her by picking something new for himself off the shelf.

"Grape-Nuts?" the fake Caroline said.

"Yeah? So what?"

"I thought you hated Grape-Nuts," she said.

It was unnerving. How did she know this? Very few people would be privy to that level of information—probably just Caroline and Gavin's mother.

But that meant...

"You okay?" the fake Caroline asked.

Gavin was suddenly feeling nauseous. His face felt hot. He was a bit lightheaded. He'd just now realized that his wife, the real Caroline—

wherever she was—was either playing along with this charade, or someone was extracting information from her against her will. That's how the fake Caroline would know Gavin hated Grape-Nuts. How had that not occurred to him until just now? What was happening to the real Caroline? Where was she?

"I'm fine," Gavin said. "Just need to eat, I think."

The fake Caroline stared at him for a long moment. Was she suspicious? Did she know what he was thinking?

"You look a little pale," she said.

She placed her right palm flat against his forehead. Apparently he felt fine. She cupped his cheek lovingly before lowering her hand.

"How's your stomach lately?" she asked.

The pills he took sometimes made him nauseous, and his stomach occasionally rumbled loudly enough to be heard in another room. It wouldn't just rumble, it would grumble and gurgle and let out all kinds of strange noises.

"About the same," he said. "I'll be fine."

"Maybe we need a vacation," she said. "It's been a while."

"What was the name of that hotel we stayed at in Cabo?" he asked.

She looked at him and grinned. Did she recognize that he was testing her again?

"The Riu Santa Fe," she said. "Wasn't that a great place? Remember when that Canadian guy climbed that palm tree and jumped into the pool? Man, he nearly ate it. I guess that's what happens when you have four kinds of booze on tap in every room."

Gavin was astounded. The level of detail they had somehow embedded into this impostor's brain was unsettling.

"It was dumb," Tanner Stockwell said. "So fucking stupid."

Eddie could hear the panic in Tanner's voice, even after he'd had plenty of time to calm down and settle his nerves since last night.

"Ain't nothing we can do about it now," Eddie said.

They were seated in matching leather easy chairs that faced each other over a glass-top coffee table.

"We're totally screwed, man."

"Hell, no, we ain't. You just need to relax."

Sunday afternoon at Tanner's house on Lake LBJ south of Kingsland, on the Burnet County side, a mile outside Granite Shoals. Damn nice place. Waterfront. Expensive. Inherited, not earned. Tanner's dad—one of Eddie's uncles—had made plenty of money selling properties just like this one back in the nineties. Then he'd keeled over dead eight years ago and left the house to his only child. Eddie, the loyal nephew, got squat out of the deal. Not one dime. Tanner, meanwhile, had the gall to bitch that the owner of the house two doors down had been renting the place out on some website. Too many loud college kids partying within earshot. Eddie wished he had Tanner's problems.

"We should just tell the truth," Tanner said. "They'll be a lot harder on us if they've got to track us down and prove what happened."

Eddie had always suspected that Tanner would crack under pressure. Real pressure—not a bar fight or a girlfriend catching him with another woman. Sure, Tanner could put on a confident front—the charismatic, good-looking dude that ruled every dance hall or beer joint he walked into—but in a situation like this? So far, he was being a pussy. Big surprise.

Eddie leaned closer and made Tanner look him in the eye. "Dude. Be calm. Hear me? Everything is under control."

After a moment, Tanner nodded, so Eddie leaned back in his chair. Of course, that wasn't the end of it. It wasn't that easy.

"What about that guy in the parking lot?" Tanner said.

That right there was the only small item of concern. A potential witness. When Eddie and Tanner had been messing with the Galaxie, a man in a tan cowboy hat, blue jeans, and boots had walked right past them on the way to his truck. Had he seen what they were doing? If so, had he gotten a good look at them?

"I wouldn't worry about him," Eddie said, getting up and going over to the bar.

"Just...don't worry about him?"

"Nope."

The eastward-facing wall of the living room was all glass, floor to ceiling. Eddie could see some loser in the middle of the lake on a Jet Ski that wasn't running. Stranded, and floating slowly to the south.

"Why not?"

Eddie popped the little mini-fridge open and grabbed two bottles of Lone Star.

"We got no idea who he was or whether he saw anything. He could've been drunk. He might not see that good at night, or maybe he was thinking about some chick he just met inside, or who knows what was going on. I didn't see a damn thing that made me think he knew what we were doing."

"Because you were down on the ground," Tanner said. "I was the one keeping watch, and I'm telling you, he looked right at me."

Eddie came back to the coffee table and handed one of the ice-cold beers to Tanner. With luck, this beer and a few more would chase away the hangover Eddie had from last night.

"Yeah, okay," Eddie said. "What did he look like?"

"Huh?"

"Describe him for me."

"Tan cowboy hat."

"And?"

Eddie sat down again.

"Green shirt," Tanner said.

"What else?"

"Probably thirty years old."

"He looked forty to me."

"Maybe he was."

"I was lying. I couldn't tell how old he was. Did he have a beard or just a goatee?"

"I think a goatee."

"You sure he wasn't clean-shaven?"

"Shit, man, I don't know. What's your point?"

"If you can't tell me what he looked like, how would he know what *you* looked like?"

Tanner didn't appear convinced.

"It was dark over there by the car," Eddie added. "He didn't see nothing. So we just need to keep our heads down and play it cool."

Tanner took a long drink of beer and didn't reply. He wasn't making eye contact. This was not the kind of response Eddie wanted.

He looked out at the lake. The idiot on the Jet Ski was still out there, now waving his arms frantically, trying to catch the attention of someone on the far shore.

"You hear me, man?" Eddie asked, looking at Tanner again. "Just play it cool. Trust me. I've done this before."

"Yeah, okay," Tanner said.

Eddie let it lie for a moment, but he couldn't stop there. He had some coaching to do. He said, "That don't mean the cops won't come poking around. They might. They'll be asking questions down at the bar, wondering who was there last night, and somebody's bound to say they saw us talking to Deke."

"Shit."

Good Lord, Tanner was a wimp. His face was white.

"You just tell 'em exactly what happened. You don't gotta lie or nothin'. He was drunk and mouthing off, and then he staggered back to his friends by the pool table, and we didn't see him for the rest of the night, which is true."

"But they'll think it was an accident, right? That's what you said."

"They won't have any way of proving it *wasn't*," Eddie said. "Unless one of us talks. But we ain't gonna do that, are we?"

"No," Tanner said. "Hell, no."

"They act tough, the cops do," Eddie said. "Make it sound like you gotta answer all their questions, even when you don't. Try to bulldog you into admitting something, even when they don't got any reason to think you was involved. You follow me? They can get downright mean. That's just the way they work. They try to rattle you, just in case you *were* involved. Then if you weren't, they say, oh, sorry, but we had to do that."

"Yeah, okay."

"If you get nervous, just blame it on the situation—you're straight as an arrow, never got into any trouble, but now the cops are asking you about a dead guy. That's enough to make anyone nervous. Blame it on that."

"I will."

"They start putting too much pressure on you, just pretend it's making you mad and you won't stand for it."

"I'm not a great actor."

"You'll do fine, man. Don't worry about it."

Eddie chugged the rest of his beer and wondered if Tanner would be able to keep his shit together.

4

Late that afternoon, closing in on sundown, Red was on the back porch again. He was hunting the squirrel, but mostly he'd come outside to escape the smell of Lysol. Billy Don hadn't had much choice but to get cleaning, just as Red had said. The trailer might've been suitable for a couple of bachelors, but not for a 17-year-old girl.

He was enjoying the peace and quiet when the back door opened and Christie stepped out.

"Hey," she said.

Oh, Christ, Red thought. *Is this gonna be a thing? Always having to say "Hey" back to this girl?*

"Hey," he said.

She was still holding the door open. "Mind if I hang out? The fumes are kind of strong in here."

Good Lord. Even the back porch isn't my own anymore.

"Sure," he said. "Come on out."

She let the door swing shut and took a seat in the lawn chair to Red's right.

"What're you hunting?" she said, nodding at the pellet gun leaning against the railing.

"Dang squirrel that's been driving me nuts," he said. "Jumping on the roof, waking me up."

"So you're gonna shoot him?"

"That's the plan."

If this little girl turned out to be an anti-hunting fanatic, Red figured he might totally lose it.

"You gonna eat him?" she asked.

"You bet."

"Gross."

"You never had squirrel?"

"No way."

"Damn tasty if you cook it right," he said. "Make a nice stew, with some taters and carrots," he said.

She turned and gave him a look like he was talking crazy.

"Ever had rabbit?" he asked.

"I don't think so."

"Possum?"

"Oh, come on. You don't eat possum."

"I've ate possum before."

"On purpose?" she asked.

"You never know what you might get around here, so prepare yourself."

"I can't wait," she said.

She was being a smart aleck, but not in a bad way. More like she was amused by the idea.

"You'll definitely be getting your fair share of deer and wild hog meat," he said. "That's about all we eat around here."

"I think I can handle that," she said.

"And maybe some ringtail coon," he said.

"You're lying," she said.

He reached for his beer on the railing and took a long drink. He almost asked her if she wanted one, but then he remembered she was just a kid. "There's all kinds of cokes in the fridge," he said. "Just grab whatever you want. No need to ask. If we run out, tell Billy Don."

"I will, thanks."

He nodded.

She said, "You didn't really want me staying here, huh?"

"What?"

"I could tell you weren't exactly on board with it," she said.

"No, it's cool," he said. "It's fine."

"But Billy Don kind of twisted your arm, didn't he?"

"Well, I'm not gonna lie. It took me a while to warm up to the idea. But it'll work out."

"I just wanted to let you know I appreciate it," she said.

Wow. A kid her age with manners? Impressive.

"You're welcome," he said.

"I promise not to be a nuisance," she said.

"And I promise to let you know if you are," Red said.

"Deal," she said. "I do have one question, though."

"Huh?"

"How am I gonna get to school tomorrow?"

"That's right. You don't have a car, do you?"

"Nope. I don't even know where the school is."

"That's right," Red said. "You're starting at a brand-new place. Think of it as an adventure."

She did not look excited by that prospect.

"How did you get to school before now?" Red asked. "Your dad take you?"

"Sometimes. Not usually."

"So how did you get there on the days when he didn't take you?"

"Rode my bike or caught a ride or whatever. If the weather was really nasty, sometimes I wouldn't go."

"You just wouldn't go?"

She shook her head.

"Didn't that piss your dad off?"

"He wasn't around that much," she said, and then quickly added, "Hey, is there a bus stop nearby?"

"Not on this road, but I think it stops at the intersection about a mile away."

"Okay, I can walk, but, uh, what if it's raining?"

"Now you're asking questions above my pay grade, but you can ask Billy Don. He'll help you figure it out, and on top of that, he'll be glad to do it. It'll make his day."

"Just like he's glad to be in there cleaning?" she asked.

Red had to laugh. "Exactly like that."

"I tried to help him with that, but he wouldn't let me."

"'Cause he knows I woulda put a stop to it. Let him do it. Doubt he's ever used a toilet brush in his life. It'll build some character, and God knows he could use some."

"So you're kind of like the boss around here?" she asked, again with that amused tone.

"Abso-damn-lutely, and don't let Billy Don tell you different," he said.

"I won't."

"He'll say he's the boss, which is an obvious lie."

He heard a soft chime and Christie pulled a phone from her pocket. Incoming text. She seemed to stare at the screen for a very long time. Then, very softly—almost too low for Red to hear—she said, "Oh, no."

"Everything okay?" Red asked.

Is this going to become a thing, too? he wondered. *Am I gonna have to ask that question a lot in the next few months?*

"It's from Sara, a friend of mine," Christie said. "Her dad works at the sheriff's office. They figured out why my dad wrecked."

Late Sunday evening, as Gavin had sex with the fake Caroline for the first time, he realized, in mid-stroke, that he was cheating on his wife.

How weird was that?

It didn't matter that she looked exactly like Caroline and claimed to be Caroline, she wasn't Caroline. So he was cheating. He knew he should feel guilty and ashamed, but the truth was, it was pretty damn hot. Hotter than it had been with Caroline for quite some time. Besides, he knew that Caroline—the real Caroline—would understand why he was doing it. He *had* to, if he was going to save her. If he didn't have sex with the fake Caroline, she would wonder why.

"Wow," she said as Gavin continued doing what he was doing. "Wooooow."

"That feels good?" he whispered into her ear. Playing coy.

He could feel her nodding quickly.

"Right there," she said. "Just like that."

"You sure?"

"Oh, yes."

"How about if I slow down a little?" he asked. "And then I do this?"

She dug her fingernails into his back. "Even...better."

"Or this?" he said.

She actually gasped. He hadn't heard that gasp in years.

What would she do if he started asking questions right now?

Who sent you here?

What did you do with my wife?

What is it you want from me?

How would she respond? Would she be able to resist answering while she was obviously in the throes of passion?

But the point was moot, because he was picking up the pace again, unable to resist, losing himself in the moment, and he couldn't talk right now even if he wanted to. The pleasure finally peaked in a mighty cresting wave that lasted and lasted for both of them, and then it slowly ebbed away.

Gavin collapsed and rolled to his right, beside Caroline—the fake Caroline—and they both struggled to catch their breath.

"Oh, my God. We should do it like that more often," she said after a moment, grasping his hand in hers. "That was amazing."

"I agree," Gavin said.

"It was like…I don't know…like the early days, when we first met. Did you feel that?"

"Absolutely," he said. "Almost…like it was the first time."

"Whatever it was, I liked it."

"Me, too."

Gavin vowed that when he was reunited with the real Caroline, he would never tell her how much he'd enjoyed himself just now. Or about any of the other episodes that were certain to occur in the forthcoming days and weeks.

5

The squirrel must have taken a different route this morning, because Red managed to sleep until 8:17, and by then, the trailer was dead quiet. Billy Don and the girl must've taken off already. Wait a sec. Now Red could hear Billy Don's Ranchero as he finished coasting down the long caliche driveway and gassed it as he turned onto the county road. They'd just left.

Red lounged in bed a bit longer—stretching and yawning and scratching—and then he got up and went into the kitchen. What he saw stopped him cold in his tracks.

There, on the counter, was a plate stacked high with pancakes. He reached out and touched a finger to the top one. Still warm. Light and fluffy and perfectly golden-brown.

Next to the plate was a note.

Mr. O'Brien,

Thought you might want some breakfast. If they cool off, you can zap them in the microwave for a minute or two. Thanks again for letting me stay here.

Christie

Well, damn. The kid was a cook. And they smelled pretty good. Red slathered the pancakes with butter and syrup and took a bite. Hell, yeah. Very tasty. Maybe the kids were learning something useful in school nowadays after all. Forget all that math and history you'd never use. Teach something useful like making pancakes and other breakfast foods.

Kind of funny that the kid called him "Mr. O'Brien." She was respectful and had manners. Another good sign.

He took the plate over to the little dinette set and sat down to finish eating.

Even more impressive than Christie's pancakes was the way she was dealing with her dad's death, and the news last night from her friend—if it was accurate.

According to the friend, Sara, one of Deke Gilbert's wheels had come off his Galaxie, which caused him to lose control and flip several times. But Red knew wheels don't just come off like that—not without some kind of mechanical failure or malfunction. The cops didn't see any evidence of that.

So that made them wonder if it had been an error on Deke's part. What if he'd screwed up and forgotten to tighten the lug nuts adequately? Red figured a guy like Deke would have to be pretty soused to mess up something like that. The dude was a car guy—a mechanic, through and through. But if he'd been drinking and working on his car...hell, anything was possible. Red had seen the look of sadness on Christie's face when she'd mentioned that the cops were wondering if that had happened.

One thing was for sure: Deke Gilbert was the best driver Red had ever seen, not counting some of those NASCAR dudes on TV. The Spicewood demolition derby had a lot of rules that prevented you from modifying your car to make it more damaging to other cars—like, say, filling your bumper with concrete. Those restrictions, in Red's opinion, put the focus on the ability to be a kick-ass driver, which is where it should be. You had to take a regular old vehicle—mostly stock, minus the glass and mirrors and some other stuff—and just plain outdrive everybody else. That's what Deke Gilbert had done six times.

Red decided he needed a big glass of milk to chase down the pancakes, and as he rose from the table, he had another thought that made him pause.

What if somebody else loosened those lug nuts? What if someone wanted Deke Gilbert to die in a terrible crash, or at least mess up his car?

Red was pondering that possibility when he was sidetracked by an incoming photo from Mandy. She had just stepped out of the shower, apparently.

He sent a text back: *when am I gonna see those beauties in person again?*

She said: *how about tonite?*

He replied: *works for me. maybe I should come to your place on account of this girl.*

He'd called Mandy last night and told her about the situation with Christie. She'd told him what a wonderful and selfless thing he was doing, and he'd informed her that he hadn't hesitated for even one second to open his home to this poor, young child in need.

Mandy said: *thanks, but I want to meet her. gotta make sure she isn't some kind of lolita!*

Red didn't understand that comment, but he pretended he did.

It had occurred to Gavin on the first day the fake Caroline had appeared that he couldn't be the only person on the planet with an impostor wife, so he'd googled "spouse replaced by a duplicate" and came up with a bunch of hits. Top of the list was the Wikipedia page for something called the Capgras delusion. Never heard of it, but the word "delusion" told Gavin it wouldn't apply to his situation.

He wasn't delusional. No chance. That would be like saying he was delusional when he noticed the sun rising every morning. He was certain the sun would rise tomorrow, and he was certain his wife had been replaced. But he read the description anyway.

Capgras delusion is a psychiatric disorder in which a person holds a delusion that a friend, spouse, parent, or other close family member (or pet) has been replaced by an identical impostor.

Jesus friggin' Christ, how weird was that? He couldn't imagine what it would be like to have your own brain fool you like that. It was draining enough to have full control of your faculties and *know* that your wife had really and truly been replaced by an impostor. He also realized that if he were to tell anyone what was happening, they would think he was suffering from this strange Capgras delusion. Then they wouldn't believe Caroline really had been replaced.

As for finding other people who'd really had a spouse replaced by a duplicate, he struck out. He literally could not find a single instance of that happening, except in movies. No help there. No advice on how to proceed.

That meant it was up to him—and him alone—to expose the impostor and find his real wife. But he had to be clever about it, because the fake Caroline couldn't be pulling off this hoax on her own, could she? There had to be some sort of network supporting her, all working to further their cause, whatever it might be.

What if Caroline's friends were in on it? Like Donna, for instance. Was she in on it? That would explain why she hadn't noticed anything odd about Caroline at the HEB. What about her coworkers at the district attorney's office? What about her mom and dad and sister? Gavin decided he would have to proceed as if he couldn't trust anyone.

But how could he expose the hoax? He thought about that for a great while.

He had all kinds of wild ideas—impractical ideas—but he kept coming back to the same basic, time-tested investigatory technique.

Surveillance.

Eddie Trask had just texted Tanner Stockwell—*you all good this morning?*—when a man's voice said, "You shouldn't be smoking."

Eddie Trask ignored it. Just kept pumping gas. Not in the mood to deal with assholes. Worrying about Tanner and whether he'd crack.

"Hey, there," the voice said, louder now. "You need to put that cigarette out."

Eddie turned slowly and saw an elderly man who'd approached Eddie's brown Chevy truck from the convenience store. White hair, blue baseball cap, using a cane. Just some random old dude who'd spotted Eddie and couldn't mind his own damn business.

"Move along," Eddie said.

"Pardon?"

"I said keep moving. It's none of your concern."

"It's dangerous," the man said, stepping closer. "So it *is* my business."

Now Eddie could see that the man's cap had "Korean War Veteran" embroidered on it, along with various military decorations or insignia or whatever the hell they were.

"It ain't a problem," Eddie said.

"Why, of course it's a problem," the man said. "You're dealing with *gasoline*."

"How many people you know that blew themselves up at the gas pump?" Eddie asked, starting to lose his patience. "Answer is none. It don't happen."

"It *could* happen," the man said.

"Well, I could blow your fucking head off," Eddie said. "It *could* happen."

He immediately regretted it. He couldn't afford for this to turn into some kind of big deal. Old man might have a damn stroke, the way he was looking at the moment. Face was beet red. Bad timing, because Eddie had an important meeting to attend—the kind where his participation was mandatory. The smart move right now would be to put the cigarette out and apologize, but Eddie couldn't do it.

The old man glared at Eddie for a long moment, and then he obviously decided it was better to let it go. He shuffled off to a sedan parked on the side of the building and drove away.

Eddie could only shake his head. That old man fought a war so he could gripe at people for meaningless bullshit? What a waste.

Eddie hadn't filled his tank completely yet, but he stopped pumping and got back into his truck. Best to scoot out of here right now, just in case the old man decided to call the cops about the threat. Last thing Eddie needed was another hassle.

Gavin drove a plain-vanilla white Ford F-150—a dime a dozen in these parts, but why take chances that Caroline's impostor would notice him?

He found an ad on Craigslist for a $1,500 Kia. The car wasn't all that pretty—yellow, with blotchy paint and some hail damage—but Gavin didn't care about that stuff. He sent a query and the seller responded in five minutes. The guy lived ten minutes south of Marble Falls and could meet anytime at the Walmart on the north end of town. Convenient.

They met at 9:45 and Gavin took the twelve-year-old car for a short drive around the parking lot. Gavin was no mechanic, but it seemed to run fine, so he paid cash in exchange for the title. His plan was to leave the Kia parked here at the Walmart and pick it up whenever he needed it.

When he and the seller were done with the transaction, he locked up the Kia and his truck and went inside the Walmart. He wasn't sure what he was shopping for, but he'd read a series of novels about some insurance fraud investigators in Austin, and he knew they used all kinds of gizmos and gadgets to make it easier to put people under surveillance.

He ended up buying a decent pair of binoculars, an inexpensive trail camera, latex gloves, some aviator sunglasses, and a Houston Astros baseball cap. The hat might've been the smartest purchase of all, because he never wore hats of any kind nor was he a pro baseball fan, and those two factors would make the cap a great disguise.

He was glad he didn't see anybody he knew, or even anyone he recognized.

He paid cash, in case the network of operatives supporting the fake Caroline was tracking his credit cards and reviewing his purchases. Sounded paranoid, sure, but better safe than sorry.

Then he went outside, donned the hat and sunglasses, and drove away in the yellow Kia, heading north on Highway 281. Thirteen miles to the county seat of Burnet.

6

"Christie said something to me on the way to school this morning," Billy Don said later, after he'd returned from dropping her off.

"I bet I know what it was," Red said.

He had already settled into his recliner for the morning, watching some old Vincent Price movie. Well, it wasn't really a movie. It was just Vincent Price reciting some creepy short stories. The first one was about some crazy dude killing an old man who had an eye like a vulture. Weird stuff.

"Bet you don't," Billy Don said from his usual sunken spot on the couch. The springs were shot, and every time Billy Don sat in it, his butt got a little closer to the floor.

"She said it's awfully damn nice of me to let her stay here in the trailer," Red said.

"Nope."

"She probably said something about me having a heart of gold."

"Not even close."

"Then she must've asked why it smells so funky every time she passes your room."

Billy Don shook his head. "She said she wants to figure out who killed her dad."

Red grabbed the remote and turned the volume down on the TV. "Do what?"

"She says ain't no way he forgot to tighten those lug nuts, which means somebody screwed around with Deke's car. She wants to figure out who done it."

"I was thinking the same thing myself earlier," Red said, "but what exactly is she thinking she can do about it? She's just a girl. She should let the cops handle everything."

Billy Don shrugged, as if he didn't really care either way, but Red knew that was bullshit. There was more to come.

"Now I've lost the plot," Red said, gesturing toward the TV.

"He buried the old man under the floorboards," Billy Don said. "You never read it?"

Red turned the volume back up. A full minute passed before Billy Don spoke again.

"Seems weird for you to say she should let the cops handle everything," he said.

"Christ," Red said, making his exasperation plain. "Are we still on this?"

"You're the one always saying the cops don't know what they're doing, and they're corrupt, and they'll do just about anything to close a case, including pinning it on the wrong guy."

"You don't agree?"

"Bobby Garza's always treated us okay, and Marlin, too," Billy Don said, referring to the Blanco County sheriff and game warden.

"They's the exception," Red said.

"Point is, if you don't trust cops in general, why would you expect Christie to leave it to them to figger out what happened?"

"I knew life would get complicated if that girl moved in," Red said.

"You damn sure never leave it to the cops when it involves *you*, like this mess a couple weeks ago with Mandy and Dub Kimble. You launched your own investigation to figure out how Dub died."

Billy Don made quotation marks with his fingers when he said "investigation."

"Had to clear my good name," Red said. "And it worked! Mandy told me everything."

"And 'member when Harley Frizzell got killed and you thought you was a suspect?"

"I *was* a suspect."

"You investigated then, too."

More air quotes around "investigated."

"They never woulda solved that one without me!" Red said.

"So you're glad you conducted your own investigations."

"Absolutely," Red said.

"In which case, why shouldn't Christie do the same thing?"

Red didn't have a good answer for that, but after a few seconds, he came up with one.

"The difference is, I'm not some tiny seventeen-year-old girl. I'm a full-grown adult with an above-average IQ and a God-given ability for deducting things."

"That may be true, Red, and you're right—she's only seventeen. It's probably more than she can handle on her own."

"Like I said."

"Plus, she's got school."

"Right."

"That's why we're gonna help her."

Red realized Billy Don had been playing him.

"What do you mean *we*?" Red said. "You got a mouse in your pocket?"

"You won't help?"

"I'm a busy man with a full schedule."

"Hard to take that seriously when you spend half the day in that chair."

"They say the best time to relax is when you don't have time for it," Red said.

"Who says that?"

"They do. Them."

"That don't make sense."

"Doesn't have to."

Billy Don shook his head in frustration. "I see what's going on. You don't think you can figure out what happened to Deke, so you're afraid to even try. I understand. You don't want to look bad."

"That reverse psychiatry ain't gonna work, either," Red said.

"You just sit here and watch TV," Billy Don said, pushing himself up off the couch with a grunt. "I'll take care of it myself. Me and Christie."

"Sounds good to me," Red said.

Billy Don trundled down the hallway to his bedroom and closed the door.

On the TV, Vincent Price was acting like a damn lunatic, swearing up and down he could hear the dead man's heartbeat. Whoever wrote this stuff must've been on drugs.

Gavin's plan, such as it was, was to park outside Caroline's office and see if the impostor went anywhere for lunch later. If so, where? With whom? Would she eat the things Caroline normally ate, or would she eat something different, something that would prove she was a phony? Shrimp, for instance, or okra, or spinach. Caroline hated all those things. If she did eat one of those things, what would Gavin do about it? Confront her and explain that he had figured out she was a phony? He didn't have an answer at the moment. One step at a time.

He'd driven less than two miles when he noticed something he hadn't noticed before—a small square of black electrical tape on the clear plastic in front of the speedometer and the other gauges. He removed the tape and saw that it had been concealing an illuminated check-engine light. That little fucker. That shitty little rip-off artist. It pissed Gavin off, but at the same time, he could admire the deception for its sheer simplicity.

Gavin glanced at the temperature gauge. All good. Then the oil pressure gauge. No problems. His automotive skills extended as far as adding coolant and checking tire pressure. He had no idea what might cause that warning light to go on. Was it urgent? What exactly was he supposed to check? He'd just ignore it for now.

He kept his speed at 65, now eight miles from Burnet, the county seat, where the district attorney's office was located. Caroline sometimes had to travel to the surrounding counties served by the DA's office, but Gavin knew she would be in the office all week. She'd mentioned it this weekend—the fact that she was looking forward to a week of peace and quiet, relatively speaking, without a lot of running around.

He pulled into Burnet at 11:08. When he reached the courthouse annex, where the DA's office was located, he decided it would be best to park in the middle of the lot, between the annex and the sheriff's office. There was plenty of room. Lots of people came and went from both buildings. Nobody would pay attention to a guy sitting in his car on the edge of the lot. They'd think he was waiting for someone doing business inside the annex. Gavin found a spot with a great view of the doors of the annex. He could even see Caroline's Tahoe parked on the west side of the building. Perfect.

He killed the engine and settled in to wait.

She might not leave for lunch, but he knew she hadn't packed a lunch today, so it was a coin toss. She might not eat at all. She did that sometimes. Just too busy to take the time.

Might as well use the time productively. He pulled out his phone and googled "check engine light." First article said it could be something costly, like a bad catalytic converter, or something simple, like a loose gas cap. Could be a faulty oxygen sensor or ignition coil. Gavin could check the gas cap later, but the rest of it…hell, he didn't even know what those things were. He was pretty sure the catalytic converter was contained within the exhaust system. It would probably cost more to fix than the car was worth, which made Gavin understand why the punk was selling the car for $1,500 in the first place.

He glanced up from his phone just in time to see the fake Caroline crossing the lot toward the sheriff's office. Jeez. A few seconds later and he would've missed her. Wouldn't have been an auspicious start to his investigation, would it?

He watched the impostor making her way on high heels across the lot, and he couldn't help noticing the sway of her hips, and that made him smile as he remembered last night. Then he felt guilty for smiling. Then he remembered that he was fully justified for having made sweet, sweet love to the fake Caroline, although, to be honest, perhaps he shouldn't have enjoyed it so much. And he did enjoy it. A lot.

It was already getting hot in the car.

7

"Be back later," Billy Don said, his keys jangling in his hand.

"Where you headed?" Red said from his spot in the recliner. He might've dozed off, but he wasn't sure. Vincent Price was long gone.

"Buchanan Dam," Billy Don said, pausing by the front door with his hand on the knob.

"Yeah?"

"Yep."

"What's going on in Buchanan Dam?"

"Good starting point," Billy Don said.

"For what?"

"You weren't listening earlier?"

"Yeah, you said Buchanan Dam."

"No, I meant earlier this morning—what I said about Deke and all that."

"I don't always commit everything you say to memory," Red said.

"Gonna run up there and stop at the Beach Club," Billy Don said.

"Get a beer before you start investigating?" Red said, and he made quotation marks with his fingers, just like Billy Don had done earlier.

"No, that's the last place Deke was before he wrecked," Billy Don said, letting go of the doorknob for the time being.

"They open this early?"

Red had been to the Beach Club once a few years back, and he'd liked it, but it was a little too far from home to be one of his regular hangouts.

"They're closed on Mondays, but I'm gonna look around."

"That's your plan? Look around?"

"Yep."

"At a parking lot and a locked building?"

"Pretty much, but I'm open to suggestions," Billy Don said. "Might even buy lunch if you wanna ride along. You don't even have to offer the suggestions. Just ride. Keep me company. Hand me a beer every now and then."

"You're trying to sucker me in to your boondoggle," Red said.

"Maybe so, but I'm planning to stop at that little Mexican food joint we stopped at that one time."

"Alberto's?"

"I don't think that's it, but something like that. It was good, I remember that."

"Antonio's? Alonzo's?"

"Got me a hankering for some of their enchiladas."

"Well, dammit," Red said.

"Now you're thinking about the enchiladas, huh?"

"Yeah, thanks to you."

"That was the plan," Billy Don said. "So you gonna get your boots on or what?"

The fake Caroline entered the sheriff's office and disappeared from view.

Gavin lowered both windows, but there wasn't much of a breeze. He was tempted to leave the car running with the AC on, but what about that check-engine light? What if something broke because he stressed out the engine?

Gavin was pondering that possibility when a brown Chevy truck pulled into the slot two spaces over from his Kia, with no vehicle in between. Gavin looked down at his phone, pretending to be occupied, but he watched the Chevy out of the corner of his eye.

The driver—a male in his thirties or thereabouts—had the window rolled down and was finishing a cigarette while talking on the phone. Gavin couldn't make out the words, but he could hear that the guy's voice was raised. Upset. Angry. Emphatically poking the air with the hand that held the cigarette.

After another full minute, the man ended the call and climbed out of the Chevy. He was shorter than Gavin expected, but broad and stout. Strong.

Then he happened to glance right at the Kia and caught Gavin looking at him. The man was homely, with small, deep-set eyes, a broad, flat nose, and hair like a Brillo pad.

He took one last drag on his cigarette, flicked the butt to the ground, then walked into the courthouse annex. For some reason, Gavin felt compelled to watch him go. Something about that guy was seriously creepy. He figured Brillo Pad was probably going in there because of some kind of legal problem.

Gavin waited some more.

Seven minutes later, Caroline came out of the sheriff's office and walked back toward the courthouse annex. She never glanced in Gavin's direction, but why would she? Gavin appreciated the sway of her hips again, but he also noticed that she moved with purpose and confidence. Like she was going somewhere important, and things damn sure better be ready when she got there. How had he never noticed that before?

Oh, wait. Damn it. It wasn't Caroline. Why did he keep forgetting that? The woman walking with such self-assurance wasn't his wife. It was the impostor.

The impostor went inside the annex, and then nothing else happened for twenty minutes.

Gavin finally decided he had to have some AC, even for just a few minutes. So he turned the key in the ignition—and nothing happened. Just some clicking noises. He stopped for a moment, then tried again. Just clicking and more clicking, getting slower. Then nothing.

Well, son of a bitch. What the hell was he going to do now? Gavin still had the seller's phone number in his phone, so he dialed the number. Got voicemail.

"Listen," Gavin said, "in case you're wondering, I'm not real happy with this car. First I discovered you'd taped over the check-engine light, which is probably a crime, and now it appears the battery is dead, or something. So unless you want me to report this to the police, you need to call me in the next five minutes and arrange to bring me a new battery here in Burnet. If you do that, I'll overlook the check-engine light. I'm a fair person and that seems reasonable to me."

He hung up and waited. Five minutes passed. Ten minutes. Fifteen.

Gavin kept watching his phone, waiting for the call, and then he looked up and the creepy guy with hair like a Brillo pad was standing beside the open driver's-side window.

"You all right?" the man asked. "You look a little freaked out."

"I'm, uh—"

"You got bidness inside the courthouse?" Brillo Pad asked.

"Uh, yeah, in a little bit. I'm early."

"Just had a hearing myself," Brillo Pad said. "What a fucking joke."

"No doubt."

"What'd you do?" Brillo Pad asked.

Gavin didn't know what to say, but before he knew it, he blurted an answer out—and he had no idea where it came from or why he said it. "Robbed a liquor store," he said. He was starting to sweat even more profusely than he had been before.

"No shit?" Brillo Pad said. "*You* robbed a liquor store."

"It was a misunderstanding," Gavin said, trying to backtrack.

Brillo Pad laughed. "Oh, right. Same here. I've been having misunderstandings all my life. First misunderstanding on your record?"

"Yeah."

"I could tell. You'll be fine. Get a good lawyer if you can afford it. That's the fucking key. They can make all kinds of shit go away. You think the prosecutor wants to go to trial? Hell, no. They want you to plead guilty to a lesser charge, so everybody can move on."

Gavin nodded, but desperately wanted to change the subject. "Hey, you know anything about cars?"

"Sure. What's up?"

"Here, listen to this." Gavin cranked the key again. It clicked a little.

"Sounds like your battery's shot to hell," Brillo Pad said. "You got jumper cables?"

"Unfortunately, no."

"Better find some."

"I will."

"Or get a new battery."

"I will."

"Or, hell, maybe it's time for a whole new car. This thing's a piece of shit."

The place was called Alfredo's Mexican Restaurant #2, because #1 was up in Lampasas, about thirty miles to the north. This one—#2—was in a tiny metal building on 1431 in Kingsland, with a caliche parking lot and a neon OPEN sign in the window.

"Alfredo seems like an Italian name to me," Red said as they ate damn tasty chips and salsa. "Or I guess it *could* be Mexican, because there really ain't much difference between Mexican and Italian, is there?"

"Just a different country that's overseas, that's all," Billy Don said. "Plus they got a different language."

"Well, I *know* all that," Red said. "I'm just saying they're a lot alike."

The interior had yellow walls with green trim and a ceiling made of acoustic tiles. They'd decided to grab lunch before heading over to the Beach Club. The restaurant was crowded, but that was because there were only maybe twelve tables.

As they waited, Red found himself eyeballing passing plates of food being delivered to nearby tables. Damn, the fajitas looked and smelled great. Maybe he'd get those instead.

"Apparently, Deke was at the Beach Club and got pretty drunk before he left and flipped his car," Billy Don said, keeping his voice low.

"Where'd you hear that?" Red asked, but he already knew.

"Facebook," Billy Don said.

Yep. Just as he suspected. Red had broken down and gotten himself an iPhone, but he refused to open a Facebook account, despite both Billy Don and Mandy urging him to do so. Next thing you know, he'd be Snapgramming and such. He had no interest in that. People on Facebook ended up like zombies, staring at their phones all day.

"If it's true, don't that just embellish the idea it was an accident?" Red said. "Maybe he was working on the car earlier that night—"

"They said he was."

"Okay, so maybe he was drinking beer while he was working on it, like anybody might do, and he forgot to tighten the lug nuts all the way."

"Maybe," Billy Don said, "but let me ask you something. You and me both been known to handle guns while we was a little bit drunk."

"Well, sure, but how'd we go from cars to guns?"

"You ever think you might screw up and forget a gun was loaded, or think it was loaded when it wasn't? Something like that?"

"Ain't happened yet."

"That you remember."

"I'd remember."

"I figger Deke was probably the same way with cars," Billy Don said. "He wouldn't have to *think* about tightening those nuts, he'd just do it. Second nature."

The waitress—a Mexican-looking gal who may or may not have fully understood English—came to take their orders and then went away. Red had changed his mind again and gone back to the beef enchiladas. The place didn't serve beer, but you could bring your own, and they'd stopped beforehand to get a six-pack of Keystone Light tallboys.

"You want my opinion," Red said—and he waited for Billy Don to interject some smart-ass comment, but he didn't, so Red kept talking— "you shoulda come up here on a day when the Beach Club is open, so you might actually could talk to some people who was there on Saturday night."

"Maybe so," Billy Don said, "but I couldn't think of what else to do, and I felt like I had to do *something* today. Christie seemed so down when I took her to school."

"Maybe she's that way all the time," Red said. "Being a teenager and all."

"Yeah, maybe," Billy Don said.

"They're weird that way, from what I hear. Especially girls."

"Seems about right."

This was strange territory for the two of them. Normally they only had to look out for themselves, and that wasn't too difficult—just remember to eat occasionally, and maybe take a shower, and try not to accidentally injure yourself. If Billy Don seemed glum about something, Red sure as hell didn't put much effort into figuring it out or lifting his spirits. *Just man up and stop moping around, for God's sake.* That was about the extent of Red's pep talk. And he wouldn't want any more than that in return if the situation was reversed.

But figuring out a 17-year-old girl? Might as well try to do a jigsaw puzzle blindfolded. Sure, she had reason to be down, what with her dad dying and having to move to a new place, but Red had no idea how to make her feel better about things.

The waitress arrived with their food.

"You ever go to the Beach Club?" Billy Don asked her as she set the plates in front of them.

"Qué?" she said.

"The Beach Club," Billy Don said. "You ever go there?"

"No," she said.

"You know the place I'm talking about?"

"Sí. Peach Club."

"No, it's the *Beach* Club," Billy Don said.

She smiled.

"Did you know a guy named Deke Gilbert?" Billy Don asked.

"Sí," she said.

"You did? You knew Deke?"

"Qué?" she said.

"You understand the question?" Red asked. "*Comprendo el,* uh, question?"

She smiled at him.

"That's okay," Red said. "I don't think she understands. She don't *comprendo.*"

She continued smiling.

"Can we get more chips?" Red asked.

"Sí. More cheeps," she said, nodding.

She went away again.

"I like her," Billy Don said.

"Yeah, your investigation is off to a good start," Red said. "She'll make a great witness."

8

After his hearing at the courthouse, Eddie Trask drove over to the Buchanan Dam Beach Club. It was closed on Mondays, but Eddie spotted a green Pontiac Firebird parked in front of the aqua-colored cinderblock building. That meant Teresa, the manager and primary bartender, was inside.

Bad luck.

He parked in a shady spot not far from where Deke Gilbert had parked on Saturday night. There was one question that had been nagging at Eddie. Where were the lug nuts? He remembered throwing them, but had he slung them from his truck as he'd driven home, or had he tossed them into the weeds somewhere here at the club? He couldn't remember for sure. At the time, he didn't think it was all that important what he did with them. But then Deke had died.

He got out of his truck and walked to the club. Pulled on the double glass doors, but they were locked. He cupped his face to one of the doors and looked inside. Dark. Couldn't see Teresa anywhere. Maybe in the office. He knocked hard a couple of times, but she didn't answer.

Eddie didn't have Teresa's phone number. She wouldn't give it out. She was a good-looking lady—blonde and full-figured—so half the men and some of the women who frequented the club had hit on her at one point or another. He couldn't blame her for refusing to share her number. She didn't need a bunch of drunks and lesbians calling her at all hours.

However, he did have the number for the phone inside the bar, so he dialed it. No answer.

Crap.

He knocked again. Nothing.

He walked around the side of the building, all the way to the back, which was surrounded by a six-foot sheet-metal fence.

Eddie couldn't see over it but he jumped and looked. Jumped and looked. Saw the big colorful beach-themed mural that covered the back of the building, plus the deck, but no Teresa. Nobody back here.

So he went back the way he'd come, and just as he rounded the corner at the front of the building, Teresa was walking to her Firebird.

"Hey, gorgeous," Eddie called out as she opened her car door. She jumped slightly, then looked back to see who it was. Eddie grinned. "Sorry. Just me."

"Yeah, I saw your truck."

He'd always gotten the feeling Teresa was a little scared of him. Or maybe she just didn't like him. She was friendly to some of the men who came into the bar, like Tanner, but she'd always been a little standoffish with Eddie.

"What're you doing up here on your day off?" Eddie asked, stopping ten feet away. She was standing in the wedge between her car and the open door, facing him.

"Just cleaning some things up," she said. "Too damn tired last night."

"I hear ya. Hey, that was a real bummer about Deke, wasn't it?" he asked, because that was exactly what an innocent, uninvolved person would say in this situation. "That must've happened right after he left here, huh?"

She let out a sigh and placed her arm over the open car door. "Yeah, and a guy from the sheriff's office already came around yesterday afternoon asking questions. Thing is, I can't really talk about it. That's what Mr. Henry's lawyer told me to do. Just keep my mouth shut."

Mr. Henry owned the bar, although he never set foot in it. Nobody had ever met him, except for Teresa. He lived in Dallas.

Eddie laughed. "Guess that's true in just about every situation— just keep your mouth shut. Always works for me. They probably just wanted to know how much y'all served him and when he left. That kind of thing."

"Can't really say," she said. "I know for damn sure I didn't serve him too much. He seemed fine to me."

"Figure they'll do a blood test and see how drunk he was," Eddie said.

"Maybe so, but like I said, I can't talk about it."

He didn't like her attitude. Kind of snippy.

"Okay, whatever," Eddie said. "That's not why I'm here, anyway. Saturday night, there was a guy in a tan cowboy hat and a green shirt. He looked a lot like a guy I used to work with in the oilfields. You happen to know his name?"

"And he has a goatee, right?"

"Yeah, that's him."

"That's Sammy Fontana. Nice guy. He just moved here a couple months ago."

"Sammy, huh? Then he's not the guy I used to work with. Thanks, anyway. Guess I'll run on. Enjoy your day off."

He turned to leave and she said, "Why didn't you just ask him Saturday night?"

He turned back. "What's that?"

"When you saw him Saturday night, why didn't you check if it was the guy from the oilfield?"

It was like she thought he was stupid or something. Like something that simple wouldn't have occurred to him.

"Because he was going into the stall while I was taking a leak at the urinal, and that ain't exactly the time for a conversation, know what I mean? Then I looked for him later and didn't see him. Good enough?"

"Jeez, don't get all uptight."

Eddie knew he should let it go, but he couldn't. He'd never had that kind of willpower.

"You know, Teresa, I've always gotten the feeling you think I'm a jerk or something. Am I right? Did I do something somewhere along the way to piss you off?"

That knocked her back a little. Not looking so smug anymore. Made her realize it was just the two of them alone in this parking lot, so she'd best keep her sass to a minimum.

"No, man, I'm just tired," she said.

"Okay, but that don't give you the right to be a bitch."

"Sorry, then, okay? I gotta go."

She slipped into the car, closed the door, and started the engine. He halfway expected her to lock the doors, but she didn't.

Eddie stayed right where he was, watching her, while she backed up and drove away. Then he spent a few minutes looking for the lug nuts.

A brown Chevy truck was pulling out of the Beach Club's parking lot just as Billy Don pulled in. Other than that, there wasn't another vehicle in sight.

"When they say closed, they mean closed," Red said. He used to go to a beer joint where the bartender would open up unofficially for hardcore regulars on the one day it was supposedly closed. He'd been hoping this place did the same thing, but no luck.

Billy Don stopped the Ranchero dead center in the lot, killed the engine, and just sat there for a moment. The community of Buchanan Dam wasn't much to begin with, but there was even less out here, about a mile from the dam itself. To the west, not quite a quarter mile away, was Reverend Jim's Dam Pub. About the same distance to the east was Rockaway RV Park. Right next door to the Beach Club was an abandoned place called the Bluebonnet Dance Tavern. Cool building, but shuttered up.

Red waited. Neither of them said anything for a full minute.

"Well," Red said. "Now what?"

Billy Don opened his door and climbed out, and Red could feel the car rise higher on its suspension. Red got out, too. It had become a nice afternoon—temperature in the seventies, with very dry air and lots of sun.

"Wish I knew where Deke parked on Saturday night," Billy Don said.

The Beach Club was a low, wide cinderblock building with no windows. The parking lot was about three times as wide as the building itself. The entrance—double glass doors—faced south, onto County Road 301, a narrow two-lane with a speed limit of 35 in front of the club. Behind the club, to the north, was the busier four-lane State Highway 29. Beyond that, even further north, was the Colorado River, where it emptied out from Lake Buchanan.

"What time did Deke get here?" Red asked.

"Why?"

"If he got here late, the lot was probably pretty full, it being Saturday night. So he probably had to park way left or way right."

Billy Don grinned. "Gotta admit, that's pretty smart."

"Told you I was good at this stuff," Red said.

Billy Don walked to the glass doors and tugged. Locked. Red was still standing beside the Ranchero, so he retrieved a fresh Keystone Light from the ice chest they'd brought along, popped the top, and took a long drink. There were worse ways you could spend a day than driving around central Texas on a warm afternoon, eating Mexican food and drinking cold beer.

Billy Don started walking a long circuit around the empty parking lot, kicking at something every now and then. Red couldn't spot a single empty beer can or any other trash.

"Found a quarter," Billy Don called out.

"Don't spend it all in one place," Red said.

Now Billy Don was passing the twin dumpsters on the right side of the club.

"Dang," he said. "Stinks."

"Imagine that," Red said.

Red sauntered off toward the left side of the club, in the direction of the six-foot sheet-metal fence that enclosed the rear of the property. He remembered that the club had a large deck in the back—even big enough for a band to set up back there and play music under the stars. Nice when the weather was cooperating.

Also to the left side of the property was a small grove of live oak trees, which was handy, because Red needed to take a leak something fierce. Too much Keystone. He stepped into the oaks and took a position behind the biggest tree trunk. He wasn't bashful, but he didn't want some uptight motorist to call the police and report him for taking a piss in public.

"Red! Where'd you go?"

"Hang on!" Red called back.

"What?"

"Taking a leak! Hang on!"

Red finished, zipped up, and just then, just as he turned, he saw something in the grass, no more than three feet away.

It was a lug nut. Shiny. Hadn't been there long.

Then he spotted another one. And a third.

"Billy Don!" he yelled. "Come check this out!"

"What?"

"The master has done it again!"

9

"I need some help with a car I bought this morning," Gavin said. He was sweating profusely from the walk over from the courthouse annex. He felt a bit queasy.

"That's what we're here for," the friendly guy behind the counter said. The tag on his O'Reilly's shirt identified him as Thomas. Late twenties, with shaggy brown hair. Tall and skinny. The only employee Gavin could see, which was fine, because Gavin was the only customer.

"Pretty sure the battery is dead," Gavin said.

The little bastard who'd sold him the car still hadn't called back. He wouldn't—Gavin knew that now—and there was nothing he could do about it.

"You got it here?" Thomas asked.

"The battery?"

"No, the car."

"Sorry, no. It's parked outside the courthouse."

"It would be weird if it was parked *inside* the courthouse," Thomas said, smiling.

Gavin grinned and nodded. "Good point."

Gavin's stomach let out a loud rumble.

"Whoa," Thomas said. "That was impressive."

"Just some medicine I'm on," he said. "Side effect."

Thomas nodded. "If you bring your car over, we can test the battery, the alternator, and the starter. That's all free, by the way. No charge for doing that."

"But I can't get the car started. It might have something to do with the check-engine light. The jerk who sold me the car had covered it with a piece of black tape."

Thomas frowned. "Really? That's pretty scummy."

"Think I should report him?" Gavin asked.

"Wow, I don't know. I guess you could, but to who?"

"The cops."

"I guess. Hey, we can check that, too, by the way."

"The check-engine light?"

"Yep. We can run a test and see why it's staying on. Of course, any repairs would be extra."

Gavin heard someone moving around in the parts room behind the counter. Another employee.

"First I need to get the damn car started," Gavin said.

"What kind is it?" Thomas asked.

"Kia."

"Kia what?"

"What do you mean?"

"What model of Kia?"

Gavin realized, much to his embarrassment, that he couldn't answer the question. "I don't, uh…"

"You don't know the model?"

"Sorry, no."

"We'd need to know the model to match a battery to it," Thomas said.

"We can't just use any battery?" Gavin asked.

"No, it might not fit, or the cables might not be long enough, depending on how the posts are arranged," Thomas said.

Gavin was a patient man, but he was getting frustrated—not with Thomas, but with the Kia. No wonder the car was yellow. It was a lemon.

"Okay, well, I'm not sure what to do. The car is dead, it's a mile and a half away, and I can't tell you what model it is."

"Can you jump it?" Thomas asked.

"Maybe, but I need someone to help me. I don't know anything about cars. I don't want to know anything about cars, to be honest, especially Kias."

"Ha. I don't blame you about that last part. Why don't we run over there and take a look?"

"You can do that?"

"Todd?" Thomas called out to the person in the parts room. "Gotta go help this guy with his battery. Back in a bit."

"Holy moly," Billy Don said.

"Don't touch 'em," Red said.

"Wasn't gonna."

"But don't."

"I won't."

"Just leave 'em where they are," Red said.

They both stood there staring for a moment.

"So what do we do?" Billy Don asked.

"Good question," Red said. "Ain't no need to rush, so let's think this through."

Billy Don nodded. "So you just got lucky and saw 'em laying there?"

"Pretty much," Red said, because he couldn't think of any way to imply it was skill that led him over to the oak grove. If he hadn't hollered that he was taking a leak, he could've said he'd come over here specifically to search the area, but too late for that.

"Think they're from Deke's car?" Billy Don asked.

"If they ain't, it's the biggest damn coincidence since—well, something really damn coincidental."

"Only just three, though?" Billy Don asked.

"That's all I see," Red said. "But that makes sense. If someone screwed around with Deke's car, they wouldn't have taken all five lug nuts off, because the wheel woulda come off before he even got out of the parking lot. They probably woulda left at least two lug nuts on there, although I bet they loosened those, too."

"So do we call the cops or what?" Billy Don asked.

Red didn't answer right away.

"Red?"

"You know how I feel about that," he said.

They both held their breath as a Jeep on the county road slowed, as if to pull into the club's parking lot, but then continued on its way.

"If we don't call 'em, do we take the nuts or leave 'em?" Billy Don asked.

"Just let me think," Red said.

"If we take 'em, I'm pretty sure that's a crime," Billy Don said.

"Messing around with evidence. But if we leave 'em, what if somethin' happens to 'em?"

"Don't know," Red said. "Just hang on."

"I can't believe the cops ain't looked around here yet," Billy Don said.

Which hadn't occurred to Red yet, so he said, "I was thinking the same thing the moment I saw the lug nuts sitting there, and it goes back to the cops being incompetent. I think that gives us our answer."

"Which answer?"

"About whether we call 'em or not," Red said. "Hell, they ain't even done their jobs so far, so why should we tell 'em what we found?"

"Yeah, I guess so," Billy Don said. "Or maybe the cops searched and just didn't see 'em."

"Irregardless, it don't make no sense to leave the nuts here. What if the person who took 'em off wises up and comes looking for 'em?"

"Why'd they leave 'em in the first place?" Billy Don asked.

"Drunk, probably. Didn't think it through. Didn't want to get caught with those nuts in their possession, because that's nine-tenths of the law right there."

"I don't think that means what—"

"We take the nuts and we hold on to 'em," Red said. "Then we can always decide later if we should hand 'em over—if we can find a cop we can trust. Agreed?"

"Yeah, I guess."

"You gotta be on board with this," Red said. "No claiming later that I talked you into it or some bullshit like that. You got a better idea, now's the time to spit it out."

"Wish I did," Billy Don said.

"Okay, then. We're doing it. Right?"

"Right."

Red bent to pick up the first nut and Billy Don said, "Hang on. You're just gonna grab it?"

"Why not?"

"You shouldn't be touching it."

Red stood up straight again. "I was gonna stick my pinkie in the center and get it that way, but if you wanna play like some sort of CSI expert, go right ahead."

"Let me run to the Ranchero and see if I got something to put 'em in."

"Fine by me, and bring me a beer while you're at it."

Gavin parked the Kia Rio—that was the model, he'd learned—near his truck in the Walmart parking lot. Thank God for Thomas from O'Reilly's. Great guy.

Thomas had jump-started the Kia at the courthouse with his own car, then Gavin had driven it back to the store for a new battery. Thomas then used some sort of gizmo to determine why the check-engine light was on. He said it was probably just a bad spark plug, or possibly a plug wire, which meant there wasn't any big rush to get that fixed, but he shouldn't let it go too long, either. Gavin tried to give him a $20 tip, but Thomas said he couldn't take it.

The drive back to Marble Falls had gone just fine, but other than getting the car fixed, Gavin didn't consider the day a big success. This surveillance stuff was harder than it appeared. The investigators in those insurance-fraud novels he read made it look easy, as long as you were persistent. And sometimes you had to be creative. Come at it from unexpected angles.

Gavin locked the Kia and got into his truck for the drive home.

What next? The idea of parking outside the courthouse annex again and waiting for the impostor to go somewhere was not appealing at all, and now that he'd done it once, Gavin didn't think the odds for success were very high. What were the odds she would go somewhere or do something that would help Gavin figure everything out? Slim to none.

He had to make something happen. But how?

Eddie didn't own a computer, but he sometimes used the ones at the Lakeshore Library, which was about ten minutes from the Beach Club, up on 261.

He went there now and it didn't take him long to track down Sammy Fontana. Found him listed in the tax rolls on the county website. Handy as hell, what with an address and everything. No wife listed on the deed, either. Fontana owned sixty acres off County Road 306, west of the lake, with several hundred feet of frontage on the Llano River. Damn. That was some expensive real estate.

Eddie did some more poking around online and found an obituary listing Fontana as a survivor. His wife had died eight months earlier at the age of 42. They'd lived in Austin at the time. No kids.

Then Eddie found an article saying Fontana had owned an importing business that had made him a wealthy man. Didn't say what he imported. Kind of a critical detail to leave out, wasn't it? Fontana sold the business three months after his wife died. The article quoted him as saying, "I need to take some time to focus on what's important."

Like drinking in a beer joint until closing on a Saturday night? Mourning his wife by chasing tail? Dude had all that money and he chose to hang out at the Beach Club?

Okay, what now?

Was Fontana a problem? There was no way to know for sure.

On the other hand, there was one really good way to make sure he *wasn't* a problem.

Eddie drove home and grabbed two beers from the fridge. Sat on the couch and guzzled one, then popped the top on the other.

Eddie knew from experience that you had to keep shit from getting out of control. You couldn't wait around to see if things were going to be okay, because, more often than not, they *weren't* going to be okay. They were going to turn to shit. Sometimes it took a few months, other times a few days, or even hours, but they turned to shit.

He downed the rest of the second beer.

What had Sammy Fontana seen on Saturday night? Nothing at all? Something? Maybe he didn't understand what he was seeing at the time, but he'd piece it together later. Could Eddie take that chance?

He went into the kitchen for another beer and continued weighing his options. The way he saw it, he didn't *have* any options. Just one.

He went into the bedroom, to the closet, and shoved hanging clothes aside to reach way to the back corner. Came out with his Marlin .30-30. He'd always loved lever-action brush guns, and this one was in immaculate condition. Had a nice Leupold scope, too. He wasn't supposed to have any firearms in his possession, but a guy had offered it in a trade for an ounce of medium-grade pot. Eddie had gotten the better end of that deal.

He cranked the lever, but just a few inches, until he could see for sure there was a live round in the chamber.

10

"How was your first day?" Billy Don asked. "Make some friends?"

"Not really," Christie said. "But there's one girl I already knew. I sat with her at lunch."

She was squeezed in between Red and Billy Don in the Ranchero. They'd picked her up from school on the way home from the Beach Club, and now they were on the county road, headed toward Red's trailer. If she'd been depressed this morning, she seemed to be doing okay now.

"This is a pretty cool car," Christie said. "Or is it a truck?"

"Little of both, I guess," Billy Don said.

"Hold old is it?"

"About forty years."

"How about your truck?" Christie said, talking to Red.

"About the same," he said. "Except for the grille guard. That's newer."

"What's that for?"

"In case I hit a rhino or something," he said.

"But you really mean deer, right?"

"Yeah," Red said. "They can dart right in front of you, and, well, it ain't pretty."

"Mind if I ask you another question?" Christie said, talking to Red.

"How did I become so incredibly handsome?" Red said.

"Well, yeah, there's that," she said, playing along, "but I was just wondering what happened to your dad."

"Oh," Red said. He hadn't been expecting that.

"If you don't mind telling me," Christie said. "You mentioned him yesterday."

"No, it's fine," Red said. "I don't mind talking about it." He let a moment pass, so his words would have the appropriate gravity. "He was a good man. Nicest guy on the planet. Never raised a hand toward nobody. But he died when I was fourteen."

"What did he do for a living?" Christie asked.

"He was a cattleman," Red said, which was close enough. Matt O'Brien had been a rodeo clown. No shame in it, but Red could still remember the way the other kids would tease him about it, calling him "Bozo Junior." As Red got older, he resented his dad for that, even though it wasn't his dad's fault. He knew that now.

"So he was like a rancher?" Christie asked.

"Kinda."

"How did he die?"

"Big ol' Brahma bull got him," Red said. That was true, and to this day, Matt was the only rodeo clown to die from a gore injury directly to the anus. Fellow clowns would still recount that story, while tightening their butt cheeks.

"That's so sad," Christie said. "I'm sorry."

"It was a rough time," Red said. "We were all filled with somberity."

"What about your mom?" Christie asked.

"Oh, she was a piece of work," Red said. "Always drank too much, and then one day she ran off with a welder," Red said. He laughed. "I got pretty good at signing her name to government checks after she was gone."

"And you don't know where she is now?"

"Last I heard was Midland, but that was a lot of years ago, and the truth is, I just don't care anymore."

They rode in silence for a few minutes.

Then Christie said, "Is it uncool that everything you just told me makes me feel better about my situation?"

Red laughed hard at that one. "Happy to be of service," he said.

Billy Don said, "But Red dropped out of school, and you ain't gonna be doing that."

Christie looked at him. "You didn't finish?"

"Thanks, Billy Don," Red said.

"I'm just sayin'," Billy Don said, which was one of those phrases he'd picked up on Facebook.

"It was two months short of graduation and I couldn't handle it anymore," Red said.

He'd attended Career Day, where they'd advised him that—based on his grades and his SAT scores—his job opportunities might be somewhat limited. Like he couldn't be some kind of scientist if he wanted to. That pissed him off enough to walk out and never come back.

"You could always get your GED," Christie said.

"No, thanks," Red said. "I'm already a successful bidnessman. Don't need no GED."

"I could help you brush up on your grammar," she said.

"Huh?"

"Never mind. Just kidding. So what did y'all do all day? Other than dropping me off and picking me up?"

"Not much," Red said, because he and Billy Don had agreed they wouldn't say anything to her just yet about the lug nuts. They'd decided they would return to the Beach Club tomorrow, when it was open, and poke around.

"Very little," Billy Don said.

"Just hung around," Red said.

"Nothing important," Billy Don said.

"Watched some TV," Red said.

Christie looked at Billy Don and then at Red. "Okaaay," she said. "That wasn't weird."

"Thanks again for the pancakes," Red said, to change the subject. "They were tasty."

"You're welcome. I was surprised you had any milk in the house, to be honest. I tried not to pay any attention to the expiration date."

Billy Don slowed and turned right into the caliche driveway and began the long, bumpy, uphill climb to the trailer.

Halfway up, Red spotted Mandy's orange Nissan truck. Then he saw that the driver's door was open and Mandy was sitting behind the wheel. She was probably smoking a cigarette. She didn't smoke much—maybe six or eight cigarettes a day—and thankfully she was planning to quit real soon. Kissing her after a smoke was kind of nasty, but it meant she couldn't bitch about him chewing Red Man on occasion.

As they reached the top in the Ranchero, Mandy got out of her truck, cigarette in hand, and waited. She was wearing a denim skirt and a royal-blue tank top that matched her eyes perfectly.

"There's Mandy," Red said.

"Wow, she's pretty," Christie said.

That made Red feel proud. His girlfriend was pretty. Damn right.

"And look at that body," Christie said. "Jeez."

"I'm looking," Billy Don said.

"Hey," Red said. "Take it easy."

"Don't make me stand next to her," Christie said. "I'll look like a stick."

"Red is attracted to her mind," Billy Don said.

"I bet," Christie said.

"Hey, it's true," Red said. "She's smart. Doesn't hurt that she can turn heads. All natural, too, if you know what I mean."

"Are we really talking about this?" Christie asked.

"You started it," Red said.

Billy Don parked in his usual spot and Red got out, holding the car door for Christie.

"Hey, darlin'," Red called to Mandy as she waited by the porch steps.

"Hey, there."

"We was just all talking about what a hottie you are," Red said.

"Y'all are sweet," Mandy said. "Oh, my God. Is that Christie?"

"Hi," Christie said.

Mandy flicked her cigarette butt to the side and walked over, saying, "Good Lord, you are adorable! You come here right now and give me a hug." Christie did as Mandy asked, and as they embraced—with Mandy obviously putting more into it than Christie was, as far as Red could tell—Mandy said, "I am so, so sorry about your daddy. That is just tragic, and if you need anything at all, you just let me know, 'kay?"

Red could tell Mandy had already had at least one vodka and OJ. Screwdrivers were her favorite drink, and she liked to carry one around in a large plastic tumbler with a travel lid.

"Thank you," Christie said.

Mandy finally stopped hugging Christie and held her at arm's length. "I mean that. Anything at all."

"She does mean it," Red said.

"That's very nice of you," Christie said.

"I'm gonna start by making you a nice supper here in a little bit. You like spaghetti?"

"How was your day?" the impostor asked as they were eating dinner at the coffee table in the living room. They had a nice maple table in the dining room, but they only used that for special occasions or when they had guests.

"Fine," Gavin said.

"Any new projects?" she asked.

She was trying to sound casual, but Gavin could tell she was really hoping he'd heard from a client.

"Terry is supposed to send me something, but nothing yet," Gavin said.

"For who?"

"A hospital down in Corpus."

Gavin's job as an illustrator was feast or famine. Sometimes he would be busy for long stretches and earn a lot of money all at once, but that didn't make it easy to enjoy the lulls without worrying that he'd never earn another dime. Right now, he was in a dry spell, which was great timing, considering the circumstances. It might take him quite some time to figure out the fake Caroline's diabolical scheme, and to locate the real Caroline.

"I know you've been getting a little fidgety," she said.

He shrugged as he cut another bite of the chicken he'd grilled earlier.

"I'm sure it'll pick up soon," she said.

"It always does," he said. "How was your day?"

"Fine. Had a hearing for this nut job who stabbed his friend in the face with a steak knife. Went right through his cheek and then his tongue and lodged in the lower jaw on the other side."

"Jesus."

"You don't want to see the photos, believe me. They were drunk and arguing about some stupid car, and the man just snapped. Based on his history, he shouldn't have even made bail, if you ask me. Only a matter of time before he kills someone, if he hasn't already. He's claiming self defense, but the victim's son was there, too, and he says that's not what happened."

Gavin didn't know how Caroline dealt with people like that all day without letting it foul her mood on a permanent basis, but somehow she remained sweet and upbeat—most of the time.

"So where'd you go today?" she asked.

"Nowhere," he said.

She stopped with a bite of chicken on her fork. "You didn't?"

"No. Why?"

"When I got home, it looked like your truck had moved."

"It's in the same place I always park it," he said.

"I know, but it looked like it was pulled forward a little more," she said.

Why on Earth would she notice something like that? *How* on Earth had she noticed?

"Oh, you're right," he said, feigning forgetfulness. "I ran up to the store a few hours ago."

"What for?"

"Huh?"

"What did you need at the store?"

"I just, uh, got some gas," he said. "For the mower. I filled up the gas can for the mower."

"But you just mowed a few days ago," she said.

"Yeah, but I used up all the gas, so I knew I'd need more before I can mow again."

Now she was looking at him as if she didn't quite believe him, but she didn't say anything else. Had she really noticed that his truck had moved, or had someone perhaps informed her that he had been in Burnet earlier today?

"That was very observant of you," he said.

"Oh, I'm very observant," she said. "I know all and see all."

What did she mean by that? He couldn't ask without appearing paranoid.

"I just needed to get out of the house," he said. "Bored, I guess."

Three years earlier, they had moved a few miles north of Marble Falls from Austin so she could take the job with the district attorney's office in Burnet, a short drive away. They'd made the decision together, although he'd certainly pointed out the drawbacks of living in such a small town. He knew she would always be too busy to worry about ways to occupy her free time, but for him, it would be—

Wait. Hang on. This was not the real Caroline. He couldn't forget that. He shouldn't be thinking in terms of "they."

"Maybe now would be a good time to start your novel," the impostor said.

"Maybe so," he said, knowing that would never happen. Not right now. Maybe not ever.

"You've got the time," she said. Caroline was always persistent, sometimes to the point of annoyance.

"Yeah, but lots of chores to do around here, too," Gavin pointed out.

"Like what?" she asked.

"We talked about building a shed," he said. "The south side of the house could use some fresh paint."

"We could hire someone to do that stuff."

"Maybe," he said. "Or I could do it."

She let it go. Finally.

"Are you sleeping any better?" she asked. "Are the new meds helping?"

He looked up from his plate and smiled. "Not really. Why? Is it obvious? Am I grumpy?"

"Not just grumpy. You just...you're not yourself lately."

Not yourself. Did she really just say that? Oh, man, the irony. The fake Caroline was saying he wasn't himself! Was she laughing inside about it?

"I'm sorry," he said. "I'm fine. Just ignore me. You like the chicken?"

11

Sammy Fontana was expecting a delivery—a new freezer to keep in the garage—so he'd left the gate open for the truck. They'd told him it would arrive between two and four o'clock, but then they'd called to say they were running late and it would be more like five.

At five-fifteen, the driveway alarm went off and he figured they'd finally arrived. Not that the driveway alarm was foolproof. Sometimes it triggered whenever a deer passed by, or even a squirrel, but Sammy had been tinkering with it, adjusting the height of the sensor beam, and he thought he'd finally found the sweet spot.

He stepped onto the porch of his cabin and waited. Would be nice to have an extra freezer. He was an avid bow hunter—a damn good one—but it had been at least five years since he'd had the chance to really get out and hunt. That was all going to change this season. He'd be hunting hard, right here on his sixty acres. Not a huge property, but all the neighbors around him had even larger ranches, including one that was five hundred acres, so there were plenty of deer to go around.

He didn't hear a truck. Didn't hear anything.

Well, crud. Maybe the alarm still needed some tweaking. Sammy had set the unit to pick up objects four feet or higher off the ground, but the sensor beam seemed to fluctuate with heat and sometimes even wind. False alarms were to be expected on occasion.

Still nothing.

The gate was only three hundred yards from the house, so if the truck had really arrived, it would be here by now.

Sammy waited another minute, and then he saw motion in some oak trees about eighty yards from the cabin. Or did he? Was it the wind blowing branches? A deer? Could've even been a bird.

He watched that area for more movement, but saw nothing.

Eddie hid behind the trunk of an oak tree and waited, holding the deer rifle with the barrel pointing toward the sky. He should've known it wouldn't be easy. What were the odds Sammy Fontana would be outside on his porch, just standing there, facing this direction? What was he doing, anyway?

Eddie waited. He wouldn't be able to hear a door closing at this distance if Fontana went inside. There was still time to bail out and regroup. Just haul ass. Try it again some other time.

He leaned slightly to his right and chanced a peek. Fontana was still standing there, but now he was looking to his left, as if he'd been distracted by something.

Okay, what the fuck. Might as well go for it. He swung the barrel of the .30-30 around the trunk of the tree and held it tight against the bark for steadiness. Brought the butt into his shoulder and held it firm. Put his right eye up to the scope and took a few seconds to find Fontana and settle in on his chest.

Easy shot at this distance. Hit him right in the sternum and that would be it. Eddie took a deep breath and held it. Began to slowly squeeze the trigger.

Fontana moved. He took a few steps to his left, as if looking for something. Or listening for something.

Now Eddie realized he was hearing something, too. A large vehicle out on the county road. Garbage truck? Road maintenance? A big rig that had made a wrong turn off the highway? Moving slowly. Then Eddie heard brakes.

Damn it.

Was the vehicle turning onto Fontana's property? What were the odds?

Sure enough, judging by the sounds, the truck was turning through Fontana's gate, and now it was beginning to navigate the long driveway.

Now Eddie had to make a snap decision. Finish what he started, or wait until later? Eddie had always been impulsive—he knew that about himself, but he'd never been able to rein it in.

He was impulsive now. He found Fontana in the sights again and worked to hold the rifle steady, the crosshairs squared right on Fontana's chest. The truck driver probably wouldn't hear the shot, and if he did, he wouldn't know where it had come from. Then he'd find Fontana lying there, but Eddie would be long gone. The cops might even wonder if the truck driver had had something to do with it.

Eddie was shaky, so he found a point of focus—the second button down on Fontana's shirt—and slowly began to squeeze the trigger.

Harder.

Harder still.

What the hell?

Jesus, he was an idiot. He'd left the hammer forward, in the safety position. He quickly yanked it back, and now the rifle was ready to fire.

He looked through the scope, but Fontana had moved again. Eddie swept to the left and then to the right, and he found his target again, but Eddie was trembling enough now that he knew he couldn't make a clean shot. What would happen if he wounded Fontana or missed entirely?

The truck was louder. Closer.

Eddie retreated behind the big oak tree again. Damn it. So stupid. He'd blown it.

He hunkered behind the tree trunk and waited for his chance to get the hell out of there.

12

When Eddie got home, there was a Crown Victoria parked at the curb out front. No lights or markings, but the license plate showed all numbers, no letters, and that was a giveaway. County-owned car.

Eddie parked in the driveway, glad his .30-30 was inside a case behind the seat. Before he even got out, here came the cop, walking up the driveway. Not a uniformed cop, but an investigator dressed in a crisp white button-down shirt, blue jeans, and boots. Trying to mimic the look of the Texas Rangers, including the white Stetson on his head. Had his badge clipped to his belt, along with a Glock.

Eddie had never met this guy, but he'd seen him around. Name was Floyd Shaddy. He'd been with the Burnet County Sheriff's Office for about a year.

"Mr. Trask?" he said.

"Yeah?"

Shaddy stuck his hand out and Eddie shook it.

"I'm Detective Shaddy with Burnet County. I tried calling you earlier."

"Yeah, I ran off and forgot my phone," Eddie said. He'd left it at home on purpose, of course, because cops could use it to track where you'd been. He hadn't wanted to leave a record of where he'd been for the past hour.

"You got a minute to talk?" Shaddy asked.

"About what?"

Eddie wasn't making any attempt to appear friendly or relaxed. A guy like Shaddy already knew Eddie's record and would not expect a warm reception. He'd expect Eddie to be nervous and suspicious and uncooperative, just on general principle.

"I understand you were at the Beach Club in Buchanan Dam on

Saturday night," Shaddy said. He was about Eddie's age. Probably six-two. Slender. Clean cut. Narrow face, with hazel eyes and sandy hair.

"I stopped in, yeah," Eddie said.

He knew he probably shouldn't answer any of this guy's questions, but it was the only way Eddie could learn where the investigation stood.

"Any idea what time you got there?" Shaddy asked.

"Nope."

"How about what time you left?"

"This is about Deke Gilbert, huh?"

"I'm just trying to piece together what happened," Shaddy said. "Talking to just about everyone who was there."

"I heard it was an accident," Eddie said.

"Sure looks that way," Shaddy said. "Did you run into Deke while you were there?"

Good chance Shaddy already knew the answer to that, so Eddie said, "Yeah, we talked for a few minutes. He was pretty wasted. Guess the blood tests will show that much."

"What did y'all talk about?"

"It was kind of hard to understand him. It was loud in there and he was slurring pretty bad. But the bottom line is, he was talking smack about the derby this coming weekend. Saying he was gonna kick my ass a fourth time."

"What did you say about that?"

"Hell, I just laughed. He was probably right. But I don't really enter it to win, I just wanna have fun. He always got so serious about it."

Shaddy looked at him skeptically. "He didn't get under your skin a little bit?"

"Honestly, he really didn't. Besides, I always figured he had an extra little advantage nobody knew about."

"Meaning what?"

"Meaning he probably found a way to skirt the rules a little."

"You're saying he cheated?"

Eddie realized he probably shouldn't have gone down this path—it made him look envious or bitter—but he hadn't been able to resist.

"Oh, I don't know. Maybe. Sure would explain a lot. How else could a guy win it six times? Not that I really care one way or the other. Long as they got cold beer afterward, I'm all good. It's a fun event. No reason to turn it into a big competition."

"Who was there at the club with you?" Shaddy asked.

Again, this was something Shaddy probably already knew.

"Tanner Stockwell," Eddie said. "Cousin of mine."

"Did y'all go together or drive separately?"

"I drove us."

"Tanner was there when you were talking to Deke?"

"He was, yeah. Don't know if he was paying attention or not. It wasn't a long conversation, and it wasn't particularly interesting. And it was loud."

Shaddy nodded, as if Eddie was being helpful, but he said, "Couple of people told me it looked like you and Deke were about to go at it. Like you were arguing about something."

He stopped there and waited for Eddie to respond.

"Really? Who told you that?"

"Some folks who saw the conversation. Why would they say that?"

"Hell, I don't know. We were probably leaning in close to hear each other and maybe it looked like something else. I can tell you for sure it was all good. Just some friendly bullshitting. I told Deke he should get a ride home. I remember that real well, saying he shouldn't drive."

Shaddy nodded again. "You see him anymore after that conversation?"

"I sure didn't."

"What time was that?"

"I really don't know. Maybe an hour before closing."

"You stayed until closing?"

"Yes, sir."

"How much would you say you had to drink?"

"I'm not sure, but I was fine to drive, I can tell you that much."

"I'm not looking to get you for DWI. Can't now, anyway. You had a pretty good buzz?"

"Sure, but I wasn't nothing like Deke. He was hammered."

"How about Tanner?"

"What about him?"

"He was drinking pretty hard, too?"

"Neither of us was drinking hard. Just Deke."

"Fair enough. But you and your cousin both had a buzz going?"

"A little one, yeah. This sure is a lot of questions if it was an accident."

"Yeah, but it's all stuff I gotta ask. I appreciate your patience. So tell me about Tanya."

"What about her?"

"She and Deke used to see each other."

"What about it?"

"And on Saturday night, she and Tanner were getting kind of friendly with each other."

"I don't know about friendly, but they was talking," Eddie said.

"You know if it went beyond that?"

"You'd have to ask them."

"Did Tanner ride home with you?"

"Sure did."

"Did she come along?"

"Nope."

"She follow you home?"

"Haven't you talked to her about it?" Eddie asked. "No, she didn't follow us home."

"Just how cozy were they getting in the club?" Shaddy asked.

Eddie grinned. "I can guess where you're going with this, but you're way off base. Tanner and Deke didn't even talk about Tanya, and there wasn't any kind of argument or nothing like that, with me or Tanner. We're peaceful guys."

Eddie remembered what he'd said to Tanner about the cops: *Just tell them exactly what happened. You don't have to lie.* But he'd already screwed up and changed the story to cover for Tanner. Stupid. Tanner was the one who'd seen Deke glaring at Tanya from across the club, and when Deke had started walking toward her, Tanner had headed him off. If Tanner hadn't done that, none of this mess would've ever happened.

"Peaceful?" Shaddy said. "Didn't you get slapped with agg assault last month? Little incident with a steak knife?"

Eddie grinned at him. "You know it was me, so why ask?"

"Just double-checking."

"You just wanted me to know you knew," Eddie said. "Trying to shake me up. Well, I ain't answering any questions about that."

"I wasn't planning on asking any," Shaddy said.

Truth was, it was pretty simple. Eddie's good friend Vic and Vic's son Ray had always acted as Eddie's pit crew for the demolition derby. Hell, they weren't just crew, they were like family. They were eating supper one night, talking about the car they were building, drinking, disagreeing about this and that, when Vic suggested maybe Eddie never won the derby because he was a shitty driver. He was just joking, but it was a damned stupid thing to say, and Eddie wasn't in the mood for it. He reacted without thinking, slamming his steak knife into the side of Vic's face. He immediately wished he hadn't done it, but fuck, things happen, you know? Why would Vic say anything that stupid if he wasn't prepared to suffer the consequences?

"The truth'll come out on that," Eddie said. "It was self-defense. Vic had a knife, too, you know. All three of us did. And what would you expect his son to say? Of course he's gonna lie for his daddy."

"I understand," Shaddy said.

"As far as this thing with Deke, I've told you all I know," Eddie said.

"It's helpful."

"I'm glad."

"Where did you park that night?" Shaddy asked.

"Where did I park?"

"Which part of the lot? To the east? To the west?"

"I knew what you meant, but it just seems like a weird question," Eddie said.

"Yeah, I have to do that sometimes—ask weird questions."

Shaddy waited again.

"I parked to the right," Eddie said. "To the east."

"Did you see Deke's Galaxie?"

"Didn't notice it."

"You or Tanner go anywhere near it?"

"Well, since we didn't see it, that's tough to answer. Guess I might've walked past it without realizing it."

"A car guy like you could walk past that old classic without seeing it?"

"I'm trying to help," Eddie said. "So why does it seem like you don't believe some of the things I'm telling you?"

"Sometimes I just need to clarify," Shaddy said.

"I think I'm about done talking," Eddie said. "Time for you to leave."

"If later on you remember anything important, give me a call, okay?"

Shaddy held out a business card, but Eddie didn't take it right away. He let Shaddy sit there for a minute, the card tweezed between two fingers. Then Eddie reached out and took it.

"Appreciate your time," Shaddy said, and he walked back to his car and drove away.

First thing Eddie did, after Shaddy was out of sight, was go inside and call Tanner, but it went to voicemail. Eddie knew better than to leave a message with too many details.

"Hey, it's me," he said. "We need to talk ASAP. Don't take any other calls before then. Just call me back as soon as you can. I'll explain everything then."

13

Red and Mandy's romance had followed the familiar storylines of a classic love story from the start…

Her live-in boyfriend at the time had been part of the crew helping Red build a tree house shaped like the Alamo in his backyard, but Dub—the boyfriend—had fallen and injured himself, which led to the threat of a lawsuit. Then he got killed in a mysterious hit and run.

Red figured that was the end of the lawsuit, but Mandy wasn't going to let it drop, and it even got to the point where she was more or less extorting Red. He finally gave her $20,000—some of the cash he had left over from a highly successful trip he and Billy Don had taken to Las Vegas, which had followed the $50,000 they'd won together in a pig-hunting contest. In exchange, she gave him some crucial information about the night Dub had been run down, which eventually cleared him as a suspect in Dub's death.

At that point, with all that cash, Mandy had gone on the run with some other guy she'd been seeing on the side—a young Mexican-looking dude who worked at the Dairy Queen and had a weird fixation on women's feet. Both of them were also suspects in Dub's death, but Red figured with them taking off together, the cops would put them at the top of the list. Goodbye and good riddance.

In the end, it turned out none of them had killed Dub—not directly or intentionally—but that didn't stop the young Mexican-looking dude from stealing the cash and hauling ass, leaving Mandy high and dry, way the hell up in Oregon. So she called the Blanco County sheriff and spilled everything she knew, in return for a bus ticket back home. The Mexican-looking dude had eventually been caught in Idaho with more than $17,000 in his possession, and that cash was returned to Mandy.

Not long after she came back to Blanco County, Mandy drove out to see Red at his trailer. She told him she'd realized he could've stiffed her on the cash, but he chose to help her out, and she was grateful. He was telling her it was no big deal when she suddenly leaned over and kissed him. Just out of the blue and totally unexpected, Mandy put the moves on him, and a few minutes later, Red finally had the opportunity to remove her low-cut blouse and see that amazing rack for himself. Worth every penny of that $20,000—and then some.

After a couple of extremely enjoyable hours in his bedroom, she threw one more curveball at him. She admitted that Dub hadn't really injured himself seriously when he'd taken that fall at Red's place, and the lawsuit was bogus. What else could Red do except laugh about it? He and Mandy had sort of been seeing each other ever since.

Yep. Just like a million other traditional American love stories out there.

"She couldn't get any sweeter," Mandy said to Red later, after they'd all eaten supper and visited in the living room for awhile. "But that girl's had a rough life, I can tell you that. Just from talking to her, I can see that, for sure. And I ain't just talking about her daddy dying."

Red wasn't wanting a lot of small talk before Mandy took her clothes off, but if it was the price he had to pay, he'd play along. Right now, they were in bed—Mandy on her back, looking at the ceiling, while Red lay on his side, facing her. He could see some side boob, thanks to the tank top, but he was doing his best to ignore it and focus on what she was saying. He knew from past experiences that women loved to accuse you of not listening.

"Sad situation," Red said. "Breaks my heart."

"It's a wonder she ain't some kind of juvenile delinquent," Mandy said. "And I know about that, because I was one myself."

"I bet you were," Red said. "A bad little girl."

"If she's made it this far—what is she, seventeen?—if she's made it this far, she just might turn into a decent, responsible adult. Seems like she's got a pretty good head on her shoulders."

Red said, "Speaking of—"

"They got no idea where her mama is?"

"Nope. She just took off, according to Billy Don."

Red began to toy with the lower hem of the tank top. Last he'd seen, before he and Mandy had come into the bedroom, Christie was studying while listening to music with ear buds, which meant she wouldn't hear any sounds coming from his room. And Billy Don's room was at the other end of the trailer, and he'd have the TV on.

"I suppose even if they could find her, what's the point?" Mandy said. "Obviously she don't want nothing to do with her daughter, which is just sad."

Red began to slide his hand under the tank top, resting his palm flat on her stomach. It was a great stomach. Smooth and flat. Still tan this time of year. Sometimes Red liked to kiss her bellybutton and—

"She got some good friends she can count on?" Mandy asked.

"I guess so," Red said. He worked his hand higher and felt the lower edge of her bra. Mandy tended to wear the kind of undergarments Red liked. Lots of interesting colors and fabrics. Silk. Lace. Skimpy, too. Push-up bras and thongs. Praise Jesus.

"Friends can make all the difference," Mandy said. "As long as they ain't a bad influence."

"You had friends like that?" Red asked.

"No, I *was* the friend like that. Drinking. Getting high."

Red reached higher and cupped her right breast. Wow. If he had been standing up, the pleasure would've been enough to make his knees buckle.

"Cutting class," Mandy said. "Chasing boys."

"Naughty, naughty," Red said.

"I got sent to the principal's office about a hundred times my senior year," Mandy said. "I thought he was an okay guy, though—until I caught the perv looking down my shirt."

"Can't really blame him," Red said. "Bet you already had big ones." He switched his hand to the other boob.

"Looking back, I can't believe I even graduated," Mandy said.

She hadn't responded to his cupping and rubbing so far, but that was okay. He was happy to keep himself occupied for the time being. She'd warm up eventually. She always did. In fact, she was usually warmed up before Red even placed a hand on her. She walked around warmed up.

"Christie was saying maybe I should get my GED," Red said, "but I don't see the point."

Mandy turned her head and looked at him. "Wouldn't that kind of feel good?"

"*This* feels good," Red said, sliding one of her bra straps off her shoulder. "That's all the feel-good I need."

"But it would feel good in a different way," Mandy said.

"I just don't see why I would ever bother with that," Red said.

"For one, I'd be proud of you. And you'd be proud of yourself."

"I'm already proud of myself," Red said. "I'm a self-made man."

"You should think about it," Mandy said. She rolled onto her side, facing him directly. "Not right now, of course. Right now, I want you to think about *this*."

She grabbed him in that special way he liked so much.

Tanner finally called back, and Eddie said, "Where the hell you been, man? I called three hours ago."

"Sorry. What's up?"

"A cop came to see me earlier. A detective named Shaddy. You heard from him?"

"Shaddy? No."

"You probably will," Eddie said. "He might not call first. They like to just show up, because they think that rattles you."

Tanner didn't say anything. It sounded like he was moving his phone around or maybe driving.

"You hear me?" Eddie said.

"Yeah, man. I'm just thinking."

"About what?"

"About how to deal with this."

"What's there to think about?" Eddie asked. "We already talked about it. You answer the questions—just tell exactly what happened when we saw Deke—but one thing has changed. The cop asked about Tanya and Deke and all that shit, and I said that never came up."

"What?"

"I covered for you, okay? I said Deke didn't say nothing about her."

"Well, he didn't."

"Yeah, but you and me both know that's why he was coming to see you."

More silence. Eddie didn't like that.

"I need to know you understand what the fuck I'm talking about," Eddie said.

"Okay, okay," Tanner said. "Just relax. It's a lot to take in. I'm just wondering why you said you covered for me, you know? That's a weird way to put it."

"All I mean is, I didn't get into the whole Tanya thing. We all know that Deke was getting jealous, but why get into that with the cops? Nobody knows how that conversation went except you and me."

"Yeah, I know, but why—"

"The bottom line is, if you hadn't been trying to screw Tanya, Deke wouldn't have gotten all uptight."

"Oh, man," Tanner said. "That's the way you see it? I don't even understand."

"Understand what?"

"Why that's even an issue. It doesn't matter why Deke came over and talked to me—whether it was about Tanya or whatever. One thing has nothing to do with the other. What matters is what happened after that. And why. And whose idea it was."

Eddie took a moment to compose himself and digest what Tanner had just said. Finally, he said, "We both did it."

"Wasn't my idea," Tanner replied immediately.

Well, fuck.

"I'm not saying that's accurate, but what difference does it make now?" Eddie replied.

"What do you mean it's not accurate?"

"We were both drinking. Memories are foggy," Eddie said.

"Mine sure as hell isn't," Tanner said. "I remember everything just fine. You said that wheel would come off before he reached twenty miles an hour. You said it would be funny."

"Why are you bringing all this up now?" Eddie asked.

"I've just—it was so stupid, but it was an accident. I've been thinking about it, and maybe we just need to tell them what happened. Or maybe get a lawyer and let him talk for us both."

"No," Eddie said. "Hell, no."

"They might be more lenient if we—"

"We talked about all this already, remember?"

"But if we try to hide it and they catch us anyway…"

"You don't know what you're talking about," Eddie said. "That stuff about being lenient is bullshit. They always want to screw you as hard as they can. Always. The only reason they're ever willing to deal is if they're not sure they can nail your ass. Understand?"

Tanner kept quiet.

"You haven't talked to anybody else about this, right?" Eddie asked.

"Of course not."

"And you're not going to, right?"

"Right, Eddie. I wouldn't do that. For fuck's sake."

Eddie wasn't convinced. He knew he had a lot more at stake than Tanner did. Eddie's record was a big strike against him. If Tanner decided to cooperate with the cops, Eddie was doomed.

"You can handle this cop? Shaddy? He's a persistent son of a bitch."

"I can answer his questions, but I can't make him believe me, can I?"

"Just be consistent," Eddie said. "That's the important thing. Don't change your story. Doesn't really matter if he believes you, 'cause he can't prove nothin'."

"I'll do the best I can," Tanner said.

Eddie had a bad feeling in his stomach.

14

In bed, watching TV while the impostor read a book on her Kindle, Gavin tried not to think about her body. Her perky breasts. Her firm butt. It was identical to Caroline's body in every last detail, but it was somehow…different. How was that possible? It made no sense.

Don't think about it. Don't think about the sex last night.

Jimmy Kimmel was doing one of those hilarious skits where celebrities read mean tweets about themselves, but Gavin couldn't concentrate. It was futile. He couldn't resist. He could already feel a tingling in his groin. An urgency.

He slowly moved his right hand across the sheets, under the blankets, and placed it on her left thigh. The same thigh he'd been touching and rubbing and fondling for 16 years, but it *wasn't* the same thigh. It was an all-new thigh on an all-new body. A fantastic body. The same, but different.

He slid his hand down to her knee and then slowly up to her hip bone.

She made a sound—a soft, surprised moan that said so much. It meant *Oh, are we doing this again so soon? What's come over you?*

He rolled onto his right side and faced her. She was still looking at her Kindle, but she began to grin, showing off those dimples that Gavin loved so much.

He placed his left hand on her stomach. No shirt or nightgown. Not this time of year. Unless it was damn cold out, she wore nothing but panties to bed. She was warm to the touch. Almost glowing. Irresistible. He moved his hand upward and began to stroke the area between her breasts. She had always liked that. Needless to say, so did he.

He was still attracted to his wife, but the desire, the drive, had mellowed with time, as one might expect. Whatever this was—this freakish attraction to her lookalike—he vowed right now, as she rolled him onto his back and climbed on top, that he would do everything he could to rekindle that same kind of passion with the real Caroline—if he ever saw her again.

Red woke at 1:17 a.m. to take a leak, and as he made his way to the toilet in the darkness, eyes all but closed because he knew the route by heart, he smelled something out of place. Familiar, but out of place, and at first, in his half-asleep state, he couldn't recall what it was.

Then he remembered.

Couple years back, he and Billy Don had met an old hippie lady who'd rubbed elbows with people like Jimi Hendrix, Willie Nelson, and Janis Joplin. She also smoked pot regularly and had given Billy Don several joints, one of which they had smoked together on the front porch of this very trailer.

Now Red was smelling it again.

Red went to the bathroom first—priorities—before walking slowly down the hallway to investigate the smell. First thing he noticed was that light was showing underneath Christie's closed bedroom door. This late on a school night and she was still up?

And the smell was much stronger here. Guess she hadn't figured out the trick of laying a rolled towel at the base of the door to stop the smoke from leaving the room. Red had done that a time or two himself when he was a kid, but he'd been smoking regular old cigarettes, like a normal American teenager.

Red reached out to knock, but then he decided against it. Did he really want to get into it right now? Would be a lot easier to wait until the morning. Or tomorrow afternoon, when she got home from school. Or, hell, he could just tell Billy Don and let him deal with it. Why did Red care what this kid did? He barely knew her. She was sweet and all, but if she wanted to ruin her life with pot, why should Red stop her?

Gavin woke at 1:43 a.m., and it wasn't long before his legs began to make him squirm. He tried to resist, but the urge to move them was overwhelming. He simply could not remain still.

He had first begun to experience restless legs about three years earlier. No way of knowing why it started—it just started, and it slowly grew more frequent and more intense over time.

Idiopathic, the first doctor said, which simply meant he couldn't identify a cause, even after giving Gavin a complete physical exam and running various blood tests. At first, Gavin thought that was a copout—surely there must be a way to determine why his legs felt that way—but he'd learned better later. The medical establishment had identified some of the risk factors—peripheral neuropathy, iron deficiency, kidney failure, spinal cord lesions—but none of those applied to Gavin.

Idiopathic, then. He hated that word.

He got up now and closed the bedroom door as he left. Might as well let Caroline—even the fake Caroline—sleep in peace. And, boy, could she sleep. Always deep, slow, regular breathing that made Gavin envious. Out like a rock. He could probably jump up and down on his side of the bed and she wouldn't budge or even twitch an eye. She could sleep that way for a full eight hours almost every night. How did she do it?

He went into the little bathroom that served the spare bedroom and took out his latest prescription. Held the little brown bottle in his hand for a moment and just looked at it. Why weren't these damn pills helping? Probably the same reason the previous four prescriptions hadn't helped.

As with some of the other meds, you had to ramp this one up slowly. Start with a small dose and increase it over a few weeks. Gavin had done that, and he'd reached the maximum dosage recommended by his doctor—and then he'd gone beyond it. So far, he'd doubled it, without his doctor's approval. Desperation and intense fatigue will make you do things like that.

Of course, he was always careful to monitor himself for side effects, because some of these drugs could cause some fairly bizarre behavior.

Compulsive gambling.

Excessive shopping or spending.

Sleepwalking.

Falling asleep while driving.

Delusions and delirium.

Suicidal ideation.

Hypersexuality.

That last one could explain his attraction to the impostor, although he suspected it was more complicated than that. If he were truly hypersexual, wouldn't he be attracted to other women—in person, on TV, in photographs, walking past on the street? He wasn't, not any more than usual. The literature also mentioned compulsive masturbation—up to a dozen times a day!—but Gavin hadn't experienced that, either.

The drugs could also cause fatigue, which was ironic, considering that Gavin was fatigued every damn day from his restless legs. Then there was constipation, dry skin, muscle weakness, memory impairment, edema, indigestion, and stiff joints. Gavin had suffered from all of those, to some degree, in the past few years. Sometimes he felt twenty or thirty years older than he really was.

If only he could sleep. He felt sure that would solve most of his problems. Even just one night—one long, blessed night—of deep, restful sleep would change his life in ways he couldn't have imagined a few years ago. But, no. Instead, he woke every morning feeling as if he hadn't slept at all, or that he'd slept only a few hours, or that he'd never reached deep sleep, but had simply dozed in a twilight state. Not genuine sleep, not in the way most people meant.

Every time he saw a new doctor or started a new prescription, he held out hope that this would be the one. But he also became less and less patient. And more willing to push the limits on his medication. Like this one. He'd read on some reputable websites that if it were going to help with his restless legs, he'd notice an improvement almost immediately. But it had been several weeks. So he had bumped it up. And bumped it again. And again, breaking pills into fragments. Now, standing in the guest bathroom in the middle of the night, he decided it was time to triple the dosage. That amount was still below the upper threshold for his condition, but it was, by any measure, a whopping amount. More than most people with restless legs needed.

Screw it.

He filled a glass of water, shook three of the pills into his palm, and swallowed them down.

15

God help him, he had sex with the impostor again the next morning. He couldn't help it. He was *drawn* to her. It didn't matter that he was totally wiped out from another poor night of sleep. When he woke up and went into the master bedroom and found her in front of the full-length mirror, wearing panties and in the process of putting on a bra, he couldn't help himself.

"Hey," she said, catching his eye in the reflection. "You get some sleep?"

"A little," he said, because that was better than forcing her to listen to his complaints for the thousandth time. And because, seeing her there, he suddenly had other things on his mind.

He stepped behind her and cupped her butt with both hands. Nuzzled her neck.

"Wow," she said, laughing. "Again? Really? You're gonna have to make it quick."

"I can do that," he said.

When Eddie woke up, he'd received an email on his phone letting all the drivers know that the derby was still on. He'd been worried they might cancel it out of respect for Deke Gilbert or some bullshit like that, but in fact they did the opposite and announced that they were specifically dedicating this year's derby to Deke's memory. Eddie got a laugh out of that. The dude was a drunk and a bar-room loudmouth. Probably a cheater, too, although Eddie hadn't been able to prove it.

That was one thing about the derby—it was damn difficult to cheat. Eddie had looked at the rules a hundred different times, and he just couldn't find a way. You were required to remove all kinds of crap from your car—door handles, mirrors, chrome, molding—but you couldn't *add* or reinforce anything to make your car stronger. You could do some minor welding on the doors, bumpers, engine mounts, and a few other places, but not on the frame. You couldn't modify the suspension. No skid plates. No tranny protectors. On and on. They basically wanted everything stock, and they inspected the vehicles to make sure the rules were followed.

Of course, the first year Eddie entered, he didn't see any reason to cheat. He knew he could kick Deke Gilbert's ass fair and square, and it really wouldn't matter what kind of car he drove. He'd seen an old Lincoln Mark IV for sale on the side of the highway near Round Mountain, so he snapped that up for a thousand bucks. Ugly as hell, and all beat to shit, but it ran just fine. As far as Eddie could tell, those 1970s vehicles—the massive "land yachts"—were ideal for this type of competition, and Deke had always won with that sort of car.

Eddie could just picture how it would all play out—he and Deke would be the last two cars running. Then Eddie would finish the cocky son of a bitch off with one huge hit after another. Unfortunately, in reality, some jerk in an El Camino scored a lucky hit early on and busted Eddie's radiator. The radiator seemed to be the weak point in most cars and the drivers did what they could to protect it.

The second year, Eddie drove up to Lampasas and bought an old Plymouth Gran Fury. That fucker threw a rod in the first two minutes of his heat. Again, bad luck, and nothing Eddie could do about it.

The third year—last year—Eddie drove up to Amarillo to get ahold of a 1976 Cadillac Fleetwood 75, which weighed an amazing three tons. Just a total beast. But every time he made a run at Deke— in reverse, so he wouldn't damage his own radiator—Deke would duck out of the way instead of taking the hit like a man. Reminded Eddie of the way Floyd Mayweather boxed. Sure, he was quick, but he didn't have the guts to go toe to toe. Plus, they weren't the only cars out there—other idiots kept getting in the way—and one of those idiots caught Eddie at just the right angle and tore his front bumper off. A lost bumper meant you could be disqualified, which is what happened, and if that wasn't the dumbest thing Eddie had ever heard, it came in a close second.

Eddie was still planning to participate in the derby this year, of course. Not just because Deke was no longer around to get in his way, but because that's what an innocent man would do. He would look guilty if he didn't enter. He couldn't count on Vic and Ray to be his pit crew, though. Not after what had happened with the steak knife. Yeah, okay, he'd lost his temper, but what kind of friend presses charges for one stupid moment? Hell, Eddie had apologized, hadn't he?

And what about Caroline McIntosh, that bitchy prosecutor trying to revoke his bail? She'd been trying to convince the judge that Eddie should be jailed until his trial. What kind of bullshit was that?

Shit, this was getting crazy. Eddie was building a list of people he had to worry about. Tanner, Sammy Fontana, and the prosecutor.

He almost had to laugh about it. What was he going to do? Kill them all? That wouldn't be so easy—not if he hoped to get away with it. Look at what had happened with Fontana.

He was letting himself get rattled. No reason to panic just yet.

The key question right now was, who was the biggest threat?

Maybe it was time for a chat with Tanner in person.

After the impostor went to work, Gavin sat down with a cup of coffee at the kitchen table. He always drank a lot of coffee nowadays. Strong coffee. All day long. It was the only way he could cope with the fatigue. And it helped him think. Cleared away the mental fog. He couldn't function without it.

He was trying to figure out what he should do next.

In those novels Gavin read, the crime-solving couple frequently used GPS trackers attached to vehicles to keep people under surveillance. Illegal, but they did it anyway. Gavin decided he could do the same thing, but then he would have to learn how to use the tracker itself and the app that came with it.

There was an easier route: simply buy a cheap used iPhone and use the Find My iPhone feature to locate the phone as needed. So that's what he decided to do, by searching through the ads online, the same way he'd found the Kia. This time, however, he turned to the Marketplace portion of Facebook, because then the ad would be connected to the person's profile, and he was pretty sure he would be able to tell if the person was a rip-off artist or not.

Didn't take long. He found an older iPhone for just $75. The price was low because the screen was cracked, but other than that, the seller—a young mom—said it worked perfectly. He met her in the parking lot at the Marble Falls Police Department and instantly felt he could trust her. The phone seemed to be in working order, so he paid her, in cash. Then he went to Walmart and bought a SIM card for a cheap pay-as-you-go plan. He activated it and made sure the Find My iPhone feature was working.

The easiest thing to do now would be to hide the phone in Caroline's car tonight when she got home. But what if she went somewhere important today? He might miss it. So he texted her—using his regular phone, not the new one, of course—and asked if she wanted to go to lunch later.

That would be a nice surprise! she replied.

Tanner Stockwell was doing some research on his computer—*how to get a plea bargain*—when the knock came at the door. He wasn't expecting anyone. Lots of friends knew where his lake house was, but most of them wouldn't just drop by without an invitation, especially on a Tuesday morning at 11:12.

He knew who it was. He could feel it in his gut. He turned around in his chair to look, and there was a man cupping his hands around his face at the front door, peering inside through the glass. The man gave him a wave.

Hell.

No dodging him now. Had to be Shaddy, and he'd done exactly what Eddie had said he'd do—he'd shown up without calling. Tanner hadn't even heard him pull up, so he'd probably parked on the street, specifically so he could pop up without warning.

Tanner rose from the chair and walked toward the door, steeling himself along the way for this encounter. Just be cool. Make eye contact. Be friendly. Don't panic. Shaddy would know that Eddie had already warned Tanner he was coming, so don't pretend otherwise, but also don't act as if he had been waiting for this guy to show up.

Tanner grabbed the knob and swung the door open. "May I help you?"

"I believe so," the man said, now wearing a white Stetson that he'd removed when looking through the window. "You're Tanner Stockwell?"

"Yes, sir."

The man extended his hand and they shook.

"Detective Floyd Shaddy with the Burnet County Sheriff's Office. You got a minute to talk?"

Shaddy was a middle-aged man. Thin. Maybe six foot two. Dressed in a white button-down shirt, jeans, and boots. Had a badge and a gun on his belt.

"Oh, right," Tanner said. "My cousin Eddie said you talked to him."

"Yes, sir, I sure did. Yesterday afternoon. Mind if I come in?"

"Oh, sure. Come on in."

Shaddy entered and Tanner steered him toward the leather couch in the living room.

"Coffee?" Tanner asked.

"No, I'm good."

Shaddy sat and Tanner took the matching leather chair at a 90-degree angle to the couch.

"So..." Tanner said, because he wasn't sure what to say.

The detective had taken his Stetson off, and he cradled it on top of his crossed knee.

"Let me ask you something," Shaddy said. "How old are you?"

"Twenty-six," Tanner said.

"Hell, that's young," Shaddy said. "Real young. You still got a lot of years ahead of you."

Tanner nodded agreeably, but what was Shaddy's point?

"I want you to think about all those years when I say what I gotta say," Shaddy said. "I talked to your cousin and he told me what happened down at the Beach Club on Saturday night—according to him. Truth is, I think he might've left a few key details out. I know you were there with him, and when I look at his record, I figure anything that might've happened was his idea. He's got a history of making bad decisions."

Tanner was starting to feel queasy, but he kept his mouth shut. All was quiet, except for the drone of one faraway boat's engine on the lake.

"You, on the other hand—clean record. You haven't done anything stupid, and that tells me you probably weren't the instigator. It wasn't your idea."

Shaddy stopped and just stared at him.

Tanner said, "I'm...uh...not sure what we're talking about."

"Well, I'll get right to it. I could ask you what happened Saturday night, but if you're gonna tell me the same story as your cousin did, you might as well save it. What I want instead is the truth. The full story. Get what I'm saying?"

Tanner could feel his palms getting damp. "Yes, sir."

"And a young guy like you is gonna get a lot more of a break if he comes clean and tells exactly what happened. You need to get in front of this now, son, before it screws you up for the long term."

Tanner was getting lightheaded. Heart slamming. It wasn't as easy to maintain eye contact as he'd hoped.

"You okay?" Shaddy asked.

Tanner nodded.

"You need me to get you some ice water?"

Tanner shook his head.

A long moment passed. The boat on the lake was gone.

Shaddy said, "You ready to talk about it?"

Tanner swallowed hard and said, "I need to think. Time to think."

Shaddy nodded, as if that were an agreeable response. He rose slowly off the couch and put the Stetson back on his head. Tanner couldn't get up yet. He was afraid if he did, he'd fall down.

"I'm a patient man, but don't wait too long," Shaddy said. "You hear me?"

Tanner nodded.

"I'll show myself out," Shaddy said.

16

When Red and Billy Don walked into the Beach Club, Red remembered why he had liked it the first time around.

Like any good beer joint, the Beach Club was cool inside, and dimly lit. Not so dim that you couldn't look across the room and see the dude who wanted to collect that fifty bucks you still owed him, but dim enough that some of the ladies you might meet could more easily pass inspection, especially if you had a few beers under your belt.

You had pool tables and a shuffleboard table over there. A long bar with comfortable stools. Big TVs on the walls to keep track of both major sports—pro football and college football. Lots of beer signage and neon lights and a juke box with a damn good selection of country classics. There were some beach-related items here and there, but not as many as you'd expect, considering the name of the place.

It was the kind of beer joint where everybody knew most everybody else, and they had a habit of turning to see who had just walked in—which is what happened that afternoon. There weren't more than a dozen people inside because it was only twenty minutes past noon, but most of the conversation stopped for just a moment when Red and Billy Don came through the door. Then it picked right back up when all of the regulars realized they didn't know these newcomers.

The bartender—a good-looking lady with medium-length red hair and a shapely figure—was waiting as they stepped up to the bar. She looked to be about thirty-five years old.

"What can I get y'all?" She placed a couple of small, square napkins on the bar.

An Astros game was playing on a TV mounted high on the wall, but the sound was muted, because music was playing on the jukebox.

Red glanced at the beer bottles displayed on a small shelf and said,

"Lone Star, please."

Billy Don said, "Ziegenbock draft."

"Well, ain't you fancy?" Red said.

"Hey, the poster on the wall right there say it's 'For Texans by Texans.' That ain't fancy."

"Whatever," Red said, because Billy Don had been using that same response on him a lot lately. Another dumb habit he'd picked up on Facebook. It was annoying as hell, so Red was happy to turn the tables on him.

The bartender set a bottle of Lone Star on Red's napkin and a full pint glass on Billy Don's napkin.

"That's a perfect head," Billy Don said, not meaning anything by it, but Red couldn't help but snort, which in turn made the bartender grin.

"What?" Billy Don said.

"Nothing," Red said.

Both men took a long drink, and then Red said to the bartender, "Haven't been in here in a long time. Really like this place. Y'all still got live music?"

"On Fridays and Saturdays, yeah," she said.

"We'll have to stop in and check it out," Red said.

"We get some good performers," she said. "And we do karaoke on Sunday nights."

Red thought karaoke might be one of the dumbest forms of entertainment humans had ever invented. He'd rather collect stamps or watch soccer. "I love karaoke," he said.

"Nobody's much good, but we have fun," she said.

"I bet you do," Red said. "By the way, I'm Red and this here's Billy Don."

"Teresa," she said.

This was going well—because Red was doing a good job, and because Billy Don was letting him do the talking, as Red had directed.

"You run this place, Teresa?" Red asked. He took a long drink from his bottle.

The trick was to ask questions without sounding like you were trying to get information. It had to sound like small talk.

"More or less," she said. "I'm the manager."

"Me and a bunch of buddies are looking for a good place to hang out after the derby this weekend," Red said. "This place should work out real nice. You get a good crowd from the derby?"

"Not really," Teresa said. "Spicewood is forty-five minutes away. The folks that live around here come back this way after it ends, but that's about it. Now, after the derby in April in Burnet, that's when we fill up."

"The one that's part of the Bluebonnet Festival?" Billy Don asked.

"Right."

"Never been to that one," Red said. "Any good?"

"It's a blast," Teresa said, "although I'm usually working and have to miss it."

"From what I hear, Deke Gilbert use to win that one regularly, too," Billy Don said.

Why is he talking so much? Red wondered.

"He won most of the races he entered," she said. "Damn good driver."

"Speaking of which," Red said, "I was tore up to hear what happened to him. What a shame that was. I was a big fan, to be honest. I went to the last five or six derbies in Spicewood. Did you know him real good?"

"Yeah, pretty good. He came in here a lot."

"They say he was in here on Saturday night," Billy Don said.

"He was, yeah," Teresa said.

"And he wrecked on the way home," Billy Don said.

"That's what they say," Teresa said.

"Damn shame," Red said.

"Hey, I got an idea," Billy Don said. "Maybe we should all drink a toast in his honor after the derby this Saturday."

What kind of nonsense was that? What did that have to do with anything?

Teresa looked at him for a long moment. "You know, that's a real nice thought. I heard they're dedicating the derby to him, so maybe I could put together an unofficial tribute afterward—like a toast and a moment of silence. Maybe have a display with some photographs. Something like that. I bet his friends would like that. Thanks for the idea."

"You bet," Billy Don said.

Got lucky, Red thought.

"Weird the way he died," Red said. "I'm not one to gossip, but I heard the cops think maybe someone screwed around with his car."

Teresa didn't seem to react one way or the other. But she did say, "They came around asking some questions. I got no idea what happened."

Red said, "The only thing I could think of, maybe one of the other drivers wanted to put his car out of commission before the derby."

"Excuse me a minute," Teresa said, and she went to check on a pair of customers at the far end of the bar.

"I told you to let me do the talking," Red said quietly out of the corner of his mouth to Billy Don.

"Yeah, you was talking just now, and looked what happened. You ran her off."

"I did not. She had to take care of them folks."

"I thought I did okay," Billy Don said.

"You're gonna blow it if you keep yammering," Red said.

"Just making conversation," Billy Don said.

"You asked for my help on all this, remember? That means doing things my way."

Wasn't much Billy Don could say about that, and he didn't reply.

Red noticed that Teresa wasn't coming back to this end of the bar. She'd finished with the other customers, but now she was washing some glasses in a sink. Pretending to be busy?

"I'd like to hear what she thinks about my theory," Red asked.

"What theory?" Billy Don said.

"About one of the other drivers screwing around with Deke's car."

"Not much of a theory."

"Why not?"

"'Cause it seems so obvious."

"Oh, really?"

"Yeah."

"Then how come you never said it yourself?"

"Well, you gotta figure if someone did remove those lug nuts—which I figure they did, based on where we found 'em—"

"I found 'em," Red said.

"Then it had to be someone who mighta held a grudge, and that would include a lot of the drivers he beat in the derbies."

"Well, Mr. Smart Guy, if you—"

"Hush. She's coming back."

Teresa approached and said, "Another?"

Both men had finished their beers.

"You bet," Red said.

"That's good stuff," Billy Don said, tipping his empty glass.

"Yeah, it has a good flavor, doesn't it?" Teresa said. "We sell a lot of it."

She put another Lone Star longneck in front of Red and then tapped another Ziegenbock into a fresh glass for Billy Don.

"Thank you, ma'am," Billy Don said.

"Sure thing."

"Gotta admit I like to watch all them real-life crime shows on TV," Red said, leaning forward, keeping his voice low, like it was a private moment between the three of them. "And now we've got a genuine mystery right here in Buchanan Dam. I'm wondering what you think, Teresa. Did someone mess with Deke's car?"

"I'm not really supposed to talk about it," Teresa said. "That's what the lawyer said."

Something told Red to keep quiet for a minute, because Teresa knew something and she wanted to share it. Maybe she'd been looking for this exact scenario—a chance to spill the beans to a couple of total strangers.

So Red waited and, thank God, so did Billy Don.

Then Teresa got a little closer and, with a low voice, said, "Truth is, I have to wonder if they're right."

It wasn't like Burnet had a broad range of first-class restaurants, but Caroline liked a place called the Highlander House of Buffet, so Gavin picked her up from the office and took her there. Gavin had the chicken-fried steak and mashed potatoes while Caroline had lasagna and a big salad.

As they ate, Caroline said, "I can't remember the last time we had lunch together on a weekday."

"Just thought I'd surprise you," Gavin said. "And while I'm at it, your car is due for an oil change—"

"I know. I've been meaning to take it in."

"I'll do it after lunch," Gavin said. "I'll take it to that quick-lube place."

"That would be very sweet, but you don't—"

"I have downtime," Gavin said. "Might as well get some things done. You can drive my truck back to the office, and then I'll come over later and leave your car."

She leaned close and kissed him on the cheek. "Thank you for taking such good care of me."

He couldn't help feeling guilty. He wasn't normally a liar. A deceiver. A manipulator. Then he remembered that this woman was not his wife, and he felt much better.

"You remember I'm having dinner with Brendan tonight, right?" she said.

"Right."

Brendan was a member of Caroline's book club—the only male in a group of ten. Gavin always wondered about that. If Brendan was looking for dates, a book club was probably better than a nightclub. He was a good-looking guy and probably ate up all the attention.

"Wish I wasn't, but I already postponed once, so I'd better go," Caroline said. "Then I'll probably need to go back to the office. Just for an hour or two, I promise."

He wasn't sure he could believe any of it.

17

"You wonder if the cops are right?" Red said.

"Yeah," Teresa said.

"Why do you say that?" Red asked. They were all basically whispering now.

"Well, because, on Saturday night, there happened to be a—"

And then she suddenly stopped talking. Red was aware of a wave of reflected sunlight flashing across the wall behind Teresa, which meant someone had just come into the club. She was looking in that direction at the new customer.

"There happened to be a what?" Red murmured.

But now Teresa was backing away and not paying any attention to Red anymore. She was too focused on the person stepping up to the bar on Red's left, four stools down.

"Hey, there, Eddie," Teresa said.

"Hey, doll."

Red looked over at this guy Eddie, who had hair like one of those scouring pads made from steel wool. Red couldn't recall the brand name right now. When Eddie turned and glanced his way for a moment, Red saw that he had small eyes sunk deep into his face. His nose was flat and broad, like somebody had smashed it with a pool stick.

Teresa turned to get him a bottle of Corona, which she placed in front of him, cap removed, on top of a paper napkin. So he was a regular, obviously. A regular with bad taste. Red hated Corona. Skunk water.

"Wonder what she was gonna say?" Billy Don said under his breath.

"Good question," Red said, "but this guy ruined it."

Red noticed that Teresa moved away from Eddie as soon as she served him. She walked the length of the bar and came around into the main room, where she proceeded to straighten chairs and empty ashtrays. Funny, because the chairs all looked pretty straight to Red, and none of the ashtrays seemed to have any cigarette butts in them.

"I don't think she likes that dude," Billy Don said.

"I picked up on that myself," Red said.

"Butt ugly," Billy Don said.

Ten more minutes passed without Teresa coming back. Red finished his second Lone Star. Eddie was just sitting by himself, watching the baseball game and being ugly. The Astros were up three to one in the bottom of the fifth.

"Getting hungry," Billy Don said. "I vote we go back to Alfredo's."

"Maybe so," Red said. He wasn't sure they could accomplish more here unless Eddie left and Teresa came back and finished what she'd been saying.

"Or we get another beer first," Billy Don said.

"Hey, I almost forgot—late last night, Christie was smoking pot in her room."

"She was?"

"Yep. You didn't smell it?"

"I don't smell nothin' when I'm sleeping."

"Even yourself?"

"What's that mean?"

"Never mind. Anyway, I'm not thrilled with her getting high in the house. Or anywhere. She's seventeen."

"How old were you when you started drinking?" Billy Don asked.

Red was about to say that didn't matter because booze was legal, but Eddie got up and walked to the back corner of the club, to the bathroom. And then, through the greatest of luck—or was it?—Teresa showed up and walked behind the bar, tending to the customers at the far end again.

When she looked this way, Red raised his empty bottle and wiggled it—the internationally recognized sign for "Need another one, please."

She nodded.

A moment later, she came down and served them their third round.

Red leaned forward and said, "So, uh, what were you saying? There happened to be…?"

"Pardon?"

"You was saying something about Saturday night, and how there happened to be...something."

She shook her head. "Sorry, I don't remember."

"But you said—"

"Excuse me a minute," she said, and she left again. This time she didn't come back.

"You think a gal like that would go out with me?" Billy Don asked a moment later as they sat in Red's truck in the parking lot. "Noticed she wasn't wearing no wedding ring. She's nice looking."

"That's what's on your mind right now?" Red said. "After everything we just learned?"

"What, uh, what did we learn?"

Red shook his head in amazement. "Sometimes I forget what kind of gift I have for figuring stuff like this out."

"You sure have a gift for bragging about it," Billy Don said.

"Ain't braggin' if it's true," Red said. "And here's what I noticed. When that dude Eddie was hanging around, Teresa didn't want to talk. Matter of fact, as soon as he walked in, she clammed up. You could tell she was nervous from the moment he showed up."

Billy Don said, "Okay, maybe that's true, but so what? Maybe he's just an asshole or something. Maybe he's got a short temper, or maybe they used to date and she don't want him around anymore. Could be a lot of different things."

"Yeah, maybe he gave her VD," Red said.

"Exactly."

"I was just kidding."

"But you never know."

"So you're saying she was right on the verge of telling us what happened on Saturday night, but then the guy who gave her VD showed up and she plumb forgot what she was about to say."

"You're making it sound stupid," Billy Don said.

"There is one other really big clue that should be obvious to anyone, including you. It has only presented itself henceforth since we came outside."

Billy Don looked around, but didn't see it. "Which is what?"

"Here's a hint. It weighs about four thousand pounds."

"An elephant?"

"Elephants weigh twice that much."

"Half an elephant?"

"That's right. Half an elephant. That's the clue."

"Now you're lying."

"Of course I am. It's that Oldsmobile Delta 88 sitting right over there," Red said, pointing to the large brown automobile hunkered in a shady spot on the other side of the parking lot. "Looks like a 1973 model to me, but I ain't no expert."

"Okay, but I ain't seeing how it's a clue," Billy Don said.

"That right there is a car for the demolition derby if I ever seen one," Red said. "Big old beast like that is perfect for slamming into other cars. Which means our boy Eddie is a driver. You think that's a coincidence? Deke Gilbert dies, and when another driver shows up, Teresa suddenly decides to stop talking about who mighta messed with Deke's car?"

Billy Don was nodding slowly now. "I get ya. Makes sense. But how do we know for sure he's a derby driver?"

Red thought about it, then said, "Take your phone out and check the entries from last year. Bet you a dollar you see an Eddie on there."

Billy Don pulled his phone from his pocket and did some one-fingered typing, following by some one-fingered sliding. It was a slow process.

Red waited.

Now Billy Don was reading, hopefully to the best of his limited ability.

Red waited some more. He grabbed a pouch of Red Man and stuffed a wad into his cheek. Found an empty beer can to use as a spittoon.

"Hmmm," Billy Don said.

"For God's sake, can't you just—"

"Oh, here it is. Hang on just a second."

Red took a deep breath and waited.

"Eddie Trask," Billy Don said. "He got disqualified last year."

"In the same division as Deke?" Red asked. "There's more than one division."

"Yep," Billy Don said. "Same division. Hang on a sec."

"What?"

"Just hang on. Looking at other years."

Red was tempted to whip out his own iPhone and take a look for himself, but he hadn't done much poking around on the Internet yet, and despite his impatience, he wasn't sure he could find the information any faster than Billy Don.

"Okay, Deke beat him two years ago, too," Billy Don said.

"Interesting," Red said.

Then, after another pause, Billy Don said, "And the year before that."

"See there?" Red said. "Think maybe a guy like that would hold a grudge?"

Billy Don looked at him. "Have to admit—you're pretty good at this."

"Only question now is, is the Eddie inside the club the same Eddie? I bet he is, but we need to confirm it."

Billy Don began messing with his phone again, typing something in. Then he held it up, saying, "This here's a photo of Eddie Trask."

It was clearly the same man, with the same scouring-pad hair, and just as ugly.

"Good work," Red said, returning the compliment Billy Don had paid him earlier. It felt weird, them being nice to each other.

Billy Don returned to his phone. "This is a mug shot, Red. From a newspaper article."

"Oh, yeah? What'd he do?"

Which, of course, led to more waiting.

Red figured Trask had been busted for DWI, or poaching, or possession of pot, or writing a bad check, or something trivial like that.

"Jesus," Billy Don said. "He stabbed a man in the face with a steak knife."

"Seriously?" Red said.

"No chill at all," Billy Don said, which was yet another expression he'd picked up online.

"So why did he—"

"It was a friend of his," Billy Don said. "Not even some stranger. Doesn't say why he did it. Just says they got into an argument."

"How long ago?"

"About a month," Billy Don said.

"What happened to the friend?"

"Says he was treated at the hospital and released the next day. So I guess he didn't die."

Red was about to point out the idiocy of that last remark, but he let it slide. "Looks like Eddie Trask is a violent son of a bitch," he said. "Just the kind of guy who might screw around with somebody's car."

"What're we gonna do now?" Billy Don asked.

"Wait," Red said.

"Why can't you answer me now?"

"No, I mean we're gonna wait."

18

After the oil change was complete on Caroline's Tahoe, Gavin idled in the parking lot and looked for a good place to stash the iPhone. He'd already made sure the phone was turned to silent mode, so it wouldn't ring or make any sort of noise whatsoever if a random call or text came to that number.

But where to hide it? Ah. He had an idea.

In the back seat, on the left side, there was a set of cup holders that popped out, providing access to the jack underneath. He tucked the phone in there and put the cup holders back in place. Perfect. Even if the impostor had a flat tire, she wouldn't go poking around in here—not if she behaved like the real Caroline, who would call Gavin if she had a flat.

So he closed the hatch and drove to the district attorney's office. Parked her Tahoe and then climbed into his truck, which was parked nearby. Immediately saw that she had left a note for him on the seat.

That was so much fun. Thank you. I know you've been restless lately, and tired, and maybe a little cranky, but it will all work out, and I am always there for you, no matter what. Love you!

That sounded exactly like something Caroline would say.

Eddie Trask drank three beers quick, sitting at the bar, in addition to the three he'd drunk in the car on the way over—but it didn't help much. Might've taken the edge off a bit, but his world was still going to hell fast.

Tanner was going to rat him out.

Eddie knew this because when he'd driven over to Tanner's to have another conversation—this one in person, to make sure Tanner understood the price he'd pay if he didn't keep his mouth shut—Eddie had seen Floyd Shaddy's Crown Victoria parked out front.

At the time, Eddie braked hard and stopped where he was, out of view from anyone inside the house. Then he backed up, turned around, and found a place on the county road where he could wait and watch for the detective's car to pass on its way back to Marble Falls. It did, not more than ten minutes later.

Eddie sat there for another ten minutes waiting for a text or a call from Tanner—but his screen remained black. What did that mean? Why wasn't Tanner immediately letting him know the detective had shown up? Was it because he wasn't going to tell him at all?

So Eddie drove slowly back toward Kingsland, hoping to hear from Tanner along the way. He stopped at a convenience store and grabbed a six-pack. Still no word from Tanner. He drove north on 1431, no destination in mind, and began drinking beer. It helped relieve the pressure, for sure.

By now, 47 minutes had passed since Eddie had spotted the Crown Victoria. He went northeast on 2342, which took him through Inks Lake State Park, and past the fish hatchery, and then he decided, spur of the moment, to stop in at the Beach Club again. Maybe somebody would know something about the police investigation. Gossip got around.

So he pulled into the lot of the club more than an hour after driving over to the lake house. Still no word from Tanner.

Eddie finally lost his patience and couldn't wait any longer. Still sitting in the car, he dialed Tanner's number, and of course the little fucker didn't answer. Eddie hung up without leaving a voicemail.

He sent a text instead.

Everything good, any visitors?

That was vague enough that it wouldn't ever be much help to the prosecution during a trial.

Eddie waited, and now he was starting to get pissed off. If that little son of a bitch thought he could squeal to the cops and get away with it, he obviously didn't know what Eddie was capable of.

He popped another beer, and just as he was lifting it to take a drink, his phone chimed. A text from Tanner.

Just got out of the shower, all good, quiet around here.

Eddie stared at his phone for a long moment. He had to resist the urge to snap the phone in two.

There was no doubt what that text meant. No doubt whatsoever. But what was Eddie going to do about it?

His frustration continued when he went inside the club and couldn't find anybody to talk to. Even Teresa seemed to be avoiding him.

"There he goes," Billy Don said.

"I see him," Red said.

"Looks kinda wobbly," Billy Don said.

"No kidding," Red said.

They were watching Eddie Trask make his way from the club to his Oldsmobile Delta 88. The surface of the parking lot wasn't in the greatest shape, but there was no doubt that Trask was a bit unsteady on his feet. It was slight, but noticeable. Trask reached the car and appeared to bump his head on the door frame as he got inside.

"So we're just gonna follow him?" Billy Don asked.

"That's the plan."

"What if he sees us? This truck ain't exactly inconspicable."

"I know, but I'll hang back. If it looks like he's getting suspicious, I'll bail out."

Billy Don didn't reply.

"You got a better idea, hot shot?" Red asked.

Billy Don kept silent.

"It would be good to know where he lives," Red said. "Or where he works. If he works. He might not, considering that it's a weekday afternoon and he's hanging around a beer joint."

Billy Don grinned. "Same as us."

"Yeah, but we both got a whole lot of cash tucked away in a safe."

Billy Don nodded. "And then what?"

"When that money runs out, we'll get some more," Red said.

"No, I mean after we follow him."

"Jeez, I don't know yet. We only just figured out who he is. For now, we're just gonna gather more information and take it one step at a time. That's how these things work."

Trask whipped the Delta 88 around in a wide, sloppy arc and drove toward the county road.

"There he goes," Billy Don said.

"I see him," Red said.

After hiding the iPhone in Caroline's Tahoe, Gavin was faced with an obstacle he hadn't anticipated.

Where would he go now? Where would he wait?

He couldn't very well drive all the way home, because if Caroline's Tahoe should start moving, it would take him at least twenty minutes to get back to Burnet. And he damn sure didn't want to wait in his truck—not for what might be eight or nine hours, depending on how late Caroline worked. Likewise, he couldn't very well go to a bar or restaurant and loiter for that long.

Then he had a great idea. He could rent a motel room. A place to hang out in comfort. Air conditioning. A TV. A bed. Even a swimming pool, if he was inclined to take a dip. It was still plenty warm for that.

There were three motels in Burnet, but one, the Arrowhead Inn, was out, because Gavin remembered that the daughter of one of Caroline's coworkers was the manager there. That left the other two, both chains—the Best Western and the Comfort Inn. He opted for the Best Western, on the west side of town, because it consisted of three buildings in a U shape and offered some parking spots that would conceal his truck from everyone except other patrons at the motel.

First he stopped at an ATM for some more cash. This little surveillance mission was getting expensive—but locating his wife would make it worth every penny.

Eddie Trask drove south to the outskirts of Granite Shoals, ten minutes outside Kingsland, where he followed a narrow residential street to a caliche driveway. After he pulled in, Red gave it five minutes and then cruised slowly down the street.

Trask lived in a rundown mobile home surrounded by a six-foot fence built with rusty corrugated sheet metal that had obviously been salvaged when somebody replaced a roof. Looking through a gap in the fence where the driveway entered the lot, Red saw at least four vehicles in obvious disrepair parked randomly on the property, with weeds growing high around them. A speedboat covered with a stained tarp rested on a trailer with twin flat tires.

"I know my place ain't exactly a palace," Red said, "but this here is a genuine eyesore."

The Delta 88 was parked in front of the trailer, right beside a brown Chevy truck, but Trask was nowhere to be seen. The street dead-ended a block later, so Red turned around and drove past the trailer a second time. He noticed that one window was covered with a plastic garbage bag and duct tape, and the steps to the porch tilted to the right.

"Wonder if he rents or owns," Billy Don said.

"How could that possibly matter?" Red asked.

"Back at the beer joint, you were all about gathering information," Billy Don said. "'One step at a time. That's how these things work.'"

"Well, hell, Billy Don, if I knew you was gonna listen to me, I'd say smart stuff more often."

"Hey, wait a minute," Billy Don said.

By now, they were well past the trailer and had almost reached 1431, where they would turn right, to go get some lunch.

"What?" Red asked.

"That truck in front of his trailer. The brown Chevy."

"What about it?"

"I saw it yesterday."

"Where?"

"When we was pulling into the parking lot at the club, it was pulling out. Remember?"

Red did not remember. "Of course I remember," he said. "I wanted to give you the chance to mention it first. You passed the test. Nice job. While you were working on that, I was one step ahead, trying to figure out what he might've been doing there. Got any guesses on that?"

Billy Don thought about it for a moment. "Maybe looking for those lug nuts," Billy Don said.

"Exactly," Red said. "That's exactly what he would've been doing there. You're learning fast, Billy Don."

19

After he checked in to the Best Western and went up to his second-floor room, Gavin checked the Find My iPhone app and saw, as he expected, that his hidden phone hadn't budged. It was still located at the district attorney's office, in the back of the Tahoe.

The map was detailed and accurate, showing each business by name. But it didn't show addresses for residences. You could see the homes in satellite view, but you couldn't see them in standard map view. A privacy thing, no doubt.

Gavin turned on the TV and lay on the bed for a moment and woke up an hour later, groggy as hell, wondering where the hell he was. Then he remembered.

He checked the app and nothing had changed.

So Gavin drove to the Dollar General and bought a swimsuit marked down to $7.99.

"Maybe they should call this place Eight Dollar General," he said to the cashier, who gave him a feeble smile.

"Nobody has ever made that joke before," she said in flat tone.

He said, "Are you seri—" before he caught himself.

She laughed at him and shook her head.

He drove back to the motel and parked inside the U, where his truck could not be seen. Not that he was worried—there were a lot of white Ford trucks like his—but why take chances? Too bad the Kia was in Marble Falls.

He went up to his room again and changed into the new swimsuit, which was a little loose. He caught a glimpse of himself in the mirror and it stopped him for a moment.

What are you doing?

For a moment, standing there semi-naked with one leg in the suit, hunched over, he had a strange and embarrassing feeling that he was wrong about everything. Caroline was Caroline. She wasn't some weird duplicate or clone or impostor. She was just herself.

But the thought didn't hold up to scrutiny.

He *knew* she was a fake. He could just look at her and *see* it. It might not be obvious to everyone—or anyone else—but it was obvious to him.

He had to stay strong. For Caroline. For their future together.

And he would. But first, a dip in the pool.

Eddie woke from his unplanned nap and lay in bed with a massive headache. He shouldn't have started drinking whiskey when he'd gotten home from the club.

He got up, head spinning, stomach lurching, and went into the bathroom. Chased three Advils down with a full glass of water, and went back to bed. When the pain began to let up thirty minutes later, he reluctantly pondered his situation yet again.

He was already in bad shape because of the steak knife incident—looking at serious time for that, unless he could get a deal—and if he added Deke Gilbert on top of it, he was well and truly fucked.

He ran through the list again.

Sammy Fontana.

Tanner.

Caroline McIntosh.

Could he remove Fontana from the list? Wouldn't he have come forward by now if he'd seen anything on Saturday night? For now, he'd go to the bottom of the list.

Now Tanner and Caroline McIntosh were basically tied at the top of the list. But the prosecutor wanted to revoke his bail, and if she was successful, Eddie wouldn't be able to do anything about either of them. What could he do about her?

The idea of killing a prosecutor—even one from a backwoods Texas county—was downright insane. A huge investigative team from the Texas Rangers would descend on the area and stay here until they had Eddie's nuts in a vice, even if they had to color outside the lines and manufacture a case against him. He'd wind up dead during the arrest, the cops swearing he resisted, or, at a minimum, he'd sit on death row for ten years before they put him down like a lame horse.

Think. Think. It was easier now, because his headache was finally gone.

What could he do to make her go away, even for just a little while?

Now he sat up enough to prop himself on his elbows. A grin slowly spread across his face.

He had an idea.

"He must rent that place," Billy Don said. "'Cause I don't see him listed in the tax records anywhere."

Red was impressed that Billy Don could snoop around online and figure stuff like that out, but he didn't say anything.

They were in the truck, cruising south on Highway 281 on their way back to Johnson City.

"He's got a Facebook account," Billy Don said. "I can't see any of his posts. Should I friend him?"

"Then you'd be able to see his posts?" Red asked.

"Maybe or maybe not," Billy Don said.

"Well, I'm glad you cleared that up."

"Depends if he has any posts I can't see because he sets 'em to where only his friends can see them. It might be that he just doesn't post nothing. Some people do that—open a Facebook account and then never post."

"Wouldn't that seem kinda weird, friending him, since you don't know him?" Red asked.

"Not really," Billy Don said. "People do it all the time."

"I don't get it," Red said. "Why would he want to be friends with some stranger?"

Red had to admit it seemed like a pretty good way to poke around in Eddie Trask's business and maybe learn some things they didn't know already.

"It's called being friendly," Billy Don said. "Socializing. It's a *social* network."

"Yeah, you're social as hell," Red said. "I've seen you nearly rip a guy's head off for nodding at you too early in the morning."

Billy Don grunted.

As they came into Johnson City from the north, Red eased the truck to the right where Nugent Avenue formed a Y with the highway.

"I'm gonna do it," Billy Don said. "Send him a friend request. Say something now if you don't want me to do it. Right now. Better hurry."

"Don't do it," Red said.

"You sure?"

"Yep. Don't tip our hand."

"Okay."

Red took a right on East Ash Drive and went under the metal arch that proudly announced you were entering LBJ HIGH SCHOOL. Red still thought of this as the "new" location for the high school, even though it had been here for years. Back in his day, all of the grades, from kindergarten to seniors, were in one building located three blocks east of the courthouse, near the Methodist church. Now that building was for elementary school only, and the "new" middle school was just to the north of that.

"Too damn many schools around here, if you ask me," Red said, as he approached the area where parents picked up kids.

"Huh?" Billy Don said.

"Where do we get the money to build all this stuff?" Red said. "From the taxpayers, that's who. Wasteful as hell."

He spotted Christie waiting at the curb and he began to coast to a stop.

Christie smiled. She appeared genuinely happy to see them coming. She even gave a little wave.

Suddenly, out of nowhere, a long-buried memory came back to Red. Nothing pleasant, either. He felt his throat tighten and his eyes began to water. What the hell was this all about? He grabbed some cheap sunglasses off the dashboard and slipped them on just as he came to a stop and Billy Don opened his door. Billy Don climbed out and let Christie get in and slide to the center of the bench seat.

"Hey," she said to Red.

Red nodded at her. The truck noticeably dipped as Billy Don got back in.

Christie continued to look at Red. "You okay?"

"Yeah, why?"

"You just, uh...never mind."

"Buckle up," he said. "Don't need to get pulled over 'cause you ain't wearing a seat belt. You, too, Billy Don. Get it together, people."

Eddie figured he could make it to the courthouse annex before everybody went home, and he was right. There were still plenty of vehicles in the lot when he drove past, but he had no way of knowing which one might belong to Caroline McIntosh. Plus, he didn't want to park in the lot, because he didn't want anybody to say they saw him there.

He drove past the annex and turned left on County Road 250. Went about half a mile, just thinking, and then he finally came up with a solution. He found a wide spot in the road and turned around.

Drove back to the courthouse annex and parked right there in the lot, just as pretty as you please. From the spot he selected, he could see to the rear of the lot, where the county employees generally parked.

Eddie walked inside and followed the signs to the tax office. Got lucky and there was nobody there except one woman behind a counter tapping away at a computer.

She raised her head and looked at him with a *May I help you?* expression.

"I'm meeting a guy here to transfer a title," Eddie said, "but he's running late. Won't be here for at least an hour and—"

"We'll be closed," the woman said.

Eddie wanted to tell the dumb bitch he knew that, but he kept it in check.

"Right," he said, "which is why I'm wondering if he and I both need to come inside to do the transfer, or can it be just me?"

Eddie already knew the answer, of course. He'd bought plenty of vehicles.

"You can do it, as long as he signs the back."

"Perfect," Eddie said. "Thanks. You're a peach."

And he left. Now, if he was ever questioned, he had a reason for his trip to the annex and for hanging around in the parking lot, waiting for his imaginary seller to show up.

Which is what he did. He waited. For exactly one hour and fourteen minutes, at which point he saw a middle-aged woman emerge from the rear of the annex and begin walking toward a Tahoe. Even at a distance, Eddie recognized her immediately from the way she moved. The purposeful strides. The way she walked with confidence—which Eddie found irritating as hell. It was Caroline McIntosh, no doubt.

She got into the Tahoe, turned left out of the annex onto Polk Street, and headed into town.

He waited for ten seconds, then fired up his truck and followed.

20

Gavin lay on the motel room bed, phone in one hand, TV remote in the other.

As far as he could tell, there wasn't a way to set the Find My iPhone app to alert him when Caroline's Tahoe began to move, so he had been checking the app every few minutes for the past hour and a half. It wasn't very late yet, but there was a chance Caroline might leave earlier than she'd anticipated, or she might run out for something to eat.

Her Tahoe didn't move during *Jeopardy!*

It didn't move during the national news.

It didn't move during the local news.

Then, just like that, it moved.

It was kind of weird, and he watched the dot for a moment, wondering if it was really true. He switched from the laptop to his phone, because his phone would be easier to manage as he drove in his truck.

Yep, the Tahoe was moving. Going west on Polk Street, toward the center of town.

Gavin hurried down to his truck and went east on Buchanan Drive, which, technically speaking, was the same road as Polk Street, where Caroline's office was located, except that it changed names somewhere around Hamilton Creek.

He passed the Highlander, where he and the impostor had eaten lunch, and then pulled into the lot at Gude's Bakery, just in case Caroline kept coming in this direction, which seemed unlikely.

Checked the app and saw that Caroline's Tahoe had just taken a left on Water Street, about three blocks away. He watched as her vehicle eased past First State Bank and the library and the antique mall, and then it stopped at the Trailblazer Grille, across the street from the county courthouse, which some people confused with the district courthouse, where Caroline worked.

He waited another full minute, but the Tahoe didn't move. So Gavin went south on West Street, then east on Jackson Street, and he crossed Main Street, and he found a spot to park on the south side of the county courthouse, where he could see the Trailblazer Grille, half a block to the northwest.

There was Caroline's Tahoe, angled into a slot right in front. Empty. Maybe she really was having dinner with Brendan, her friend from the book club.

Gavin put on the Houston Astros cap and aviator sunglasses he'd bought at the Walmart in Marble Falls yesterday morning. Then he sat there quietly, with the AC running, just waiting.

Ten minutes passed, so it probably wasn't a to-go order.

Then Gavin saw a familiar person walking toward the restaurant from the north. It was Brillo Pad, the ugly guy Gavin had encountered at the courthouse annex the day before. What were the odds of that? Then again, this was Burnet, Texas—population six thousand. It wasn't that unexpected to see the same people again and again.

What *was* unexpected, however, was when Brillo Pad walked right up to Caroline's Tahoe, quickly opened and closed the rear passenger's-side door, and walked away. It happened so fast, Gavin wasn't sure what he'd just seen.

The guy had opened the back door…then closed it almost immediately. Had he thought it was someone else's vehicle—maybe a friend or family member's—but when he opened the door, he realized he'd made a mistake?

And now he was walking away, just as calmly and coolly as he'd approached the Tahoe in the first place. He reached the corner and turned right, to the west, and was out of sight a few seconds later. There was no indication that anyone inside or outside the restaurant had noticed him at all.

Gavin wasn't sure what to think.

Twelve minutes later, the first Burnet police officer arrived. Followed by another. And another.

Gavin was gripped by panic, and his first impulse was to race over there and tell the police what he had seen. Then he remembered yet again that the woman driving the Tahoe was not his wife.

So he simply sat and watched.

Caroline McIntosh was enjoying the first bite of her club sandwich when a uniformed officer from the Burnet Police Department entered the restaurant, glanced around, and then approached her table. Caroline had always had a good relationship with all of the officers, but on this occasion, she could sense that something wasn't right.

"Hi, Caroline," the officer said when he reached the table.

"Hi, David. This is my friend Brendan. He's in my book club."

The men shook hands.

David said, "Caroline, I'm really sorry to interrupt your dinner, but can I speak to you outside for a minute?"

"Everything okay?" Caroline asked.

"We should talk outside," David said.

Then Caroline felt a sudden panic that gripped her from head to toe. "Is Gavin okay?"

"It has nothing to do with Gavin. Sorry, I should've said that right up front."

"Brendan, please excuse me for a minute. Please go ahead and eat. I'll be right back."

She was wrong.

Eddie couldn't resist watching his handiwork from a distance.

He'd walked south, then west, then north, and back east again, and now he was standing on the south side of the library, smoking a cigarette, and he had an unobstructed view of the Tahoe from here.

One marked unit had parked behind it, blocking it in. Two more units had arrived and parked in other spots. Now a fourth unit arrived, and when the officer stepped out, Eddie recognized him as the captain, although he couldn't remember his name at the moment. That meant they were bringing out the big guns—taking Eddie's call seriously.

But they had to, didn't they? That's what made the plan so good. They couldn't just let it slide.

When Caroline stepped outside, she knew something was seriously wrong. Several more officers were waiting, and one unit had her vehicle blocked in. And here came Sebastian Widmann, the captain. He wouldn't be here unless...

Unless what? She couldn't imagine what was happening.

Sebastian approached her. Lots of bystanders had gathered—many people Caroline knew—but they were keeping their distance.

Sebastian kept his voice low. "Caroline, I'm just going to tell you straight up what's happening. We got an anonymous call about twenty minutes ago. The person claimed he has bought cocaine from you on multiple occasions and that we would find some in your vehicle."

Caroline's jaw fell open.

"You know that's not true," she said. "It's obviously not true."

"What we need to do right now is search your car," Sebastian said. "I know you know this. We can't just let it go. Will you give us consent to search?"

"Of course I will," Caroline said. Then she added, "Oh, God. Wait."

"What?"

"It's unlocked," she said. "I left it unlocked. Anybody could've gotten in there."

Sebastian nodded. "And rest assured we will make a note of that in the report. We're also looking for security cameras in the area."

"If anything is in there..." Caroline said, *then somebody else put it there.*

"Let's just take this one step at a time, okay?" Sebastian said. "We'll see what we've got and go from there. I still have your consent, correct?"

"Absolutely. You may search the vehicle."

What else could she say? There had been plenty of times over the years, in front of juries, when she had implied that if a suspect failed to give consent to search, well, they must have something to hide, right? Now she was in that position herself—either give consent or appear guilty—and the irony was hard to stomach.

The fiasco was drawing a larger crowd than Eddie had expected, and he was loving every minute of it.

He reached for the phone in his pocket, wanting to take some photos, but he remembered he'd left his regular phone at home. He knew the cops would suspect a set-up, and they'd start by checking to see which cases the prosecutor was working on right now. If he made the list of suspects, which seemed likely, he didn't want them tracking his phone and finding he'd been in the area just prior to the call.

So he'd brought along an old back-up phone—a cheap, untraceable phone—just to make the call he'd made earlier to the cops. That phone didn't even have a camera.

So he just watched. And laughed.

Sebastian came back less than four minutes later, and Caroline could tell the news was not good.

"What did you find?" Caroline asked.

"About a gram of coke in a vial," Sebastian said quietly. "On the floorboard in the back, behind the passenger seat."

"Like somebody opened the door and tossed it in?" Caroline said.

"Yes, exactly like that," Sebastian said. "We're looking for witnesses."

"But you have to proceed as if it might be mine," Caroline said.

"You know that I do," Sebastian said.

She was beginning to feel embarrassed and humiliated. Would

anybody in the law enforcement community believe the coke was hers? Some people might. She was squeaky clean, but she herself had prosecuted people who had appeared squeaky clean. Her boss would believe she was innocent, but he'd probably put her on administrative leave just the same. Otherwise, it might appear that Caroline had gotten a break the average civilian wouldn't get.

Sebastian continued. "At this point, I've stopped the search and we've got a flatbed on the way. I have to take it in. It's a safety issue."

She could read between the lines. Since someone had tampered with her Tahoe, there was no telling what else might be in there. More drugs, sure. That was a possibility. But so was an explosive device. Or dangerous chemicals. Some grudge-holding scumbag she'd prosecuted might want to take it out on her, the cops, and even the forensic techs.

"Somebody stuck it in there, Sebastian," she said. "It's not mine. The vehicle was unlocked."

"We'll dust for prints and swab for DNA," he said. "The vial and the vehicle. What I want you to do right now, without making it obvious, is look around at all the people who are watching us. See if anyone in particular catches your eye—but let's keep talking at the same time."

Caroline began to discreetly check faces, but by now there were dozens. Some people were gathered on the sidewalk nearby, while more were watching from across the street, near the county courthouse. There were gawkers everywhere on the block—all the way from the shops and offices on Jackson Street to the library on Washington Street. Some people were too far away to make out.

"Can you think of anyone who might want to ruin your day?" Sebastian asked.

Caroline had to laugh. "That's a long list. You know that."

"Anyone recent? Any ugly cases you're working on right now?"

She continued scanning the crowd. Friends. Neighbors. Acquaintances. Strangers.

"Nobody jumps to mind—not anymore than anyone else," Caroline said.

"Okay," Sebastian said. "But I'll want you to make a list of anyone that might be worth checking."

Caroline nodded. "I can do that."

"I have to ask you something else," Sebastian said.

His tone caused her to look at him again.

"Any chance the coke is Gavin's?" he asked.

The question hit her hard, because it was so unexpected—even though it shouldn't have been. It was only natural for Sebastian to wonder. After all, he didn't know Gavin all that well.

But the question also hit *her* hard because she realized she was wondering if the answer was yes. It would explain so much about the way Gavin had been behaving recently.

21

"Did you talk to her about getting high?" Mandy asked Red.

"Not yet," Red said.

"Why not?"

"Didn't come up," Red said.

"Really? It didn't come up?" she said.

"Nope."

"That's 'cause things like that don't just come up. You have to *bring* them up."

Red didn't answer.

They'd finished supper a few minutes earlier, and now Red and Mandy were sitting on the back porch while Christie was doing the dishes. Nobody had asked her to do them. She had just gotten up and started clearing the table. Mandy had offered to help, but Christie said no, she could do them. That wasn't normal teenage behavior, was it?

"She seems like a great girl and all," Mandy said, "but that don't mean you should let her slide on other stuff. Like smoking pot."

"She ain't my kid," he said.

He was drinking a cold beer and Mandy had a tumbler filled with vodka and orange juice, her standard drink.

She said, "Maybe not, but this is your home, and while she's in it, she should respect your rules. If you don't want her smoking pot in your trailer, she shouldn't do it. But you gotta let her know."

Red didn't know what to say. He wasn't used to having this kind of conversation. He had no idea how to handle a teenage girl, or even how to talk about the situation. It was strange. He felt pity for all the men out there with wives and kids, because they had to live through this hell on a regular basis. On top of that, none of this was his responsibility.

"Billy Don!" Red yelled.

"He ain't here," Mandy said.

"Where the hell is he?"

"He left while you was in the bathroom. Said he was gonna go drink a few beers in town."

"He's the one who should be dealing with this," Red said.

"Yeah, right. He can barely take care of himself."

"In my defense, I ain't exactly got dad experience, so I don't know what I'm doing."

"But you can fake it until Christie moves out."

Red could hear water running through the drainpipes under the trailer, which meant Christie was still cleaning dishes.

"Assuming I even wanted to do that—which I don't—how would I go about it?"

Mandy thought about it for a minute. "I'm no expert myself, not having kids, but I figure being a good parent means you just think about all the bad stuff from your childhood, and then try to make sure she doesn't go through the same crap."

Red could tell from Mandy's speech that the vodka was starting to kick in.

She continued. "Hell, you're already doing that just by letting her stay here. Her dad died, and so did yours, so you want to help her through it. That's what's called empathy."

"You mean sympathy?"

"No, empathy. It's a little different."

Wow, she really was buzzed, making up words and everything. He let it go.

"Where did you learn this stuff?" Red asked.

"It's just common sense," Mandy said. "Think about it. If you got burned by a stove, wouldn't you warn your kids about playing with the stove?"

"But I don't have kids."

"If you did, though."

"Of course I would, but maybe just once, because if they can't figure it out from that, then maybe they need to learn from experience."

"Okay, that's a little less empathy, but it's still empathy—not wanting them to get burned. Like I said, if you wanna figure out what kind of parent you'd be, just think about all the bad crap that happened to you when you was a kid. Then teach from that."

"I'm not sure it's that simple," Red said.

"Maybe, or maybe not, but it's sure as hell got something to do with it. Bet I can prove it, too. Tell me a bad memory from when you were little."

Red grinned. "Just one? I got so many."

"First one that pops into your head," she said. "Don't think about it, just start talking."

Red's grin began to fade.

Gavin was still sitting in his truck, watching the commotion in front of the Grille, essentially mesmerized, when his phone rang.

Oh, Jesus. The impostor was calling. Of course she was. He was too panicked to answer. He let it go to voicemail. Earlier he had seen her riding away with Sebastian, the captain, who was probably taking her back to the station for an interview. Wanting to question her about... whatever was going on.

What exactly had Brillo Pad put into Caroline's Tahoe? He had opened the door, tossed something inside, then closed it, all in about a second. So the item wouldn't have been a weapon. Wouldn't have been any kind of explosive or chemical. Gavin guessed it was probably drugs. That made the most sense.

The funny thing was, Brillo Pad was still hanging around, and nobody had looked twice in his direction. From Gavin's parking spot on the south side of the county courthouse, he could look past the west wall of the courthouse and see Brillo Pad leaning against a lamppost, just as casual as could be, outside the library. He was even smoking a cigarette. He looked like he was—

Finally Gavin heard a tone indicating that a voicemail was waiting. He listened.

Hi, honey. Maybe you've seen it on Facebook already, but I need to tell you what happened tonight. I went to dinner with Brendan and while we were eating, somebody called Burnet PD and said I had drugs in my car. They said they knew this because I'd sold them drugs in the past. Of course, none of this is true, and I don't think anybody here believes it, but they asked for permission to search the car, and I didn't really have any choice but to say yes. They did find something, though...the Tahoe was unlocked. I'm about to sit down with Sebastian right now and talk about it, but after that, I'll need you to come get me, because they impounded the Tahoe. They can't arrest me since I wasn't immediately in possession, and I don't think they would anyway, because this is obviously the work of someone trying to screw me around. They haven't found any witnesses yet, but there are some security cameras in the area, and we are hoping one of them had the Tahoe in the frame. We'll see. Anyway...that's what's happening. I'm just trying to keep a positive attitude and not freak out too much. I'll text or call again in a little bit, okay? I hope it isn't too late. Love you. Everything is fine.

The weird thing was, the voice *sounded* like the real Caroline, not the impostor. He wanted to believe it, but it simply didn't make sense. He wasn't going to allow himself to be fooled.

Gavin had no idea what to do next, but he took comfort in the idea that he didn't have to *do* anything. Well, he had to give the impostor a ride home later, but right now, he didn't have to worry about telling the cops what he'd seen.

But he was curious about Brillo Pad. Was he a criminal being prosecuted by Caroline, and had what he'd done tonight been an act of vengeance?

In the event that Gavin was able to locate his wife sometime in the future, he'd want to clear her name. She would, too, obviously. He needed to identify Brillo Pad.

Red said, "When I was in the fourth or fifth grade—maybe ten or eleven years old—my mom was supposed to pick me up from school one day, but she didn't show up. I waited and waited out by the street, but she just never came. I was getting ready to walk home, which would've been about seven miles in the dark, when a friend's mom drove past and saw me sitting there. By then it was about six o'clock and she'd come into town to get some stuff for supper. Anyway, she pulled over and asked if I was okay, and I had to tell her I sure could use a ride home, because my mother hadn't shown up to get me."

He paused to take a long drink of beer. Mandy was staring into the distance as the sun began to set behind the hills.

"Instead of taking me home, she took me to her house instead, and fed me supper, and helped me and my friend do our homework, and then I slept there that night, and that entire time, you'd think my mother would be out looking for me, but she wasn't. Of course, nobody had cell phones back then, so all my friend's mom could do was call my house over and over, but nobody ever answered. So I went to school the next day, and afterward, my mom finally showed up—and she never said a word about why she didn't pick me up the day before. We never talked about it. We both just acted like it never happened. Truth is, she might've been so out of it, she didn't even realize what she'd done."

They both sat in silence for a moment. The whinny of a screech owl carried from somewhere nearby.

"It wasn't really a big deal," Red said. "Makes me laugh now, to be honest."

"But you aren't laughing," Mandy said.

"I meant, you know, like a finger of speech. I think it's kind of funny."

"But I bet you didn't back then."

Red didn't say anything.

"And I bet you wouldn't want Christie to feel the same way."

Now he remembered how he'd felt for the past two days, watching the clock, wanting to make sure they weren't late to pick Christie up. He hadn't realized why that was so important to him until now.

"She's older than I was at the time," he said. "Hell, she's almost an adult. If something like that happened to her, she'd be fine."

"But I bet you and Billy Don were on time today, huh? Yesterday, too."

Red shrugged. "Just worked out that way."

She leaned over and kissed him on the cheek. "You're a good man, despite all your obvious flaws."

"Like chasing easy women?" he said.

She elbowed him. "Good thing you ain't too bad in bed," she said.

"Otherwise I might find some other scrawny redneck to hang out with."

Red was grinning again. He was just reaching for a boob when the porch door opened and Christie poked her head out.

22

Brillo Pad dropped his cigarette butt to the sidewalk, ground it out with his heel, and walked around the southwest corner of the library, heading north, away from the turmoil in front of the restaurant.

Gavin backed out of his space and went east to Pierce Street, where he turned left, going north. He went through the intersection at Washington Street, and as he reached the red light at Polk Street, he could see Brillo Pad one block to the west, now turning left.

When the light changed, Gavin did the same, easing along slowly, but he was still moving quite a bit faster than Brillo Pad and had no choice but to pass him as he walked past the Family Dollar store. They were now a block and a half north of the Trailblazer Grille.

Gavin made a snap decision to pull into the corner store on the right side of Polk, rather than passing through the green light at Water Street, which was the busiest north/south route through town.

Just as Gavin found an empty parking spot angling toward Polk Street, Brillo Pad took a left and cut between the Family Dollar and Salem's Jewelry. The sun was setting and it was getting harder to see Brillo Pad clearly.

Gavin stayed where he was for the moment, just watching, wondering what he should do, and then he remembered the binoculars he'd bought at Walmart in Marble Falls. He quickly grabbed them and watched as Brillo Pad approached a truck on the far side of the jewelry store parking lot. He climbed into it and backed out, and Gavin saw that it was the same aging Chevy Brillo Pad had been driving yesterday afternoon outside the district attorney's office. This time, Gavin wrote down the license plate number. That should do it. That's all Gavin needed.

When he looked up from the notepad, Brillo Pad had driven

between the Family Dollar and the jewelry store. Now he was waiting to pull onto Polk Street. When traffic broke in both directions, Brillo Pad drove diagonally across Polk to the nearest entrance into the corner store parking lot.

Then he pulled into the spot right next to Gavin and glared at him.

"This is a pretty good list," Sebastian said, "but it sounds like you haven't dealt with any of these people in a while. Months or even years."

"That's true," Caroline said.

"And you don't have any reason to think any of them suddenly decided to come after you?"

"I do not. I would be surprised if they did."

They were in an interview room at the police station. Based on the questions Sebastian had asked so far, he was focusing his efforts on figuring out who might've planted the cocaine in her car, rather than building a case that the coke was hers. But she kept wondering about Gavin, and she assumed Sebastian was, too. Did the cocaine belong to Gavin? As far as Caroline knew, Gavin had never even *seen* cocaine. He had smoked pot on a handful of occasions, and he drank beer regularly, but nothing harder. Still, she knew very well that people could surprise you. She learned that every day on the job. Maybe Gavin was secretly a cokehead. It could happen.

"You can't think of anyone more recent that has an ax to grind?" Sebastian asked.

She tried to stop thinking about Gavin and concentrate on that question. "Everything's been pretty tame lately. Oh, there is one guy who got a little upset when I asked the judge to revoke his bail."

"What's his name?" Sebastian asked.

"Eddie Trask," Caroline said.

"You wanna explain yourself?" Brillo Pad asked.

He'd gotten out of his Chevy and was standing outside Gavin's window.

"Oh, hey," Gavin said. "It's you again."

Brillo Pad placed both hands on the bottom of the open window and leaned in close. "What the fuck're you doing?"

"About what?"

"Why are you following me?"

"I'm not following you. I just, uh, I pulled in here to buy a Coke. I didn't even see you until just now."

"Why do you have binoculars?" Brillo Pad asked.

"I hunt."

"Yeah, right. You're a hunter."

"I am."

"You ain't no damn hunter. What do you hunt?"

"You name it."

"When does dove season start?"

"It already started."

"Yeah, but when does it start? It's the same date every year."

"I have a bad memory."

"How about deer season?"

"I don't keep track. They always announce it on the news."

"Why are you wearing sunglasses this late?"

"I have a thing with my—"

"And why the fuck is my license plate number written on that note pad?" he said, pointing.

Gavin froze. Now he was screwed.

"You a cop?" Brillo Pad asked.

"No, I'm a freelancer illustrator."

"I don't know what the hell that is."

"I create images for a living."

"Like what? Drawings?"

"Sometimes. Ever seen those billboards with the penguin playing tennis?"

"Yeah."

"Those are mine."

"Dumbest shit I've ever seen. Why are you following me?"

"I'm not. I promise. This is all a coincidence."

Brillo Pad lifted the hem of his shirt just enough to expose the butt of a semi-automatic pistol protruding from his waistband. "Hand me your keys."

"This really isn't what it—"

"Hand me your keys or I will shoot you in the fucking face—and I will like it."

Gavin slowly pulled the keys out of the ignition and passed them out the window to Brillo Pad.

"Now you're gonna get out of your truck and get into mine," Brillo Pad said. "Real slow, and without making any kind of scene."

"This isn't what you think it is," Gavin said.

"Just get out," Brillo Pad said.

"Am I interrupting anything?" Christie asked.

"No, sugar, we're just out here enjoying the evening," Mandy said. "Come on out."

Christie let the door close behind her and took a seat beside Mandy.

"What're y'all talking about?" Christie said.

"You," Red said.

"Oh, yeah? Not a very interesting topic."

"You'd be surprised," Red said. "I got some good gossip."

"Only if you're making stuff up," Christie said.

"Oh, I don't need to do that," Red said. And before he even thought about it, he added, "Like the fact that you was smoking pot in your room the other night."

A silence fell over the porch. Christie was staring straight ahead.

"Look," Red said, "I ain't got no big problem with it, but right now, you're not an adult, and if you get caught, they might try to stick you in a home or something, so that means you better not do it. Plus, me and Billy Don could get in trouble, probably. You understand?"

"Yeah, I do," Christie said. "I'm sorry."

Well, that was simple, Red thought. *She didn't even deny it. Maybe this parenting stuff is easier than I figured.*

The silence returned for several seconds.

"Red was saying earlier how much he appreciates the way you help around the house," Mandy said.

"Yeah, that's true," Red said. "I was saying that, too."

"I only help when I'm high," Christie said. "That's just a joke, by the way."

More silence. The automatic porch light came on.

"I don't smoke it regularly," Christie said. "Like maybe ten times total in my life. But a friend gave me some because she knew I was kind of stressed out lately."

"There are better ways to deal with stress," Mandy said. "And I realize I look like a hypocrite sitting here with a big ol' screwdriver. But that's the way it is right now, and in two months, you can tell both of us to go to hell."

"I wouldn't do that," Christie said.

"I know you wouldn't," Mandy said.

"We both know that," Red said.

A fox barked in the distance.

Christie said, "Actually, speaking of gossip, Sara said the cops think they know who messed around with my dad's car."

Red leaned forward to see around Mandy. "Who's Sara again?" he asked.

"My best friend. Her dad works at the sheriff's office."

"Kids talk about all kinds of stuff," Mandy said. "Half the time it's just all made up."

"Sara doesn't do that. Plus, there's another kid who has a cousin who lives on the same street as the guy who might've done it, and he said a police detective was parked in front of that man's house yesterday afternoon."

"Where was this?" Mandy asked.

"In Granite Shoals," Christie said.

"Well, there you go," Mandy said. "Half the people in Granite Shoals got the cops talking to them on a daily basis for one thing or another. Buncha drunks and degenerates up there. That cop coulda been there about anything."

"But this guy drives in the demolition derby," Christie said. "He isn't just some random guy. He couldn't beat my dad, and everybody says that pissed him off."

Maybe it was the beer talking, but Red figured it was time to reveal what he and Billy Don had learned in the past few days. If some high school kids were talking about it, there was no need for Red to keep his investigation secret anymore, was there?

"What's his name?" Mandy asked.

Before Christie could answer, Red said, "I'm gonna go out on a limb and say you're talking about Eddie Trask."

Christie and Mandy both looked at him.

"What the hell, dude?" Christie said. "How did you know that?"

When Sebastian suggested they take a short break, Caroline went into the hallway and checked her phone. Nothing from Gavin. That was weird. No voicemail. No text. Why hadn't he replied somehow?

She sent a text. *Please call me right now.*

She waited a full minute. No response.

She hurried down the hallway to the break room and found Sebastian in there, alone, pouring a cup of coffee.

He saw the look on her face and said, "You okay?"

"Can you ask the SO to send a deputy to my place ASAP?" she said.

"What's going on?"

"I can't get ahold of Gavin," she said. "Whoever put that coke in my vehicle tonight—who's to say they didn't go after Gavin?"

Sebastian said, "I'll call right now."

23

This dude Gavin was freaking crazy. That was the only conclusion Eddie could reach. It had taken him a while to figure that out, because he seemed normal at first.

"Who are you?" was the first question Eddie had asked, followed by, "Why are you following me around?"

"My name is Gavin McIntosh," the man had said, which Eddie had confirmed by checking the driver's license in his wallet. "My wife works for the district attorney. She's a prosecutor."

Then it finally sank in. *Caroline fucking McIntosh*. The woman who was trying to revoke Eddie's bail. The woman Eddie had tried to frame for drugs an hour earlier. This was her husband.

Eddie was holding the .40-caliber Smith & Wesson he'd bought for $150 out the back door of a pawnshop, without any papers. He pointed it at Gavin's head. "What did you see? Be honest or I will blow your face off."

"What did I see...tonight?" Gavin asked.

"Yes, tonight. Outside the restaurant."

"Uh, I saw you open and close her car door real quick," Gavin said. "Then you walked away."

They were inside Eddie's trailer—Gavin on the couch, Eddie standing.

"You saw me, huh?" Eddie said.

"Yeah."

"Did you recognize me? Don't lie."

Gavin nodded.

"Did you know what I was doing?"

"Not at the time, no. But then cops began to show up."

"And where were you?"

"Parked on the south side of the courthouse."

"Just watching?"

"Pretty much."

Eddie stared at him for a long moment, but the man's faced showed nothing.

"You sure as hell know what I'm gonna ask next," Eddie said.

"Actually, I don't."

"You got no idea?"

"I'm afraid not."

"Why didn't you tell the cops what you saw? I planted drugs in your wife's vehicle and you didn't step up? That don't make any sense. And why were you sitting there watching in the first place?"

"Okay, I'll tell you, and just bear with me if it seems a little weird."

"Spit it out."

"One day last week, I woke up and my wife, Caroline, had been replaced by an exact duplicate."

Eddie stared at him for another long moment, waiting for the punch line. Gavin said nothing more.

"The hell're you talking about?" Eddie said.

"The woman in bed with me was a clone," Gavin said. "An impostor. She looked like Caroline, but it wasn't her."

Eddie had no idea how to respond to that. Was this guy for real?

"Who did it?" he asked.

"I don't know. I've been trying to figure that out and find my wife. There has to be some sort of network supporting the impostor. It could just be something local, or it might stretch around the world. There might be thousands or millions of impostors out there."

Eddie came very close to laughing. He had a full-blown psycho on his hands. That, or a crack head. Dude didn't look like a druggie, but you never knew. Or maybe he was one of those whacked-out conspiracy theorists, like one of those people who thinks we never landed on the moon.

"If this clone is an exact copy of your wife, how you can tell it's not her?"

"I'm not really sure how to answer that, except that I can just tell."

"You can tell just by looking at her that she's a clone?"

"Maybe not technically a clone, but an impostor or a duplicate. Doesn't really matter what you call her, does it? The bottom line is that she is impersonating my wife, and she looks exactly like her."

Over the years, Eddie had heard all kinds of strange stories and tall tales in beer joints all over Texas, but this topped them all.

"Do other people know she's been replaced?" Eddie asked. "Her friends and kinfolk?"

"You would think so," Gavin said, "but I'm the only one who seems to see the difference. I know it sounds odd. If it wasn't happening to me, I wouldn't believe it."

"So is she, like, human, or what?" Eddie asked.

He was still holding the gun, but he saw no sign that Gavin would give him any trouble.

"Honestly, I don't really know," Gavin said. "I mean, she *feels* human and everything."

"Like her skin and everything else?"

"Yeah. All of it. Everything."

"Wait a second."

"What?"

"Are you saying you had sex with this clone?"

"Well, I mean, yeah, I kind of had to, you know? I couldn't suddenly stop having sex with her or she'd know I knew she wasn't my wife."

By now, Eddie was intrigued by what was going on in this poor idiot's head. Obviously, there was no impostor, but Gavin didn't know that, and he chose to have sex with a woman—or a robot or whatever—that he *thought* had replaced his wife. How frigging bizarre was that?

"How was it?" Eddie asked. He couldn't resist.

"The sex?" Gavin asked.

"Yeah. Was it good?" Eddie could tell that this dude, despite being crazy, was reluctant to talk about something so personal.

"It was weird," Gavin said.

"But good, right?"

"I mean, sure, I guess."

"So this basically gave you a perfect chance to cheat on your wife, huh?"

Now Gavin looked embarrassed or ashamed or something. What a wimp.

"I didn't have any choice," he said.

"Come on, man. You can admit you liked it. Nothing wrong with that. I bet it was like going back to the old days when you first met her.

Hot and sweaty, right? Doing it all the time, and she actually seems to enjoy it."

Now Gavin grinned sheepishly. "That's exactly what it was like, to be honest."

"I bet it was. Holy shit, that has to be frigging nuts. Did the clone do things your wife normally wouldn't? Oh, wait. She couldn't do that, could she? That would be a giveaway. This gets complicated fast, huh?"

"It does, yeah. I have to say it feels good to talk about it."

"So you haven't told anybody?"

"Not a soul."

"Not even your closest friends?"

"Nope. Nobody."

This was, in short, amazing news. It meant Eddie no longer needed to worry about Gavin as a witness against him. If this lunatic told the cops he'd seen Eddie put something into Caroline McIntosh's car, eventually all the craziness would spill out, and the cops would know they couldn't trust what Gavin was saying. It was a hell of a lucky break for Eddie, for sure.

He said, "I'm gonna go get a beer. You stay right here. Don't get off this couch. If you get up, I'll hear you, and then I'll—"

"I won't," Gavin said.

So Eddie went into the kitchen, listening carefully, and opened the refrigerator, and right then, out of the blue, he realized the solution to all his troubles might be sitting in there on his couch. An idea was forming.

He grabbed two beers and went back into the living room. He handed one to Gavin, who took it, surprised, and said, "Thank you."

Eddie sat in a ratty upholstered chair and placed the handgun on the padded arm. He drank some of his beer, still letting the idea swirl around in his brain. If he went forward with it, there would be no going back. But what did he have to lose? Right now, he was in the biggest mess of his life, and he might not be free much longer. He had to act now, while he had the chance.

So he said, "Now that we've talked about your situation a little bit and I know I can trust you, I need to be honest," Eddie said.

"About what?" Gavin said.

"Everything you just told me about your wife? I knew all that already."

"What are you talking about?"

"Me and you are on the same side. I know all about the impostors and the network."

Now Gavin was looking at him with suspicion.

Eddie said, "See, I needed to be real cautious, just to make sure you weren't going to double-cross me. There are a lot of players in this game, and most of 'em will gladly stab you in the back. But I can tell you're different."

"I am. I promise."

"I can't tell you everything I know, not right now, but I can tell you that you're right about your wife. She's been replaced."

"Oh, my God. I knew it!"

Eddie almost felt guilty about the look of relief that washed across Gavin's face. On the other hand, it was entertaining as hell to watch this kook jump at this nonsense.

"But I've got some good news for you," Eddie said, leaning forward to put emphasis on what he was about to say. "I can help you fix everything. I can help you get your wife back."

"Nobody answers the door at your house," Sebastian said, coming back into the interview room. "But Gavin's truck isn't there. He might've run into town for something."

"But he still hasn't answered my texts."

"I wouldn't worry just yet."

"Something isn't right," Caroline said. "He keeps his phone on him most of the time, but especially when I'm working late, because he knows I'll call or text before I head home. I always do, and he answers within a minute or two. Always."

Sebastian sat down again. He took a deep breath and said, "I need to be honest with you."

"Please do."

"Let's assume for a minute that the cocaine was his," Sebastian said.

Caroline started to object, but then she decided to hold off.

Sebastian said, "It probably wouldn't take long for word to reach him that your vehicle was being searched on the town square, and he'd know we'd find the coke, and he'd be smart enough to know a deputy would show up at your house looking for him. His first impulse would be to take off—even if only for a couple of hours, until he can get his wits together and come up with a story. He also wouldn't answer his phone."

"I just can't even imagine that scenario," Caroline said. "Now I'm wondering more and more about Eddie Trask."

"We're gonna check him out," Sebastian said.

"Thank you."

"As for Gavin, you haven't seen any signs of drug use?" Sebastian asked.

Caroline hesitated. She knew she needed to be honest. "He hasn't been himself lately. Nothing drastic, but something's been bothering him. I thought it was because his business has been slow lately..."

Sebastian nodded. "Could it be more than that?"

The silence lingered as Caroline contemplated that question. Sebastian waited patiently. Caroline finally said, "I still say no. Something else is going on. That coke isn't his. Have you found any security cameras that might help?"

"Unfortunately, no. There are a couple in the area, but none that were aimed directly at your Tahoe. Right now, I've got someone reviewing footage from a camera around the corner, but the quality isn't good. Blurry as hell. You can't make out people walking by."

Caroline had no idea what to do next. Her phone was resting on the table, screen dark. Why wasn't Gavin answering? She was on the verge of crying.

"Should I go home?" she asked. "If someone did something to Gavin..."

Sebastian's phone buzzed with an incoming text and he checked it. Caroline could tell from his expression that he was reading something important.

He sent a quick reply, then looked at Caroline. "Was Gavin planning to be in Burnet tonight?"

"No. Why?"

"We just found his truck parked at the Valero on Polk."

24

After Red told Christie and Mandy the full story—finding the lug nuts, then talking to the lady bartender at the Beach Club and seeing how she reacted when Eddie Trask came in, and figuring out that Trask was a derby driver—he felt damn pleased with himself. It was, all in all, an impressive display of investigative work on his part, and Billy Don even contributed a bit. Not a lot, of course, but some. Enough to mention, but just barely.

Red sat back and waited for the praise. The way both of them were looking at him, they were obviously overwhelmed by his genius.

"What the hell were you thinking?" Mandy said.

"What?" he said.

"You *took* the lug nuts?" she asked.

"Yeah, but we—"

"Don't you watch any of those real-life crime shows?" Christie asked. "You should've left them right where they were and called the sheriff."

"I can't believe you did that," Mandy said, shaking her head.

"You might've screwed everything up," Christie said.

"They'll have to take your word for it," Mandy said, "and no offense, darlin', but your word ain't exactly rock solid—at least, not to the cops."

Red said, "But I put 'em in a bag without touching them. The lug nuts, not the cops."

"They have a very methodical process when they collect evidence," Christie said. "Now, if it ever comes to trial, this guy will be able to say the evidence can't be trusted because you handled it first."

"They might even try to say you planted the evidence," Mandy said.

"I wasn't anywhere near the Beach Club that night," Red said.

"And where would I have gotten the lug nuts in the first place? It ain't like I could just use any old lug nuts. They'd need to be lug nuts from that specific vehicle."

"Are you sure about that?" Mandy asked.

"Probably."

"They might say you know the person who did it and you're covering for them," Mandy said. "You got the lug nuts from them."

"Yeah, and that might be enough to create reasonable doubt," Christie said. "That's all they need to do—make the jury have a tiny little bit of doubt."

"See?" Mandy said. "She knows how it all works."

"I've been doing some reading about the legal process," Christie said.

Mandy said, "You go, girl," and put out her fist and Christie bumped it with hers.

Red quietly drank some of his beer and thought about what they'd said, feeling kind of stupid, which in turn made him mad. Who died and made these two ladies experts on the law?

On the other hand, he had to admit that the cops never seemed to believe him about anything, so why would they believe him about the lug nuts? Maybe he should've considered that more before he'd collected them. And then, if Trask ever did get charged and got a lawyer—even a free one assigned by the court—that lawyer would try to make it look like Red and Billy Don couldn't be trusted. He'd smear them both with the truth, and why was that allowed?

"Hey, Red?" Christie said.

"What?" It came out a littler sharper than he meant it to.

"I appreciate that you did all that," Christie said. "I should've said that first. I'm sorry. I think it's great that you and Billy Don have been looking out for me, trying to figure out what happened. He wasn't much of a dad, but he was *my* dad, and I'd like to know how he died."

Red nodded but didn't say anything.

"Sounds like the kids at school might be right," Christie said. "But how is anybody going to prove it?"

"The bartender," Mandy said.

"What about her?" Christie asked.

"I bet she knows something," Mandy said. "Red said she was just about to say something interesting when Eddie showed up and suddenly she didn't want to talk no more."

"Maybe she just doesn't like Eddie," Christie said.

Red liked where this discussion was heading. He'd figured Mandy and Christie were going to make him call the sheriff's office and tell his story to them, but that wasn't coming up, at least not yet.

"It was more than that," Red said. "I asked if she thought someone messed with Deke's car, and she said she thought they might be right—meaning the cops—and that's when Eddie showed up and ruined everything. Even after he'd gone into the bathroom, she acted like she didn't remember what she was gonna say."

"If she knows something, why hasn't she told the sheriff?" Christie asked.

"Probably scared, or she don't wanna get involved," Mandy said. "I can tell you from personal experience that it ain't always easy to speak up and do the right thing."

Christie looked at her, curious.

"Long story for another time," Mandy said.

"Aw, man," Christie said.

"We need to focus on this," Mandy said. "It ain't all that great a story anyway."

Red knew she was downplaying it—it was a great story—but he didn't want the conversation to get sidetracked, so he didn't say anything about it.

"The bartender," Mandy repeated. "Speaking of which…" She rattled the ice in her glass.

Red rose out of his chair. "Allow me," he said.

"What a gentleman," Mandy said.

"True," Red said. "Plus I gotta take a leak. And when I get back, we're gonna figure out what we should do next."

Tanner Stockwell checked all the locks in his lake house for the second time, including the windows. He'd checked them once already, but he'd been so distracted while he was doing it, it was possible he'd missed one. All locked up tight, and the floodlights mounted at each corner of the house were on. The curtains were all closed.

He wasn't an idiot.

He was aware of the danger he was in. He understood that his cousin would go to great lengths to avoid a stint in prison. If Eddie began to suspect that Tanner was going to cooperate with the police, all hell would break loose. In Eddie's view, Tanner would quickly go from a partner in crime to a rat that needed to be exterminated.

It was possible Eddie would reach that conclusion—that Tanner was a problem—before Tanner had even made up his mind what to do. So he needed to be prepared.

Now he retrieved the .38 from his nightstand and placed it on the coffee table, where he could grab it quickly, if needed.

First thing in the morning, he'd make the call. Tell that detective he was willing to talk with a lawyer present.

"You should get a motel room," Sebastian said at nearly midnight.

Caroline had been sitting in the interview room for hours, just waiting. Waiting for Gavin to respond. Waiting for Sebastian to say they'd located him. Waiting for some bit of news that would make this hellish night come to an end with as little heartbreak as possible.

"You think I'd be safe at home?" she asked.

"I can't make that call for you," Sebastian said. "I can send a deputy with you to search your house, if you'd like. All I can tell you right now is that everything looked fine when Larry went out there a few hours ago. Doors were locked, no red flags that he could see."

No red flags. That meant no obvious signs of a struggle, such as a big pool of blood on the front porch or bullet holes in the front door. But where was Gavin? Had someone taken him?

"Thanks, but no," Caroline said. "I wouldn't be able to sleep at all."

"You need a ride to a motel?" Sebastian asked.

"If you don't mind."

"Which one?"

There were only three in town. One, the Arrowhead Inn, was managed by the daughter of one of Caroline's coworkers, but Caroline decided she wanted some privacy for the time being.

"I guess the Best Western," she said.

Teresa was having the dream again, and she understood that it was a dream, but at the same time, it seemed so real.

It was just as vivid as it had been the night before. She was with Sammy Fontana on the side of the building, hidden among the trees, going at it like teenagers in the dark. Totally unplanned, but she couldn't help herself, and God was it hot. She'd experienced nothing like it.

She could still feel the rough bark on her back as she braced herself against the trunk of an oak. Sammy grunting in her ear. Warm beer breath on her neck. The alluring scent of his aftershave.

She really and truly had never done anything like this before. That's what they all say, right? But she wasn't lying. She'd never had a one-night stand in her life, much less a quick romp with a customer who'd invited her outside to see his new truck. They both knew it was just a ruse, but she played along, telling the drinkers at the bar she'd be back in five minutes.

What would Sammy think of her after this? There was no doubt they'd been attracted to each other since the first time he'd walked into the club—the subtle glances, the flirtatious remarks, the way he seemed to hang around for a chance to talk to her—and she'd been hoping something would come of it. Something beyond a fling. Had she just scuttled that possibility forever by coming out here with him?

But wait. This wasn't real. Just a dream.

And everything that had followed. What she'd seen. What she'd heard. One of the men in the dark laughing as he repeated that old phrase...

Righty tighty, lefty loosey.

But it was just a dream.

Eddie tried to keep his explanation as simple as possible, and he claimed there was a lot of information he wasn't allowed to share and even more he didn't know, but the bottom line was simple: Gavin McIntosh could get his real wife back if he was willing to kill two people.

Tanner Stockwell and Sammy Fontana.

How frigging brilliant was that? Convince the lunatic to take care of all of Eddie's problems for him.

"The thing is, they ain't even real people," Eddie repeated. That was the key. "Not anymore. They was replaced a few months ago, too, and their duplicates—which ain't human—are running the show."

"What exactly is the show?" Gavin asked. He kept squirming around. Couldn't seem to sit still.

"All I can say is, even if I told you what it was, you still wouldn't understand it. That's how fucking crazy and weird it is. Plus, if I told you, I'd be signing my own death warrant. That is the ultimate crime—sharing that particular piece of information. Nobody has ever done that and lived."

Eddie had never thought of himself as particularly creative, but damn, he was coming up with some good stuff. And he sounded sincere.

"I've never even heard those names before," Gavin said.

"That don't surprise me," Eddie said. "They're the top dogs in the organization. You take 'em out and the whole thing comes tumbling down. That, my friend, is how you get your wife back. Not only that, you'd be rescuing the real Tanner Stockwell and Sammy Fontana. They would be grateful, for sure. I would be, too, as well as thousands of other people."

Gavin was obviously thinking about it. Was he believing it all? Hard to tell.

"I have so many questions," he said.

"And I probably can't answer most of 'em," Eddie said.

He said, "One thing I don't understand…"

"What's that?"

"If you're part of the organization, why are you helping me? Aren't you committing treason?"

"Because," Eddie said, and then he took a moment to appear emotional, even though he was really buying time to come up with answer. "Because my sister was replaced, and I want her back. I don't like to talk about it much, but one day I noticed my sister had been replaced by an impostor, and it totally freaked me out. She looks like my sister and she sounds like my sister, but it's not my sister. Damn it, I want my real sister back."

That seemed to satisfy Gavin.

Eddie was getting tired. "You'll sleep in here," he said. "That window is nailed shut. I'll be sleeping on a cot, right outside the door."

"I'm not going anywhere," Gavin said. "But I doubt I'll be able to sleep. I get restless legs and I don't have my medicine with me. Not that it works."

"Restless legs? What is that bullshit? Just go to sleep."

"I'll try," Gavin said.

As Eddie closed the door, Gavin said, "Hey, one more question. If those guys replaced your sister, why haven't you gone after them yourself?"

"Tanner and Sammy? Man, I'd love to. I'd love to make those bastards pay for all the suffering they've caused. But I'm always being tracked. They'd know where I was and what I was doing before I even got started. But someone like you—you have a much better chance. You're not on their radar yet."

Eddie stopped talking now, before he said something that would ruin it all.

He waited. Gavin said nothing.

"Got any more questions?" Eddie asked.

Gavin shook his head.

"Then what I need to know is, can I count on you?"

After a long moment, Gavin nodded. "Yeah," he said. "You can count on me."

"Then let's get some sleep and we'll figure out a plan in the morning."

25

"I can't believe y'all made a plan without me," Billy Don said, squinting into the sun as he drove eastward the next morning. When he reached Highway 281, he turned north.

"You snooze, you lose," Red said.

"I wasn't snoozing, I was drinking," Billy Don said.

"You drink, you stink," Red said.

"That don't make sense."

"I know. It was just a observation."

They were in Billy Don's Ranchero, heading toward Trask's place in Granite Shoals. There was a chance Trask had noticed the Ranchero on Monday, when they'd pulled into the Beach Club parking lot just as he'd been pulling out. But there was also a chance he'd noticed Red's truck yesterday, when they'd followed him from the Beach Club to his trailer. So they'd flipped a coin and decided to take the Ranchero.

"Run it past me again," Billy Don said.

"Weren't you listening earlier?" Red asked.

"Not really, but in my defense, most of the stuff you say ain't worth paying attention to," Billy Don said.

"Try to keep up this time," Red said. "It ain't really all that complicated. Smart, but simple. All the best plans are."

"You get any sleep?" Sebastian asked on the phone.

"Not much."

"Sorry to hear it."

"I keep worrying that he's going to call and I'm going to miss it."

Caroline was having a tough time keeping her composure. Everything had been fine—or relatively fine—just 24 hours earlier. How had it all gone to hell so quickly?

"Wish I had some news for you," Sebastian said. "But we are looking hard and we won't stop. We processed his truck last night and didn't find anything useful."

"Somebody had to have taken him," Caroline said. "He wouldn't just run away."

Sebastian didn't say anything. Caroline knew Sebastian had seen it all, including husbands who had disappeared without the slightest warning. Wives, too, for that matter.

"How did he leave the Valero?" Caroline asked. "After he parked his truck there, how did he leave? Did he walk away or what? Did someone give him a ride, or force him to come along? If so, who was it? Do they have security cameras?"

"Inside, yes, and aimed at the pumps, but not where Gavin's truck was parked. It appears he did not go inside."

"Damn it."

"Floyd Shaddy is going over to Eddie Trask's place this morning. We want to rule him out as quickly as possible."

"Thank you," Caroline said.

"Based on what you told me about him last night, I'd say he's a long shot."

"Me, too, to be honest, but I just don't know."

"I'll keep you posted."

"I appreciate it."

"You need anything?"

"No, it's just that I don't know what to do or where to go."

"Understandable."

Caroline's boss had put her on leave until the investigation into the cocaine possession could be concluded one way or the other. It wouldn't look right for her to work on cases while she herself was a suspect in a crime.

"I'm going to go home," Caroline decided.

"Let me know if you hear from Gavin," Sebastian said.

"Of course."

They disconnected, and Caroline called Donna, her friend from book club, to ask for a ride home.

Ten minutes later, Caroline was in the motel lobby to check out and get a receipt.

The clerk—not the same one from the night before—said, "Interesting. You're the second McIntosh that stayed here last night. Y'all having a family reunion or something?"

Caroline had been digging for her credit card, but that stopped her cold.

"Who was it?" she asked.

"I'm not really supposed to—"

"It's a family member of mine, so what's the harm?" Caroline said. "Probably a cousin, but I didn't know they were staying here, too."

"Hang on a sec," the clerk said, checking the computer. He tapped away on the keyboard and Caroline couldn't help drumming her fingertips on the countertop impatiently.

The clerk finally said, "Gavin McIntosh. That your cousin?"

The knock on the door came at 8:21 that morning.

Eddie didn't want to peek out the window beside the door, but the curiosity built, and built, and he looked. Floyd Shaddy was standing on the porch looking at him. Fuck.

So Eddie unlocked the door and swung it open about twelve inches. His left hand, behind the door, was holding his Smith & Wesson.

"I told you two days ago I was done talking," Eddie said.

Detective Shaddy said, "I'm not here about Deke Gilbert, or even about the incident with your friend Vic."

"I don't care why you're here, I got nothing to say."

"Does that mean you don't know where Gavin McIntosh is?"

Eddie frowned. "Not only don't I know *where* he is, I don't know *who* he is."

"His wife is Caroline McIntosh. Does that help?"

"Caroline McIntosh," Eddie said. "That lady at the DA's office?"

"That lady is an assistant district attorney," Shaddy said. "She's the one who asked the judge to revoke your bail at your hearing on

Monday. You pretending not to remember that?"

"Oh, I remember. So what?"

"You've got a pretty good reason to be pissed off at her," Shaddy said. "And now her husband has disappeared."

"She seems like a bitch," Eddie said. "Maybe her husband figured he could do better and hauled ass."

"Just to be clear, you're saying you don't know Gavin McIntosh?"

"That's what I'm saying."

"Any chance you were at the Valero on Polk last night in Burnet?" Shaddy asked.

So they'd found Gavin's truck. Not a surprise.

"I stopped in for a six-pack but remembered I had beer at home, so I didn't go inside," Eddie said.

"That's quite a coincidence, seeing as how we found Gavin McIntosh's truck there."

"Small town," Eddie said.

"Not that small. How about the county courthouse?" Shaddy asked.

"What about it?"

"Were you down in that area last night?"

"I think we're done for now," Eddie said. "I got stuff to do. Nice of you to stop by."

Eddie began to close the door.

"We've got video," Shaddy said.

"Of what?"

"Of everything you did last night."

"I couldn't give a rat's ass," Eddie said. "You got shit."

"You should come down to the station with me and talk about it," Shaddy said.

"Sounds like fun, but I'll pass."

"How about I come inside and we clear all this up?"

"You want to come inside my house?" Eddie said, grinning. "You think I got the prosecutor's husband tied up or something? Maybe I got him handcuffed to a pipe under a sink?"

"Wouldn't hurt to let me look around, would it?" Shaddy asked.

Eddie made a show of turning halfway back toward the interior of his trailer and talking in a louder voice. "Hey, Gavin? You in there? Holler out if you want this hero to save you." Then he cupped one hand around an ear, waiting several seconds. Then he said to Shaddy, "Sorry,

I'm not hearing nothing."

There was no question that the signature on the receipt matched. Gavin McIntosh.

Caroline recognized his smooth, flowing cursive. Masculine, but precise and very legible.

The clerk had hesitated when she'd asked to see it, but when she'd identified herself as an assistant district attorney, he'd become more cooperative. That alone could get Caroline reprimanded, if not fired. She'd abused her power to get information that had nothing to do with her job.

"Do you have video from when he checked in yesterday afternoon?" she asked.

The clerk nodded and began to bring it up on his computer.

This was all so bizarre. Why had Gavin come to Burnet and rented a motel room? Caroline could think of only one explanation. He was having an affair.

But what did any of this have to do with the cocaine in Caroline's Tahoe? Was that unrelated? She suddenly felt lightheaded and overwhelmed.

"Wait, hold on," Caroline said. "I don't want to see it."

The clerk looked up at her, confused.

"I need to call someone at the police department," she said. "Give me a minute."

She stepped outside and had to fight the overwhelming urge to simply collapse to the ground and give up. What the hell was happening? None of it made any sense.

She texted Donna and said she didn't need a ride home after all. She was going to be here awhile. Then she called Sebastian Widmann.

Gavin came very close to calling out, but he kept his tongue. Eddie had told him that nobody could be trusted—not even the cops. Was he lying? Eddie had said that if the cop knew Gavin was in here, Caroline would be lost forever.

"Then it shouldn't bother you if I look around," Shaddy said.

Gavin, pressed flat against a wall in the hallway, couldn't see him, but the detective sounded like someone who had dealt with liars and con men for years. He had a no-nonsense tone to his voice.

Eddie laughed. "All you people have ever done is screw up my life. You think I'm gonna let you waltz right in here and poke around in my business, you've lost your mind."

Gavin could simply shout, "I'm in here!" Then he could sort everything out later. Figure out who was an enemy and who was a friend.

"I could get a warrant," Shaddy said. "And in the meantime, post a deputy outside to keep an eye on the place."

"Yeah, good luck with that," Eddie said. "What's your probable cause?"

There was no response.

"See, you can't just push me around," Eddie said. "I know my rights."

"I could post a deputy anyway," Shaddy said. "Don't need a warrant for that."

"Go for it. What do I care?"

Gavin could hardly bear the tension. Was this a looming disaster or a tremendous opportunity that he was about to let slip away?

"You ever used cocaine, Eddie?" Shaddy asked.

That must've been what Eddie planted inside Caroline's Tahoe. They hadn't discussed that yet. If Eddie was an honest and trustworthy man, what was he doing with cocaine? That didn't make sense.

"Hell, no," Eddie said. "I'm clean as a whistle. Always have been."

"Got any cocaine inside your house?" Shaddy asked.

Gavin's heart was thundering. He felt that his breathing was ragged and loud.

"Not a chance," Eddie said. "I wouldn't even know where to get it."

And right then, Gavin's stomach rumbled and gurgled with an amazing intensity for five full seconds.

"Who's in there?" Shaddy called out.

26

Eddie brought the pistol around the door and leveled it at Shaddy's chest. Shaddy didn't budge. Didn't flinch. Hell, his expression didn't even change, and Eddie had to give him credit for that.

"Get in here," Eddie said, stepping back and opening the door wider.

Shaddy didn't move.

"Right now!" Eddie said.

Shaddy seemed to understand that he had no choice. He walked inside slowly without saying a word. Eddie closed the door and locked it. He saw that Gavin was watching from the hallway. Just standing there like an idiot.

"What are you doing?" Gavin said.

"Get on the floor," Eddie said to Shaddy.

"You're making everything worse," Shaddy said.

Probably true, but what could Eddie do now? Just give up? Between the assault on Vic, the death of Deke Gilbert, and now this little fiasco, Eddie was facing decades in prison. Screw that.

Eddie said, "If you're gonna make me repeat everything twice, I'd just as soon shoot you in the back of the head and get on with other things. Now get on the fucking floor."

Shaddy slowly got to his knees, then placed his palms on the carpet and eased forward until he was flat on the floor.

"Put your arms straight out," Eddie said.

Shaddy complied, but he said, "Dispatch knows I'm here."

"Shut up," Eddie said. He leaned down and removed the holstered semi-automatic on Shaddy's hip. Then he stood up and looked at Gavin. "What the fuck is wrong with your stomach?"

"It just happens," Gavin said.

"Not the best timing in the world. Here."

He held out the detective's pistol.

"I don't want it."

"Take it."

Gavin hesitated.

"Take the damn thing."

Gavin reached out and took the pistol. "Are you a duplicate?" he said to the detective.

"What?" Shaddy said.

"My wife was replaced by a duplicate and I've been trying to find her," Gavin said. "I figure if you're a real cop, you'd be willing to help me, but if you're a—"

"He's not gonna help you," Eddie said. "He's a duplicate. Can't you tell?"

Gavin stared hard at the cop. "I can't. I can't tell. He just looks like a real person."

"It don't matter," Eddie said. "We ain't got time for it. You'll just have to believe me—he's a duplicate."

Shaddy's left cheek was flat on the carpet, and he was watching the two men, but he didn't say anything.

"I'm sorry," Gavin said to the detective.

"Stop with that bullshit," Eddie said.

"We're not hurting him," Gavin said. "You could be wrong."

"What the fuck are you—"

"What if you're wrong? You could be wrong. I'm not taking that chance."

"Shit," Eddie said.

Now Eddie was regretting giving Gavin the gun. "Well, fuck. There's a roll of duct tape in the tool box under my bed. I need you to grab that."

"Which room?" Gavin said.

"The one at the end of the hall," Eddie said. "There's a red toolbox under the foot of the bed."

Gavin disappeared down the hallway.

"You're throwing away the rest of your life," Shaddy said.

Eddie could only laugh. "Well, it hasn't been all that great up 'til now, so what do I care? Plus, we got all these duplicates running around. Don't you know about that?"

"What's wrong with him?"

"You just lay there," Eddie said, "and be glad he's here. Smug fucker like you deserves worse than you're gonna get."

The cell phone on Shaddy's belt began to ring. "See that? They're already looking for me."

"Not likely," Eddie said.

He put one foot on Shaddy's back, then bent down and took the detective's cell phone. Checked the screen—and froze. There was no name listed, meaning the caller wasn't in Shaddy's list of contacts, but Eddie recognized the number.

"Son of a bitch," he said.

Tanner was calling Shaddy.

"Well, crap," Red said when they spotted the unmarked Crown Victoria parked in front of Eddie Trask's trailer.

The plan was already coming apart. He'd been hoping Trask wasn't home. Not only was he home, apparently, but he was getting a visit from the law.

"You want me to drive past or not?" Billy Don said, bringing the Ranchero to a halt in the road.

Red couldn't help being curious, so he said, "Yeah, okay. Might as well."

Billy Don gave the Ranchero a bit of gas and slowly cruised past the Crown Victoria, which was parked in the open gate, so that no other vehicles could come or go from Trask's property. Red didn't see anybody inside the Crown Victoria or outside the trailer.

"Maybe they's arresting the sumbitch," Billy Don said, "and that'll be the end of it."

They were past Trask's place now, heading for the dead end at the end of the block.

"Doubt it," Red said.

"How come?"

"They'd have a lot more manpower out here if they was arresting him," Red said as Billy Don slowly turned around. "Hell, I had three deputies pull me over one time just because I had a taillight out."

"You was drunk, and it started with just one deputy trying to pull you over."

"Yeah, because of the taillight."

"But it ended up being three of 'em because you wouldn't pull over."

"Only because I didn't realize they was back there."

"Because you was drunk."

"You're just in the mood to argue, ain't you? Because that's—"

"Hang on," Billy Don said, tapping the brake. "Someone just came out of the trailer."

Billy Don coasted to the right-hand side of the road, stopping in the tall grass in front of a trailer two lots down and across the street from Trask's place.

Red had binoculars ready, and he raised them. "I see some guy, but I don't know who it is. Oh, wait. Now there's Trask coming out behind the other guy."

Both men walked over to the cop's Crown Victoria and stood there for a few seconds, looking at it and talking.

"Where's the cop?" Billy Don asked.

"No idea," Red said.

"This is weird. That other dude don't look like a cop."

"If that guy's a cop, I'm a ballet dancer."

Red kept watching as Trask got into the detective's car, started it up, and drove it out of sight behind the trailer.

"What in the holy hell?" Red said. "What are we seeing?"

"He just drove the Crown Vic behind the trailer," Billy Don said.

"I *know* that. But what does it mean?"

Billy Don didn't say anything.

A moment later, Trask reappeared, coming around the side of the trailer. He and the other guy walked over to Trask's big Delta 88 and climbed in, Trask behind the wheel.

"I got a bad feeling about this," Red said.

"You thinking what I'm thinking?" Billy Don said.

"I hope not. What are you thinking?"

"That those two guys did something to the cop, and now they're hauling ass."

Red hated it when Billy Don reached the same conclusion he did, because Billy Don wasn't all that sharp, and what did that say about Red?

"We gotta follow 'em," Red said as the Delta 88 reached the gate and turned left onto the street.

"Instead of going inside?" Billy Don said. "The cop might need help. He could be dying in there."

Red thought about it as the Oldsmobile got further away. Then he quickly hopped out of the Ranchero and said, "I'll go inside while you follow them. Go!"

Billy Don nodded and stepped on the gas.

Sebastian exited the motel office and walked over to the bench where Caroline was waiting. He sat down beside her.

"Okay, if it makes you feel any better, he was alone when he checked in. I saw the video."

"But you don't know if he was alone in the room."

"No way of knowing for sure."

"Did he ever check out?"

"No," Sebastian said. "The room is still his until noon. He could come back at any minute, although that seems unlikely."

"How did he pay?" Caroline asked.

She already knew the answer.

"Cash."

"No paper trail," Caroline said.

"On the plus side, we're done processing your vehicle and I'm having it brought over here as we speak."

"You find anything else?" Caroline asked. "Couple of pounds of heroin? Weapons-grade plutonium?"

Sebastian grinned. "Not really, but we did find an iPhone in the compartment where the jack is stored."

Caroline turned to look at him. "You found a phone in there?"

"Yep. It was password-protected, but the battery was fully charged, so it probably hasn't been back there very long. Did you or Gavin lose a phone recently?"

"No. Maybe one of the employees from the Quick Lube lost it. That's all I can figure."

She'd told Sebastian earlier that Gavin had taken her to lunch the day before and had the oil changed in her Tahoe. That was the last she'd heard from him—when he'd texted after returning her Tahoe to the parking lot outside the DA's office.

"We'll check with the manager and see if that's the case," Sebastian said. "I know those places usually check the air in your tires, so maybe they check the spare and make sure the jack is in working condition, too." He paused for a moment. "Or Gavin had a second phone for some reason."

"A burner phone," Caroline said. "You can use that phrase if you want to. I know how this all looks and there's no need to sugarcoat any of it."

"I'm sorry, Caroline," Sebastian said. "It's just that things look worse every minute. First the coke, and then he disappeared, and he rented a motel room, and now we learn he might've had a secret phone. Obviously something doesn't add up."

"I know," she said. "I know."

"And you don't have any idea what's going on?"

"Not the first clue," she said. "I'm hoping you'll figure it out and tell me."

"There's one other possibility that occurred to me. I'm wondering if he was using the phone to track you. That would explain why it was hidden in the back."

Caroline wasn't sure what to make of that. She said, "At this point, everything that is happening is such a disconnect that I don't even know what to say."

"Does that seem like something he would do? Track you?"

"Absolutely not, but none of this is normal. Everything that is happening is straight out of Bizarro World. How am I supposed to make sense of any of it?"

They sat in silence for a moment.

Sebastian said, "We pulled some fingerprints off the rear passenger door, but they were yours and Gavin's. Couldn't pull any prints from the underside of the door handle. We haven't found any helpful video footage from any of the businesses nearby. Truth is, we're kind of at a dead end, for the time being. That will change if and when we hear from Gavin."

"I hope that is very soon," Caroline said. "I can't go on like this much longer without losing it."

"That brings up a question," Sebastian said. "If he did take off willingly, any ideas as to where he might go?"

"I've been thinking about that, but if you take away his truck, how would he get there?" Caroline said. "It's not like we have a public transportation system around here. You can't even get an Uber. He would've had to walk somewhere."

"Unless, as you mentioned this morning, he went with someone else—either voluntarily or by force."

27

Red stopped at the open gate for just a moment and looked around. He wasn't all that clear on the law, but he knew that once he stepped onto the property, somebody might just decide to wing a shot at him. But his gut told him there wasn't anybody inside, except maybe the cop.

Red stepped through the gate and began walking toward the trailer.

"Hello?" he called out loudly. "Anybody home?"

No response. He walked faster.

"Hello?"

He reached the porch and quickly climbed the wooden steps, feeling them bounce slightly under his boots.

He rapped hard on the door.

"Hello?"

He rapped some more, then waited.

Was that a grunt inside the trailer? Or was he imagining things?

"Somebody in there?"

There it was again. A definite grunt. Somebody injured?

Red tried the knob and found it locked. Well, crud.

"Whoever's in there—don't shoot me, okay? I'm coming in!"

He took two steps back, then charged the door, left shoulder first, and slammed into it hard. It gave way.

"Where are we gonna go?"

"Don't know yet," Eddie said.

"They'll come after us. All of them. The entire network."

"Yep."

"Then why are you smiling?"

Eddie realized that, oddly enough, the tension was gone. A weight had been lifted from his shoulders. No more dancing around, worrying that the cops might come grab him at any minute. After all these days of worry, he finally felt free. Maybe for the last time. He knew that.

Then he noticed the old Ford Ranchero in the rearview mirror.

He was pretty sure it was a Ranchero, judging by the grill. Forty yards back. Not gaining. Eddie knew he had seen that vehicle somewhere recently, but he couldn't remember where. Someone following him? Eddie realized he was probably being paranoid, but why take chances? He pulled to the side of the road.

"What?" Gavin said.

"Just hang on," Eddie said, his eyes on the rearview.

Gavin turned around and looked. "That car back there?"

The Ranchero was getting closer, but it slowed, and then it stopped. Not on the side of the road, either, but right in the road. It was just sitting there, about twenty yards back. Eddie couldn't see the driver well enough to make out any features. Was it somebody he knew?

"What's he doing?" Gavin asked. "Who is that?"

"You think I know?"

"Why are we stopping, then? Shouldn't we keep going?"

"Just shut up for a second."

"Is that somebody you—"

"Shut up!"

Gavin shut up.

Eddie continued watching. That wonderful free feeling from just moments ago was now gone. The Ranchero didn't move, but it couldn't stay in the street forever. Eventually somebody would come up behind the Ranchero and expect it to move out of the way.

Eddie gave the Delta 88 a bit of gas and eased back onto the road. The Ranchero began to follow again. Eddie swung the wheel right, braked hard, and stopped on the side of the road again. The Ranchero stopped in the street, now less than fifty feet behind Eddie's car. There was too much early-morning glare on the windshield for Eddie to see the driver. One person inside or two? No way of knowing.

"Son of a bitch," Eddie said.

Gavin kept turning around and looking.

"What the fuck is he doing?" Eddie said. "He think I don't know he's there? How dumb is this moron?"

Eddie waited some more. He could feel his blood pressure rising. He reached under the seat for his pistol and rested it between his thighs, upside down, barrel pointing forward. Gavin still had the cop's gun.

Gavin said, "You could back up and see what—"

"Shut up," Eddie said.

He was on the verge of totally losing it.

"Stop telling me to shut up," Gavin said. "I'm sick of it."

Eddie looked at him. This guy was suddenly becoming a hard-ass? Great. Maybe Eddie shouldn't have given him that gun. Eddie shook his head, meaning it wasn't worth his time right now, and looked at the rearview mirror again.

The Ranchero hadn't budged. Eddie's heart was pumping. The back of his neck was hot. His forehead was sweating. Why did everything always have to go to shit?

Right then, a cloud blocked the rising sun and the glare on the windshield vanished. Now Eddie could see the driver—the huge dude from the bar yesterday. Same guy, right? Had to be. No way was that a coincidence. Who was he? Did it matter now?

He buckled his seat belt. This was going to be an unexpected moment of fun.

"Hang on tight," he said.

"What?" Gavin said. "What're you gonna do?"

Instead of answering, Eddie took a deep breath. Then he dropped the transmission into reverse and immediately floored the gas, tires screaming as he roared toward the Ranchero.

When Trask pulled to the side of the road the first time, Billy Don figured he'd been spotted, but he didn't know for sure. Maybe Trask had forgotten something back at the house. Maybe he was stopping to take a phone call.

So Billy Don just stopped and waited.

When Trask pulled over a second time, Billy Don knew for sure he'd been spotted, and he wasn't sure what Trask would do. Just sit there awhile? Drive away quickly? Drive away slowly?

Should Billy Don keep following?

So many questions.

If they got out of the Delta 88 and came at him, it would be two against one, but Billy Don liked a good fight. Hard to find one nowadays. Too many guys were wimps. Hell, you couldn't even kid around on Facebook without someone getting all worked up. Bunch of snowflakes, always so sensitive—and some of the things they said really hurt his feelings.

Billy Don was wondering how he should respond to such mean people when he heard tires squealing and the massive Delta 88 was suddenly coming backward at him at a high rate of speed.

Yeah, he hadn't been sure what Trask might do, but he hadn't expected *this*.

He fumbled for the shifter on the column, but there wasn't enough time.

All he could do was watch as the rear end of the 88 got closer, and then it smashed into him hard, and because he wasn't wearing his seatbelt, Billy Don was thrown forward, his chest slamming against the steering wheel.

Suddenly he couldn't breathe. Couldn't do anything but gasp. Could only watch as the Delta 88 pulled forward slowly, about ten yards, and stopped.

Billy Don managed to reach up and shift the Ranchero into reverse, and just as he moved his foot toward the accelerator, the Delta 88 came screaming at him a second time. Billy Don still hadn't caught his breath, but the impact wasn't as bad this time, because the Ranchero rolled backward with the hit.

And by giving it a little gas, he kept rolling away from the Delta 88.

Ten yards. Twenty. Thirty.

Now he'd caught his breath. He was ready. It was his turn.

He dropped the Ranchero back into drive and gunned it, just as Trask had apparently decided to continue on his way. The Delta 88 began to move forward, but Billy Don had a jump on him, and the Ranchero quickly ate up the empty space between the two vehicles.

He plowed into the back of Trask's car with a surprising amount of force, and he could see both men's heads snap backwards.

Steam began to shoot from underneath the Ranchero's hood. A busted radiator—the price he'd just paid to ram Trask's car, and worth every penny.

He looked down at the temperature gauge—still normal, for the moment—and when he raised his eyes again—Trask was climbing out of the Delta 88.

With a pistol in his hand.

Eddie flung the door open and stepped from the Delta 88, the Smith & Wesson dangling loosely from his hand.

The Ranchero lurched as the big man shifted into reverse.

"Too late now, scumbag," Eddie muttered to himself.

He raised the pistol just as the Ranchero's tires began to squeal.

Then he opened fire as the Ranchero began to roar backward.

The door gave way easily and swung all the way open, slamming against the wall at the end of its arc. Red stood in the doorway and waited for a moment, almost flinching, hoping he wasn't about to get shot.

The door opened directly into the living room. He saw lots of ratty furniture, but no people. He'd been inside enough mobile homes to recognize the layout. To the right was a doorway that likely led to the kitchen. To the left was a hallway that ran against the back wall of the trailer, and there would be three or four rooms off that hallway.

"Hey!" Red said.

And he heard the grunt again, this one longer and more desperate.

Then he heard squealing tires outside. Followed by a crash. Then, not long after that, a second crash.

Red was torn. Go outside and see what was happening?

Then he heard a third crash.

Then gunshots.
One.
Two.
Three.
Followed by the sound of yet another crash.
The grunter would have to wait. As Red hurried toward the door, he heard Trask's Delta 88 roaring away.

Billy Don wasn't sure what he'd hit. A fence? Another vehicle? He hoped he hadn't hurt anybody, but otherwise, he didn't really care.

He was too busy worrying about the bullet hole. It was bleeding. And he was getting lightheaded.

Damn. He sure hadn't expected Eddie Trask to do that.

The windshield in front of him had a neat little hole in it. He looked in his mirrors to see what was back there, but it was hard to tell what he was seeing.

Woozy.

Damn.

Someone was at the driver's door now, talking to him.

"You okay?" Red asked, breathing hard.

Billy Don was nodding. Or was he?

Red opened the door and leaned in to get a better look at him. "Jesus."

"No chill at all," Billy Don said.

"What?"

"Trask had no chill at all," Billy Don said. He thought it was funny. Something else he'd picked up from Facebook that would piss Red off.

Red took his phone out and dialed three numbers.

28

Gavin hadn't said a word in several minutes, until he asked, "Who was that guy?"

"Another member of the network. Another duplicate. Not a real person."

Eddie was doing his best to conceal how rattled he was. When he'd fired the shots, he'd been fine, but now, his hands were trembling and he felt nauseous.

"Did you know him?" Gavin asked.

"Saw him at a bar yesterday. Him and another guy."

"That's the only time you saw him?"

"Yep. But he was following me then and he was following us just now."

Eddie knew he didn't have much time. Somebody would report the shooting, possibly the big man himself, if he was still alive. Cops would arrive at Eddie's trailer in minutes. They'd find Shaddy inside. That's why Eddie had immediately driven east on 1431, away from Granite Shoals, and why he'd chosen the Delta 88. None of the local cops had seen him driving it, whereas they'd all seen his truck multiple times over the years. Problem was, the big man could describe the vehicle—again, if he was still alive and conscious.

"How did you know he was a duplicate?" Gavin asked.

"Same way you could tell your wife had been replaced. You could just look at her and tell, right?"

"Yeah, but that was my wife," Gavin said. "I couldn't tell with the detective."

Eddie shrugged. "I don't know, man, I can just tell. I've been aware of the network longer than you have, so that's probably it. I've been around more duplicates."

Gavin didn't say anything else.

Eddie hung a left and went north on County Road 122. This was a narrow, sparsely traveled road that ran parallel to Highway 281, which was about a mile and a half to the east. This county road would cross FM 1855 about three miles ahead. They could go east on 1855 to 281, or continue north on County Road 121, which would peter out about a mile later, past a rock yard and a quarry.

Was it better to run or to hide?

Once the cops found Shaddy, they'd be out in force—including at least one chopper in the air and dozens of cops on the ground. They'd use dogs in the daytime and infrared radar at night. News of the manhunt would spread quickly, across the county and then around the state. Eddie's mug shot would be everywhere, along with Gavin's driver's license photo. The cops would offer a reward for tips leading to their capture. It would be a huge fucking deal.

Run or hide?

Caroline pulled into her long driveway and proceeded slowly toward the house. Why was she nervous? There was no reason to be nervous. Nobody was waiting inside for her, and if anybody was, it would be Gavin.

But he wouldn't be there.

And he wasn't.

When she opened the front door, instead of letting the silence spook her, she searched every room of the house. Nothing was missing or out of place. All the doors and windows were locked. There were no hidden notes or clues of any kind.

She went to the keypad and armed the alarm. Expensive system, but Gavin had insisted they install it. He knew her job carried some risks, even though she'd reassured him that the odds were slim that anything would ever happen.

It was nearly one o'clock, so she poured herself three fingers of Garrison Brothers over ice and sat down on the couch. Then turned on some soothing music, low. The AC kicked on, then shut off again.

She thought it might be wise to phone the neighbors on either side and let them know what was going on, although they probably already knew. The homes out here each sat on several acres, and the dense walls of cedar and oak between the homes created privacy, but the neighbors could still keep an eye out for Gavin—or anybody else who might approach the house. She'd call them later.

She sent a text to Sebastian Widmann. *All good here. No Gavin. Plz let me know if you hear anything.*

He replied three minutes later. *Will do.*

She set her phone on the coffee table. So far, she had received a combined total of forty-three emails and voicemails from members of the media. She wasn't ready to comment yet. What would she say? She had adjusted the settings on her phone so some of the more persistent callers wouldn't ring through anymore.

She sipped some bourbon and wondered whether her life would ever be normal again.

Red had been inside an interview room a few times before. He'd been questioned by cops plenty of times, and he'd been asked to go back to the station nearly as many times, but usually, he told them to forget it. He knew his rights. They couldn't force you to talk. Couldn't force you to go anywhere unless they had a warrant. This time he was willing to talk, because this time was different.

For starters, he wasn't guilty of anything. Not as far as he knew.

And second, he wanted to tell them everything he knew because of what had happened to Billy Don. The bullet had hit him about an inch above his left nipple. There was blood, but not as much as Red would have expected.

"I've seen pigs bleed a lot more than this and live," Red had said to him while they waited for the cops and the ambulance.

"You always know the right thing to say," Billy Don said, trying to laugh, but coughing instead.

Red pressed a wad of Dairy Queen napkins to the wound, all the time wondering what was directly behind the left nipple. Not the heart, obviously, or Billy Don would've been a goner for sure. A lung? Any major arteries? No idea. Truth was, Red knew more about the insides of a deer than of a human.

Billy Don said, "If I die—"

"Shut up," Red said, and then he'd finally heard the sirens. When he looked down again, Billy Don was unconscious.

After the ambulance had left, Red had talked to several deputies at the scene, telling them everything he knew, including the fact that he'd seen Eddie Trask come out of the trailer with some other dude. Then, knowing that Shaddy was probably inside, Red had kicked the door in, then heard tires squealing, and gunshots, and an engine roaring, and so on.

That was more than an hour ago, and Red had been waiting for thirty minutes in this stupid room inside the Burnet County Sheriff's Office, which told him Trask's place must've been just outside the city limits, otherwise the Granite Shoals city cops would be handing it.

Ten more minutes passed, and Red had had enough, and just as he stood up to get out of there and go to the hospital, the door opened and in came a slender middle-aged guy wearing jeans, boots, and a dark-blue polo shirt. A badge was clipped to his belt. A detective, obviously, but Red didn't care who he was.

"About damn time," Red said. "How long do you think I'm gonna sit in here waiting?"

"I apologize for the delay," the cop said. "My name is Glen Tuggle. I'm an investigator with the sheriff's office. I need to get your statement and ask you some questions."

"Yeah, if you're lucky," Red said. "First I need to know what the hell's going on with Billy Don."

Tuggle pulled out a chair and sat down across from Red.

"Last I knew, he was in surgery."

"Is he gonna live?"

"I'm afraid I don't know the answer to that."

"You're gonna need to find out."

"I will, but right now, two dangerous men are on the loose, so I would appreciate it if—"

"Nope," Red said. "You want anything more from me, you'll call the hospital right now for an update. Until then, I ain't saying one more damn thing. Lock me up if you have to. I don't care."

Tuggle stared at him for a moment.

Red said, "That's my best friend. What would you do if your best friend got shot?"

Tuggle nodded slowly, then said, "Fair enough. I'll be right back."

The detective got up and left the room, closing the door behind him.

Red looked at his phone but nobody had called or texted. He'd called Mandy earlier, while he was waiting, and given her a quick rundown on what had happened. She was on her way to the hospital. They hadn't told Christie yet. She was in school.

Three minutes later, Tuggle came back in and sat down.

"He's still in surgery, but beyond that, we just don't know anything. Sorry I can't tell you more."

Red figured that the simple fact that Billy Don was still alive nearly two hours after being shot was a good sign. The big man was a tough son of a bitch. He'd been shot once before, in the stomach, and that had happened just two days after he'd been bitten by a rattlesnake. Of course, Billy Don had bitched and moaned about both injuries, but the bottom line was that he'd recovered quickly from both. Being such a big, stubborn bastard must've helped.

Red nodded his thanks. "How's that other detective doing?"

Red hadn't gone back in the trailer after calling 911, because he was too busy tending to Billy Don.

"Just fine," Tuggle said. "Now, I want to hear your full story, but first I want to talk about the two men you saw come out of the trailer."

"Eddie Trask and some other guy."

"What did the other guy look like?"

Red described him. Just an average guy with blondish hair and glasses. Probably the kind of guy that women considered "cute." Looked and dressed more like an Austinite than a Blanco County resident. He'd been wearing cargo shorts and some kind of hipster loafers.

"You didn't see the actual shooting?" Tuggle asked.

"No, but I heard it. It was either Trask or the other guy that did it."

"How do you know that for sure?"

"Because there wasn't anybody else around."

"Think you could pick either man out of a photo line-up?" Tuggle asked.

"I think so, yeah. Eddie Trask, for sure. Probably the other guy, too."

"Then let's give it a try," Tuggle said.

He'd brought a manila envelope with him, and now he opened it and extracted a small stack of documents. He gave Red some instructions first—saying that the suspect might not even be in the line-up, and talking about how a person's features could change over time, and some other bullshit. Then he put six photos on the table and asked if Red recognized anyone.

"That's Trask right there," Red said, tapping one.

"Where do you recognize him from?"

"Saw him two hours ago coming out of his trailer."

Tuggle circled Trask with a pen and had Red sign and date beside it. Then he placed six more photos on the table.

"That guy right there," Red said, before Tuggle even asked. "He was with Trask earlier."

Tuggle paused for a moment to text something to somebody.

Then he circled the photo and again had Red sign and date it.

"Who is he?" Red asked.

"We'll get back to that," Tuggle said. "What were you doing outside Eddie Trask's place?"

Red grinned, because by now he had come up with a version of events that was better than the truth. He didn't need to tell this cop they'd been planning to plant evidence at Trask's place.

"I'm guessing somebody told you me and Billy Don found some lug nuts outside the Beach Club," Red said. "I mentioned that to a deputy outside Trask's place earlier."

"I got the basics, yes."

"And that we collected them into a Sonic bag," Red said.

"Right."

"We was real careful," Red said. "Didn't touch 'em with our hands or nothing like that."

"That's good," Tuggle said. "Real good. And why were you over at Trask's this morning?"

"Well, we'd been trying to decide what to do with those nuts," Red said. "I don't mind telling you—without meaning no offense—that I ain't real fond of the cops. I've had some bad experiences, and I figured we'd do just as well keeping those lug nuts 'til the time was right."

"Okay," Tuggle said. "Good. And..."

"What was we doing at Trask's?"

"Right."

"It's actually pretty funny," Red said. "See, we had a plan. A great plan. Clever as hell. But then we saw the Crown Vic outside, and the plan sort of went to shit."

"What was the plan?" Tuggle asked.

"Ever heard of that mystery writer Edgar Allan Pope?"

"Poe?"

"Right. And you remember that story he wrote called *The Tattletale Heart*?"

"*The Tell-Tale Heart*?"

"That's the one," Red said. "It all started from there."

29

The phone rang, jolting Caroline awake. She hadn't even realized she'd dozed off on the couch, but clearly she had, still exhausted from her lack of sleep the night before. The bourbon obviously hadn't helped.

She quickly grabbed her phone off the coffee table and checked the caller. Sebastian Widmann.

"What's up?" she said.

"You okay?" Sebastian said.

"Just a little groggy from a nap," she said. "What's going on?"

"Gavin has been spotted, but you're not going to like where he was last seen—if our witness is correct."

"Tell me," Caroline said. "What is it? What's happening?"

"Brace yourself, okay? He and Eddie Trask are currently on the run, after leaving Floyd Shaddy bound up in Trask's trailer."

"What are you talking about?"

"Floyd went over there to question Trask, remember? We don't know exactly what happened, but according to our witness, one of them—either Trask or Gavin—fired some shots and wounded a man named Billy Don Craddock. You know him?"

"I don't think so. Please, Sebastian, please—start at the beginning and tell me what you're talking about. I'm so confused."

"Okay, sorry. The witness is named Red O'Brien and his friend is Billy Don Craddock. They were going over to Trask's place for some unspecified reason when they saw Trask and another man, ostensibly Gavin, come out of the trailer. O'Brien picked Gavin out of a photo line-up."

"And what happened?"

"O'Brien and Craddock knew that Floyd was inside because they saw his car outside. So when Trask and this other man left, Craddock followed them while O'Brien went inside the trailer to look for Floyd. Apparently Trask and Gavin saw Craddock following them and one of them fired several shots at him. He's in surgery right now."

"This is crazy," Caroline said. "There's no way it's true. Are you saying Gavin was going along with Trask willingly?"

"That's what it sounds like."

"I don't believe it," Caroline said.

"I'm sorry, Caroline," Sebastian said.

"Either it wasn't Gavin," she said, "or Trask was forcing him to go along with it."

Caroline could tell from the ensuing silence that Sebastian didn't believe her. She didn't blame him.

Then he said, "There's more."

"What is it?"

"Floyd said Gavin was saying some very strange stuff—talking about how you'd been replaced by a duplicate."

Caroline hesitated. Every piece of information she shared might be helpful for Sebastian's investigation—or it might be used against Gavin in the future. But she had no choice.

She said, "Earlier this week—or maybe it was late last week—Gavin made an odd remark about me being replaced by a duplicate. He wondered where the real Caroline was. When I pressed him on it, he dismissed it as a bad joke. He never said anything about it again. I thought he was kidding."

"Okay," Sebastian said, and he imparted so much with that one word. That one *Okay*—the way he said it—meant he realized they were dealing with a man who wasn't completely in control of his faculties. Or maybe she was imagining it. Maybe she was on the verge of losing it herself.

"The alternative was that he was having some kind of break from reality, and I didn't see any other sign of that," Caroline said. "He did not seem delusional to me. A little out of sorts lately—maybe a little depressed, but that's it. Nothing else unusual. So I let it go."

Sebastian said, "I'm not sure what to think of all this."

"You're being kind," Caroline said. "You think Gavin is a nut case, and possibly a drug user, or maybe both, and he's mixed up with Eddie Trask, and now they've gone off the rails together. That's sure how it looks. Even I can see that."

Sebastian took a deep breath. "We just need to talk to them both," he said.

"Any idea where they went?" Caroline asked.

"We're looking for them right now," Sebastian said. "They're driving an old Delta 88, so that should be fairly easy to spot."

"We can't stay here," Eddie said. "Sooner or later somebody's gonna come looking this way."

They'd driven north on County Road 121, past the quarry. There wasn't much up here except raw undeveloped land and a few scattered outbuildings. The damn road wasn't even paved. Eddie had found a small grove of oak trees off to one side of the road and pulled the Delta 88 right into the middle of them, the low-hanging branches scraping both sides of the car as he plowed his way through.

Gavin couldn't decide if it was a brilliant hiding spot, or a terrible one. They would be well-hidden from a search helicopter, but if a deputy drove up this way, he would probably see the tire marks through the tall grass, and that would lead him to the car tucked underneath the trees.

"We don't have a lot of options," Gavin said.

An hour earlier, he'd understood why they'd taped the detective up and fled—it made sense—but now he was wondering if that was the wisest choice. Was the detective really an impostor? Gavin was starting to wonder if Eddie was as good at spotting impostors as he claimed to be.

"Gotta think of something," Eddie said.

"I don't know this area at all," Gavin said.

"If we go straight north about two or three miles, we'd hit Park Road 4. We could walk over there easy. Ain't hardly nothing between here and there. A few houses on acreage, but we can go around them. You know that road?"

"Sort of."

"It runs from 281 to the cave."

"Which cave?"

"Jesus frigging Christ, are you serious? Where are you from?"

"We just moved out here a few years ago from Austin," Gavin said. "But is this what you want to do? Argue about minor bullshit?"

"It's Longhorn Caverns," Eddie said. "People come from miles around to go there. It's a goddamn *tourist* attraction."

"So what?" Gavin said.

"That means it's got a lot of people coming and going who ain't from around here. And *that* means they're less likely to know about two dangerous dudes being on the run."

"Oh," Gavin said.

"This is why you need to just listen to me and do what I say," Eddie said. "Let me do the thinking. I'll get us out of this."

Gavin wondered about the man in the Ranchero. Had he been hit by any of the shots? Who was he? Had he called the police afterward? Was he alive?

"There might not even be a search going on yet," Gavin said.

"What did I just tell you?" Eddie said.

Gavin was really starting to dislike this guy.

Thirty minutes after leaving the sheriff's office, Red sat with Mandy in a small waiting area near the emergency department. They had the room to themselves, which was nice. There was a larger waiting room around the corner, but it was filled with people yammering and crying and Red couldn't deal with that. The whole place smelled like cleaning fluids and possibly vomit. It was all depressing as hell, but Red couldn't help but grin when he remembered what he'd told Glen Tuggle.

The detective had indicated he was familiar with the short story in question, but Red reminded him what it was about.

"It's the one where a guy kills an old man who has an evil eye, and then he hides him under the floorboards, but he—"

"Keeps hearing the old man's heartbeat," Tuggle said, getting kind of impatient.

"Or he *thinks* he does," Red said, "and that was the genius of it. See, nobody else heard it, but the storyteller guy did, and that's because it wasn't really there. You knew that, right?"

"Yes."

"After awhile, it drives the guy crazy."

Red was happy to explain the gist of the story to the detective, because Red had a knack for understanding literature. He didn't need a bunch of schooling for that. It just came natural.

"And?" Tuggle said.

"I had this great idea that we could do the same thing to Trask."

Red waited for Tuggle to ask what the idea was exactly.

"How so?" Tuggle said.

"Okay, we was gonna take some lug nuts—not the lug nuts we found, but some other lug nuts—and start putting them in places where Eddie Trask would find them. We'd put one in his mailbox, one on the dashboard in his truck, one on his doormat, and so on. We was gonna drive him crazy, just like that story, until he couldn't handle it any more and confessed."

Red knew that a detective like Tuggle wouldn't tell Red how smart he was—they weren't supposed to do that sort of thing—and he didn't. Instead, Tuggle simply said, "That's why you were going over there earlier? To start on this plan of yours?"

The admiration in Tuggle's voice had been evident, and remembering that moment now made Red feel pretty good, until he also remembered how the plan had led to disaster. Who would've guessed that crazy redneck would've started shooting like that?

There had been no update on Billy Don's status for quite some time. Still in surgery—that's all anybody would say. Red and Mandy mostly sat in silence. Doctors and nurses passed by every few minutes, all hurrying this way and that.

"Turned out y'all were wrong, by the way," Red said. "Not that it really matters."

"Wrong about what?" Mandy asked.

"About me and Billy Don collecting those lug nuts at the Beach Club. The detective said it wasn't that big of a deal, as long as they have them now and me and Billy Don don't change our story on where we found them or how we gathered them. They can even swab 'em for DNA, since we didn't touch 'em, but he said we shouldn't get our hopes up about that."

He left out the part where Tuggle told him they should've called the sheriff's office the moment they'd found the lug nuts, and that Red shouldn't do anything that misguided in the future.

"So y'all ain't gonna get in trouble for that?" Mandy asked.

"Don't look like it," Red said.

"That's cool. I'm glad."

"I just wish we'd hear something about Billy Don," Red said. "I feel like I got him into this mess."

Mandy reached out and put her hand on Red's knee, which made him feel better.

"Hey, what's directly behind your left nipple?" Red asked.

"The rest of my boob, silly," Mandy said.

"No, I mean with Billy Don," Red said. "That's where the bullet hit him—about an inch above his left nipple. I was just wondering what else it might've hit."

"Hmm," Mandy said. "I'm not sure. Probably a lung."

"If he was gonna die, you figure he woulda died already?" Red asked.

"Jeez, don't be morbid," Mandy said.

"Sorry," Red said. "I just figure he's got a pretty good shot at this point. That wasn't the best choice of words, was it? 'Shot.'"

"All we can do is wait and see," Mandy said. "Think good thoughts."

Twenty more minutes passed.

Mandy said, "Maybe I should go get Christie and tell her what happened. Before she gets out of school, because word's gonna get around fast. We don't want her hearing it from some random kids. They'll get it all wrong and she won't know what to think. You want me to do that?"

"Go get her out of school?"

"Yeah. And tell her what happened."

"Do you mind?"

"Not at all."

"That's probably a good idea."

"Will you call if you hear anything? Or text?"

"Of course."

Mandy stood up and slung her purse over her shoulder.

"You okay waiting here alone?"

"Yeah, I'm fine," he said.

"I'll bring her back over here, unless I hear from you before then," Mandy said. "Or should I take her to your place?"

"Home is probably better," Red said. "She's already had a lot to deal with lately. She don't need to be up here worrying."

"Wow," Mandy said. "You're good."

"Huh?"

"Remember that talk we had on the porch?"

"Last week about space aliens?"

"No, last night, about being a dad."

"That was just last night? It seems like a week ago."

"You were all worried you wouldn't know what to do, but here you are, looking out for Christie like you've been doing it for years. I'm proud of you."

Red could feel his face getting warm. Mandy leaned over, placed her hands on his shoulders, and gave him a long kiss on the mouth. Her boobs were right there for the groping, but he figured that might ruin the moment.

Mandy said, "He's gonna be fine."

Red nodded, even though he wasn't so sure.

"I'll text you later," she said.

He nodded.

Mandy stood up, proceeded down the hallway, away from the small waiting area. Red whistled in appreciation as she walked away.

Five minutes later, she texted him a photo.

She'd gone outside to her little orange Nissan truck, pulled her shirt up and her bra down, and snapped a photo of her left boob, and she'd included a message. *See? I was right.* She followed that with one of those little faces—the one where the guy is winking and sticking his tongue out at the same time.

Hell of a woman. If Red wasn't careful, he was going to get used to having her around.

Red wrote: *Gonna save this pic for later, if you know what i mean.*

Mandy said: *You dont need it, you got the real thing. Two of em!*

Red sent a thumbs-up.

Fifteen minutes later, a doctor in scrubs walked into the waiting area and said, "Mr. O'Brien?"

Red stood up, more nervous and jittery than he'd been in years.

"Yeah?"

The doctor introduced himself. Then he began to speak in a low voice, going into great detail about what had happened during surgery, including some "unforeseen complications," and as he talked, Red began to cry. He just couldn't help it.

30

It was typical central Texas terrain. Gently sloping caliche-covered hills. Lots of oaks, cedars, and elm. Lots of waist-high grasses. Yucca and sotol. Gavin spotted some madrones, too, and he wondered if the landowner even knew they were there. They weren't rare or anything, but they also weren't common. Just a novelty of sorts. Beautiful trees.

He noticed that Eddie was breathing heavily and his shirt was already damp with sweat. They were passing a small livestock tank, and it made Gavin realize how thirsty he was. Parched, actually. He was tempted to scoop some of the water into his hand and lap it up, but that probably wasn't a good idea.

"I've been thinking," Eddie said. "Probably better if we don't keep carrying that cop's gun around."

He held out his hand. Gavin was reluctant to hand it over. It was surprising, but he'd gotten used to carrying the pistol around. Made him feel secure.

"You don't want to get caught with that on you, believe me," Eddie said.

Gavin passed it to him.

Eddie immediately turned and tossed the gun into the stock tank, where it landed with a splash.

Was Eddie really wanting to get rid of the gun for the reason he stated, or did he want Gavin unarmed?

Caroline's phone rang again, but this time she was awake.

"Hey, Brendan."

"Hey. I just heard everything that's going on," Brendan said.

"Pretty crazy, huh?" Caroline said, trying to keep it light, but she was on the verge of crying again.

"I'm not sure what to say, but I wanted you to know that I'm sure everything will work out."

She laughed. "At this point, I can't imagine how. And I bet it's the talk of the town."

"If it's any help, I don't think anybody believes any of it. The cocaine part. Everybody knows that wasn't you."

"It's good to hear that."

She didn't ask what everyone thought about Gavin being on the run with a guy like Eddie Trask.

"Do you need anything?" Brendan asked.

"That's sweet, but I'm okay."

"You sure? I mean it."

"I'm just staying home."

"I hate to think of you being all by yourself there."

"I'll be fine. Really. We have a security system."

"Do you have a gun?"

They'd walked about a mile when Gavin had an idea.

"How far are we from Marble Falls?" he said.

"You really are clueless, ain't ya?" Eddie said.

"How far?" Gavin said.

"Probably five or six miles," Eddie said. "Back the other way."

Gavin stopped walking, so Eddie stopped, too.

"Remember that Kia I was driving the other day?" Gavin said.

"What about it?"

"It's parked at the Walmart in Marble Falls. I bought it two days ago. Nobody—not even my wife—knows I own it. I haven't even transferred the title. I've been using it to keep an eye on my wife's impostor."

Eddie didn't say anything, but he was plainly contemplating the possibilities, despite the fact that he'd told Gavin to leave the thinking to him.

"Long way from here to there," Eddie said.

"I can walk it. Can't you?" Gavin couldn't help taunting him a little.

"Not talking about that," Eddie said. "Talking about lots of people and buildings and vehicles along the way, especially the closer we get to town."

"But we still don't even know if they're looking—"

"Hang on," Eddie said, listening for something. "Come on."

He started jogging toward a clump of cedar trees, so Gavin followed, and then he heard it, too—the faraway *thump-thump-thump* of a helicopter.

"Hurry!" Eddie said, pushing his way through the dense branches.

Gavin, following close behind him, could smell Eddie's body odor and it reminded him of rancid meat.

They reached the center of the trees and sat on the ground, knees drawn up to their chests, arms wrapped around their legs, making themselves as small as possible.

The helicopter was getting closer. It seemed to be moving along at a steady pace, occasionally slowing to take a closer look at something the pilot had spotted on the ground. Judging by the sound, Gavin figured the chopper wasn't any more than a hundred feet off the ground.

It got closer.

And closer still.

And then it stopped.

"Don't look up," Eddie said. "Don't even move."

Gavin was tempted, but he kept his head down. A small part of him *wanted* the helicopter to see them down here. Why was that?

At this point, each *thump* sent a vibration through Gavin's body and he could feel the wind pushing downward from the helicopter blades. His hair was swirling in all directions. The limbs of the cedar trees were swaying and thrashing violently. Gavin felt exposed, but he didn't know if he was actually visible or not.

Was the helicopter directly above them, or was it off at an angle? An angle would mean the pilot had less chance of seeing them.

What would happen if they were spotted? Would the chopper land somewhere nearby? Or would it simply fly in place until deputies arrived in vehicles? That seemed more likely. If Gavin and Eddie tried to run, there would be no way to elude the chopper.

Then, finally, Gavin could tell that the chopper was moving again. The thumping became less intense. The wind decreased. The cedar branches danced more gently.

"Just hang tight," Eddie said.

Gavin peeked from the corner of his eye and saw that the helicopter was moving east. Slow, but moving.

They waited and after a full minute, the *thumps* were several hundred yards away.

Eddie poked his head around a branch and grinned. "See, I fucking knew they was looking for us. I was this close to shooting at him."

"You were going to shoot at the helicopter?" Gavin said. "Without even knowing if a duplicate was flying it?"

"If he spotted us, yeah. Why the hell not? Nothing to lose, right?"

Red was back in the waiting area when he received a text from Mandy.

Shes refusing to go home, says she wants to come up to the hospital.

Thats fine, bring her, Red replied.

He was feeling much better now. Those tears earlier had been tears of relief. Billy Don wasn't out of the woods just yet, but things looked pretty good, despite the complications. Red had texted Mandy earlier with the update.

Twenty-three minutes later, Mandy texted that they were in the parking lot, and a few minutes after that, Red saw Mandy and Christie walking down the long hallway in his direction.

He rose from his chair and went to meet them.

"Hey," Red said when they were thirty feet away.

"Hey," Mandy said.

And by then, Christie had closed the distance, and without saying a word, she wrapped her arms around Red and held him tight.

"You okay?" Red said.

"I'm sorry," she said. He could tell she was crying. "I'm so sorry.

None of this would've happened without me. It's my fault for getting y'all involved."

"That's not true at all," Red said.

He looked at Mandy, and she sort of shrugged, as if to say she hadn't expected this response from Christie either.

"Some scumbag shot Billy Don, and that's not your fault at all," Red said, and at that moment, something dawned on him. "If it's anybody's fault, it's mine, because it was my stupid plan."

Well, shit. That was true, wasn't it?

Christie continued to hug him tight, and Red patted her back, and before long, Mandy came over and wrapped her arms around both of them.

"We need to think ahead," Gavin said.

"About what?"

Gavin noticed again that Eddie was winded and struggling to keep up. Out of shape. All those damn cigarettes he smoked. But after the helicopter had flown away, he'd agreed that they should try to make it to Marble Falls for the Kia. Without a car, they had no chance at all.

"If we make it to the car, where are we going to go?" Gavin asked.

They hadn't heard the helicopter in five or six minutes. It had moved on.

"Ain't nothing changed," Eddie said.

"What do you mean?"

Eddie stopped walking. He obviously had a hard time talking while he was walking. Too much strain on his lungs.

"We still need to deal with my cousin, remember?"

"Tanner?"

"Right. And Sammy Fontana."

"You mean their duplicates," Gavin said.

"Right. Duplicates."

"But I figured…"

"You figured what?"

"That we were scrapping that plan."

"Why would we?"

"Oh, I don't know. Maybe because we've got half the state looking for us."

"I don't like a smart mouth," Eddie said. He glared at Gavin and Gavin glared right back. Eddie said, "If we take out Tanner and Fontana, we won't have to worry about anything else. We won't have to run anymore."

"They'll be watching your cousin's place," Gavin said.

"Doubt it. That's even further away than Marble Falls."

"Doesn't seem like a good choice."

"You don't like it?" Eddie said. "You got a better idea?"

"Not right now."

"If you come up with one, be sure to let me know."

"I will."

Eddie began moving again. Gavin followed. He didn't have any other choice at the moment, especially now that he wasn't armed.

But a few minutes later, he stopped walking again. "Okay, I have a better idea," he said.

31

They approached the house from the south, because there was nothing between the house and the county road that ran behind it. No neighbors, just thick woods.

Gavin's watch told him it was 9:23 in the evening. The sun had set and the moon hadn't risen yet, so it was almost pitch dark. They needed to move extremely slowly now to avoid stumbling over the rough terrain. They couldn't even use the flashlights on their phones, because Eddie refused to turn them on. Said the phones could be tracked if they were turned on, and he was probably right.

It had been a damn long day, and Gavin was thirsty and tired, but he could tell Eddie was utterly exhausted. Gavin was still amazed they had managed to walk all this way—probably at least eight or ten miles total—without being spotted. Eddie had had to stop a dozen times throughout the day to catch his breath and smoke a cigarette, which was more ironic than Gavin could stand. Then Eddie had run out of cigarettes, and his mood had soured accordingly.

That's why it had been so difficult to change Eddie's mind about going to his cousin's house. Eddie wasn't one to listen to reason.

But Gavin had finally convinced him that the cops *would* be watching Tanner's house—because fugitives often run to friends or family members for support. Which was totally true, and Eddie knew it, and eventually he gave in. Then he asked a good question.

"So where the hell can we go? You got any bright ideas?"

"As a matter of fact, I do," Gavin said.

"Where?"

"My house."

Eddie's lungs were actually wheezing. Maybe, on top of the cigarettes, he was an asthmatic and didn't know it.

"What the fuck are you talking about?" Eddie said. "If the cops are watching Tanner's house, they're sure as hell watching your place."

"You'd be right, except for one thing," Gavin had said. "There's a big difference between Tanner and Caroline."

"Which is what?"

"I'm guessing the cops don't know Tanner particularly well, and they don't know whether he would rat you out, so they have to assume he wouldn't. But they know my wife. She's a prosecutor, for Christ's sake. She wouldn't hide me, and they know that."

"Your own damn wife wouldn't hide you?"

"Nope. Neither would her duplicate, if she always behaves the same way Caroline would. She'd know that hiding me might be a short-term solution, but it would never work for the long term. I—and she—would eventually get caught, and our lives would both be ruined for a very long time. So, yeah, she wouldn't hide me, because turning me in would give me much better odds. She would do whatever it takes to defend the hell out of me in court. She knows the system. She'd know that even if I'm guilty of something, that doesn't mean shit. What can the cops prove? That's what matters. Hiding me would be dumb. She'd know it. The cops would know it. And they'd know *I* know it. So they won't expect me to show up there, looking for a place to hide—which is exactly why we should show up there."

After Gavin had made his case, Eddie had stared at him again for a long moment.

Then he'd said, "Goddamn, I think you're right. But even if they ain't watching your house, how are we gonna stop her from turning you in?"

"We're not going to give her the chance," Gavin said.

Now they were less than forty yards from the rear of the house, and Gavin couldn't remember ever being so nervous.

Would the impostor know about the Remington shotgun hidden in the master bedroom closet? Would she know how to use it? Even Caroline might not remember exactly what to do. Gavin had shown her the basics a few years earlier, but she wasn't much into guns. Neither was he, really. He'd bought the shotgun for home security.

"You sure you don't want me to turn the security system off?" he asked.

"Hell, no," Eddie said. "Soon as you turn your phone on, the cops'll know."

Gavin wasn't sure if it worked that way, but he didn't know that it *didn't*, so he went along. He could get to the alarm keypad and disarm it.

Eddie motioned and they moved forward, picking their way slowly through the brush and trees.

"You don't got no damn dog, do you?" Eddie whispered.

"No," Gavin said.

Now he could see that all of the blinds were lowered in the rear windows. Caroline rarely lowered those blinds—no need to—but these were special circumstances, weren't they?

They stopped for a moment at the last clump of trees behind the house, roughly fifty feet from the back door. Gavin would use his key, then disarm the keypad, and then they'd find the impostor and get the truth out of her once and for all.

"About damn time," Red said.

Billy Don's eyes had flickered open briefly several times in the past ten minutes, but this time, they'd remained open long enough to lock onto Red's and stay there.

"You look like hell, if you're wondering," Red said. "Not that you were any great sight to behold before all this mess."

Red wasn't sure what time it was. Last time he'd checked it was nearly nine o'clock, but he'd dozed off since then, sitting in the chair beside the hospital bed. Didn't really matter what time it was, though, did it?

"In case you don't remember real good, you got shot. You remember that?"

Billy Don made the slightest nod.

"Okay, good," Red said. "By the way, you got a tube down your throat at the moment, so you can't talk. That right there is a goddamn blessing if you ask me. I asked the doc to go ahead and sew your mouth shut, but he didn't follow my instructions. Anyway, you got shot, which we covered already, but you don't know what happened after that, do ya?

Billy Don let out a slight grunt.

"Well, you had surgery, and that's because the bullet caught you right above your left nipple, and then it tore up part of your lung. Not all of it, but some of it, and they had to go in and clean that up, I guess. You with me so far?"

Billy Don nodded slightly again. He was connected to various machines that beeped occasionally. Red could make out some of the information on one screen: blood pressure, heart rate, breaths per minute, and some other number that lingered around 97%. It all looked pretty good, but what did he know?

"Apparently, you bled pretty good, but you had a good surgeon—I could tell, because he was one of those Middle Eastern dudes. He had to give you several units of somebody else's blood. The good news is, the bullet went through the windshield before it hit you, and that slowed it down more than you'd expect, so it was more of a ricochet than anything else. Didn't even pass all the way through. The point is, later on, when you want to act like you're so damn tough for living through it, just remember it wasn't that big a deal to begin with, okay?"

Billy Don grinned a little, or maybe it was a wince, and he closed his eyes. Red thought maybe he'd gone back to sleep, but then he opened his eyes again.

"They pulled the bullet out and that was about it," Red said. "Didn't hit anything else major. I told the doc it mighta been better if the dude woulda shot you between the eyes, because then it wouldn't have hit anything at all."

Red could hear a couple of nurses talking in the hall, but, in general, the ICU had been quieter than it had been all day. He'd heard and seen some things earlier that had made it clear several patients on the unit were in worse shape than Billy Don.

"Oh, you also smashed into somebody's trailer with the Ranchero, so it's a good thing you're insured. You backed into that son of a bitch going about thirty miles an hour. You shouldn't worry about that right now, though. We'll get your car fixed."

Red looked at the window for a long moment. The skies were clear and a waning quarter-moon was floating on the horizon.

He turned back to Billy Don.

"Mandy and Christie was up here earlier, and they came in to see you, but I sent them home a little while ago. Figure you'd want to know.

The truth is, all of us thought you might die, and that about tore me up. I won't ever admit this to anybody, and don't expect me to repeat it, but you mean a lot to me, you big, dumb bastard."

Billy Don grunted again, and Red knew he was saying he felt the same.

"Let me ask you something, Billy Don. There was two guys out there. You remember which one shot you?"

Billy Don nodded.

"Was it Trask?" Red asked.

Another nod.

"You're sure?"

Billy Don nodded and grunted at the same time. This was like saying he was one thousand percent sure it was Trask.

"You're not loopy from the surgery or the drugs or something like that?" Red said.

Billy Don shook his head slightly.

"Did that other guy have anything to do with it?"

Billy Don shook his head.

Red said, "I picked both of 'em out of a photo line-up. Wanna know who the second guy was? He's the husband of a prosecutor in Burnet County. Can you believe that shit? The cop seemed like he didn't want to tell me who it was, but it's all over the news now anyway. His name is Gavin McIntosh. Not the cop, the husband. They're looking for him and Trask all over."

Billy Don's eyes drooped again and stayed that way for several seconds. Time for Red to let him go back to sleep. But just one more thing first.

"I'll tell you something right now, between me and you," Red said, speaking more quietly now, and leaning in close. "Trask is a dead man. That's all there is to it. That ol' boy don't know it yet, but he ain't got much time left on this planet. You with me on that?"

Billy Don, eyes halfway open, nodded again.

"And no matter what anybody says later, this conversation never happened," Red said.

Billy Don smiled.

32

Gavin remembered that he'd been meaning to oil the hinges on the back door, because they squeaked. Nothing he could do about that now. Caroline slept with a fan beside the bed and the TV on, so that should mask the sound from the door.

Eddie was standing right behind him as he slipped the key into the deadbolt and ever so slowly turned it. All of the sounds seemed enormously loud, but he knew that was just how he perceived them. The deadbolt made a slight *thunk* as it opened fully. Gavin removed the key, then turned the knob and opened the door. The hinges did squeak, but not quite as badly as he expected.

He now had two minutes to disarm the alarm.

They both stepped inside, and Gavin closed the door behind them as quietly as possible. They were standing in the small, tiled entryway at the rear of the living room. Gavin had described the layout of the house to Eddie earlier.

There was enough ambient light from various electronics—including the TV, the cable box, and the DVR—that they would be able to move around without stumbling. Gavin was surprised Caroline hadn't left a few lights on. Sometimes she got a little spooked when she was home alone at night. Then again, maybe the impostor didn't worry about that sort of thing.

Just as Gavin began to take a step, he heard a snore. What the hell? Caroline wasn't a snorer. Ever. Not even when she was congested from a cold. But what if the duplicate was a snorer? Wouldn't that be weird? Would the people who created the duplicates have any way of knowing if any particular person was a snorer? Was the attention to detail that great? If it was, they'd screwed up, because Caroline shouldn't be snoring.

There it was again. A long, pronounced snore.

Eddie looked at him, his expression saying, *Is that her?*

Gavin sort of shrugged.

Another snore. Where was it coming from? Sounded like it was right here in the living room. Certainly wasn't all the way in the master bedroom.

And another snore. Somebody was sleeping on the couch.

The impostor? Did impostors even need to sleep, or was that something they pretended to do with people around? If it wasn't Caroline's impostor, who was it?

First things first. Gavin made a gesture that said, *Wait just a minute,* and then he stepped very carefully and slowly across the carpeted floor, around the couch, and he paused for a second...

He couldn't make out any features of the person on the couch—just a long, shadowy lump under a blanket—but it appeared the person was facing the cushions. Maybe.

So, as the snoring continued, Gavin tiptoed the rest of the way to the alarm keypad on the wall near the front door. He raised his right hand, and as he was about to enter the code, he remembered that the unit would emit a small beep with each number entered. Well, crap. Would that wake the person on the couch?

Gavin could see Eddie's silhouette across the dark room, waiting, and now he spread his hands, like, *What are you waiting for?*

Gavin took a deep breath, then punched the four-digit code.

Beep.

Beep.

Beep.

Beep.

The snoring did not stop.

Gavin exhaled.

Thank God.

Then the overhead lights in the room came on, and he heard the impostor say, "Hello, Gavin."

She was standing by the hallway, wearing a nightgown, and aiming a shotgun at him. His Remington shotgun.

"Caroline," he said. "I'm just—"

"Quiet," Caroline said. "I don't want to hear it."

Then the figure on the couch stopped snoring and mumbled,

"Where? What's going on?"

"It's okay, Brendan," Caroline said, as the man on the couch sat up straight.

"Brendan?" Gavin said.

"Gavin?" Brendan said.

"What the hell are you doing here?" Gavin asked.

"Keeping her safe—from you," Brendan said, with some attitude.

"Nobody fucking move," Eddie said, and Caroline flinched, because she hadn't seen him yet by the door. Eddie was aiming his pistol at her. "Put the shotgun down," he said. "Right fucking now."

Caroline pointed the barrel downward.

"No, on the floor. Put it on the floor."

She bent and gently placed the shotgun on the carpet, then stood back up.

"Well, now," Eddie said, smiling. "Ain't it great that we could all get together like this? You and me ain't had much chance to socialize."

"It's lovely," Caroline said.

Apparently her duplicate had the same sarcastic wit Caroline always had in stressful situations.

Brendan began to get off the couch, but Eddie swung the pistol toward him and said, "Nope. Stay there. Don't get up."

Brendan remained seated.

"He's an impostor, too, if you're wondering," Eddie said to Gavin. "Can you tell?"

Brendan said, "Dude, what are you—"

"Shut up," Eddie said. "I can tell just by looking at him. Her, too. You were right all along."

Gavin didn't say anything.

"You hear me?" Eddie said.

"Yeah," Gavin said.

"Go get the shotgun," Eddie said.

"What?"

"Get the shotgun."

Gavin slowly made his way across the room and stopped four feet away from Caroline. Then he had to remind himself yet again that the "woman" in front of him was not Caroline. She wasn't even a woman. She was a duplicate.

Right?

When he looked at her now, he *saw* Caroline—sort of—as opposed to just yesterday at lunch, or the day before, when he could just look at her and tell it wasn't really Caroline. But now...he wasn't so sure.

She was looking at him with such tender eyes, and they began to fill with tears. "Are you okay?" she asked quietly. "It's really me."

"I—"

"Grab it," Eddie said. "Don't let her fool you."

Gavin looked at Caroline for a moment longer, her eyes pleading with him for...something. Then he bent over to get the shotgun.

Because his eyes were focused downward on the Remington, he didn't see what happened next. He wouldn't be able to accurately describe to the police how everything unfolded. Not that they would believe him anyway.

He was leaning down, and as his fingertips brushed the stock of the shotgun—

Boom!

Boom!

Caroline screamed. Gavin instinctively dropped to the floor, shoulder first—

Boom!

—and rolling onto his back, now cradling the shotgun across his chest.

Boom!

He heard breaking glass. The squeak of the door hinges.

Boom!

Gavin raised his head off the floor and looked for Caroline, but she was gone. A person hurried toward the open back door. Brendan.

He ran outside and—

Boom!

Gavin rose to one knee and looked around, but now the room was empty. What should he do? Where should he—

Brendan stepped back into the house and immediately leveled a revolver at him. "Drop it! Don't move! Drop it right now!"

"Where's Caroline?"

"Drop it!"

Gavin placed the shotgun on the floor.

Now he heard Caroline's voice from the bedroom. She was on the phone, calling 911. Alive. She was alive.

He realized with some confusion that he felt an enormous amount of relief.

Relief that she was alive, even though she was an impostor.

Relief that Eddie Trask was gone.

But what was going to happen now?

Seven minutes elapsed before the first deputy's vehicle arrived, followed by half a dozen more. It was the kind of response one might expect when a shooting takes place at the home of an assistant district attorney, whether or not she was on administrative leave.

"Were all of those shots yours?" Gavin asked as they waited. Brendan had made Gavin sit on the couch with his hands placed flat on the cushions on either side of him. Brendan was standing in front of him.

"All but one," Brendan said.

He was remarkably calm, considering the circumstances.

"You gonna tell me what you're doing here?" Gavin asked.

"I insisted on coming over, so she wouldn't be alone tonight," Brendan said. "She said she didn't need me, but I came over anyway."

"And you brought a gun?" Gavin said.

"Yep. Had it under the pillow."

Brendan still had the gun in his hand. He wasn't pointing it at Gavin, but it was clear from his body language that he was ready to use it again, if necessary. He was intent on making sure Gavin sat right where he was until the deputies arrived. Fine. Gavin was ready to tell the full story to the police. He'd freely answer all their questions.

"Did you hit him?" Gavin asked.

"I don't know," Brendan said. "I don't think so."

Gavin saw no blood anywhere. How could that be? How many shots had been fired? Seven? Eight? Caroline had not come out of the bedroom yet. Gavin wasn't sure why, but he suspected that she simply couldn't bear to face him.

"Trask might be dead outside," Gavin said.

"Yep," Brendan said. "He might be."

"Or not. Did you lock the door?"

"Of course."

"That's not my wife in there," Gavin said. "Are you aware of that? She's an impostor. She's got you fooled."

Gavin saw what could only be pity in Brendan's eyes, but before Brendan replied, Gavin heard a siren. As it got closer, Brendan said, "Probably best if you lie down on the floor with your arms spread before they come inside. So they don't shoot you."

Gavin did as he was told.

33

Red drank a beer. Mandy drank a screwdriver. Christie drank a Dr Pepper. It was Thursday night and they were seated in lawn chairs around the fire pit in Red's backyard, nearly twenty-four hours after the shootout at the assistant district attorney's place up in Burnet County.

The night was still and quiet, except for the dancing of the flames and the popping of the cedar stumps as they burned. Red could hear a nightjar calling again and again.

"What I still don't understand," Red said, "is why they ain't caught him yet."

"You know," Christie said, "we really ought to work on your grammar."

"Ha," Mandy said.

"You keep saying that," Red said.

"Because it's true."

"Maybe so, but leave my grandma out of this," Red said.

Christie grinned. Mandy did too, but she shook her head and said, "You need better material."

"But no foolin'," Red said. "Why ain't they caught him? The guy was on foot. They brought in a couple of dogs, and then more helicopters this morning, and about a hundred people to search, and still they ain't found nothing. How is that even possible? I can't hardly drive for two minutes with a broken taillight before the cops are all over me. So how does that guy get away like that?"

Nobody said anything, but it was one of those questions you ask when you don't really expect an answer. Red couldn't remember the word for it. Something about an oracle.

The silence stretched for a long moment. A cold front had passed through earlier this afternoon, and now the temperature was in the fifties. Damn nice weather. Crisp and clear.

"And how does that dude shoot at him fifteen times without hitting him?"

"He shot fifteen times?" Mandy asked.

"That's the word on the street."

"Which street?" Mandy asked.

"All I know is they didn't find any blood," Red said. "They said he was armed and dangerous. That's about it."

Red wondered what kind of weapon Trask had. Just one handgun—the one he'd used on Billy Don? Or did he have others? How much ammo? That would be helpful information if Red managed to track Trask down, although that wasn't looking likely at the moment.

"What kind of bird is that?" Christie asked. "Whippoorwill?"

"Nearly," Red said. "It's a chuck-will's-widow. They're kinda related. They don't usually call this late in the year."

"I like it," Christie said.

Red nodded and took a drink of beer. "I wonder where he is now," he said.

"Over in those trees somewhere," Mandy said.

"Not the bird. Eddie Trask."

"Oh. He could be a thousand miles away by now," Mandy said. "I would know about that sort of thing."

Christie looked at her. "You ever gonna tell me that story?"

"Maybe, but not tonight."

"Why not?"

"I don't want you to think less of me," Mandy said, laughing. "At least not yet."

"I'm sure I wouldn't," Christie said.

"The important thing right now is figuring out where Eddie Trask mighta run off to," Red said. "I mean, wouldn't you like to know? I sure would."

"I know you would, honey, but you're gonna have to let it go," Mandy said. "Probably for the best, because if you caught up to him, I hate to think how that might end."

Red wanted to repeat what he'd said to Billy Don—that Trask was a dead man—but he knew it was smarter not to tell a lot of people what you were planning to do.

"Billy Don looked real good this afternoon," Christie said.

"Yeah, he did," Mandy said.

And it was true. He'd looked much stronger and more alert. He still had a long recovery ahead, but now the doctors said he was going to make it for sure.

Red had spent almost the full day at the hospital, and at one point, some woman from the financial department tried to get Red to sign some documents saying he'd vouch for Billy Don and make sure the bills all got paid. Red had laughed and laughed about that one. "Sure, lady," he'd said. "Can I sign it with any name I want?" She'd pointed out that Billy Don didn't have health insurance, and Red had pointed out that the hospital's slogan was "Compassionate Care For All," and it said so right above the front door, at which point the lady stuttered and stammered and said she'd come back later.

They still couldn't say when they'd cut Billy Don loose, but it would be several more days, at a minimum, and maybe a week. Billy Don seemed to be enjoying it, because he could loaf around in bed, watching TV, and have food brought to him. There was even one cute nurse who seemed to be flirting with him every time she came around.

"Chicken one day, feathers the next," Red said.

"What?" Christie said, laughing.

"Just something my mama used to say. Means things can be going real good, and then suddenly everything goes to hell. I don't know why that popped into my head. Guess 'cause everything was going okay until Billy Don got shot."

It was kind of relaxing to watch the sparks from the fire swirl straight upward and disappear into the night sky.

"But the reverse can be true, too," Christie said. "Believe me. Feathers one day, chicken the next."

Red nodded. "Yeah, I guess that's true. If you're lucky. Didn't work that way for us when I was a kid. Or today."

Mandy said, "Red?"

"Huh?"

"What she's trying to say—and you aren't picking up on—is that you and Billy Don helped her out of a tight spot. You helped her turn things around."

Red looked at Christie, who was grinning in the light from the fire.

"Oh," he said.

"Thank you," Christie said.

Red just nodded and looked at the fire, because if he wasn't careful, he might get a little choked up again, and what the hell was happening with all that lately?

"What else did your mom say?" Christie asked.

"Well, all kinds of stuff," Red said. "Most of it wasn't that clever. Usually, it was, 'Hey, bring me another beer.' Or, 'You got any money for gas?' Real memorable stuff."

"Tell me about her," Christie said. "I mean, if you want to."

"Really?" Red said. "You want to hear about her? She didn't win any mother-of-the-year awards."

"I know, and I'm just trying to figure out how a woman like her could have a son who turned out so well," Christie said.

It was so damn sweet of her to say, Red had to pretend he'd gotten an ash in his eye.

Caroline was back home again, curled in a ball on the sofa, after the forensic techs from the sheriff's office had finally finished processing her home earlier in the afternoon.

Jesus Christ on a crutch, could this week have been any crazier? Unbelievable. First her Tahoe had been impounded and processed, and then her house had become a crime scene, and all because her husband appeared to be having some sort of mental breakdown. Or was he on drugs that had caused a break from reality? Did it matter either way? Right now, the short answer was no.

She missed the hell out of him, though, regardless of what the future might hold.

Weird situation. She couldn't visit him in the jail because she was a witness against him and was on the list of people who weren't allowed to see him. Maybe the only one. That was for the best, because she didn't want to compromise the case. Ultimately, no matter what the situation, she was going to tell the truth about everything Gavin had said and done.

Her phone vibrated on the coffee table, but she didn't recognize the number, so she ignored it. Probably yet another reporter.

Then she realized it was a call she was expecting. She quickly answered the phone and said, "Angela?"

"Hi, Caroline. I'd ask how you are, but based on the voicemail you left me, I already know. What is going on down there?"

Angela had been Caroline's college roommate for a time, and they'd remained good friends ever since, despite the fact that Angela had lived in Sacramento for the past thirteen years.

"Oh, God, Angela, I don't know. I just—"

Caroline had to pause for a moment and gather herself.

"You take all the time you need," Angela said. "I'm happy to help however I can. You know that."

The line was silent for a moment. Angela had always been a good listener—one of the traits that made her a good psychiatrist.

Then Caroline said, "Something is happening with Gavin, and for the life of me, I don't know what it is. Everything is coming apart. I don't know what to do."

"Just start from the beginning," Angela said. "And tell me everything."

34

On Friday morning at 10:45, the same damn Jet Ski was out on the lake again, and judging by the sound of the engine, the moron driving it hadn't fixed it right. This time the guy was wearing a wet suit, and he'd need it if he fell into the water. The temperature had dropped twenty degrees with the first cold front of the fall. The water temperature would still be fine, but getting out would be chilly as hell.

Tanner had been watching the news—and ignoring phone calls, and staying locked up inside the house—and he knew it was long past time to get the hell out of Dodge. Just pack some shit and take off, at least until they caught Eddie. Or found his corpse. That would be the preferred outcome, as far as Tanner was concerned. Might solve all of Tanner's problems.

He'd called that detective on Wednesday morning, but he hadn't answered. Tanner left a voicemail, but Shaddy never called back, and that was because, by then, Eddie had already trussed him up like a calf. Eddie and some other guy, apparently. Just minutes after that, Eddie shot a dude outside his house in Granite Shoals. Tanner still didn't know what that was about. Why had Eddie shot him? Whatever the reason, it showed that Eddie was desperate and would do whatever was necessary to get away.

The Jet Ski engine died. That idiot deserved to be stranded again.

Tanner sat for a moment longer and realized he'd made up his mind. Okay, then. Might as well get on with it.

He went into the master bedroom and pulled a gym bag out of the closet. Three or four days' worth of clothes should do it. If Eddie was still loose after that, Tanner would have to ponder his next move. But for now, leaving made the most sense. Hell, he could even have fun with it. Fly out to California or down to Florida. Stay at a nice hotel and drink margaritas around a swimming pool.

Tanner got the bag packed, then made one last round inside the house, checking that all the doors and windows were locked. When he reached the front door, he heard a vehicle passing by on the quiet street out front. He peered through the little window in the door and saw that it wasn't anything to worry about.

It wasn't Eddie's ugly truck, or any other vehicle he might drive. Just some little yellow car. Looked like a Kia. Tanner didn't recognize it. Maybe it was somebody who'd rented the party house two doors down.

Tanner double-checked the app for the security cameras around the house—front porch, back porch, and one in the living room—and saw that everything was working fine.

He went through the kitchen and into the garage. Tossed the gym bag into the passenger seat of his red Camaro ZL1, then slipped into the driver's seat. Maybe he'd just drive somewhere, instead of flying. That way, he had total control, and there would be no paper trail of his whereabouts.

Hey, maybe New Orleans. He'd met a girl from New Orleans this summer—a smoking-hot associate professor at Tulane. Her name was Steff.

He punched the button on the garage door opener with one hand and grabbed his phone with the other. Send Steff a quick text and see if she was up for a visit. If she wasn't, there was still plenty of fun to be had in New Orleans. Plenty of other women.

Its Tanner. You busy tonight? he asked.

He started the engine. Loved that deep, throaty rumble. Supercharged 6.2 liter V8 engine.

He shifted into reverse, and when he swiveled his torso around to see where he was going, holy shit, here came Eddie walking up the driveway, not a damn care in the world.

Tanner had no idea what to do.

Gun it? What if Eddie didn't get out of the way? Just run over him?

It didn't matter now, because Eddie had almost reached the garage, and that meant Tanner had run out of time.

Eddie entered the garage, slipping between the Camaro's fender and the garage door frame. He stepped right up to the driver's side door and tapped on the glass—with the butt of a handgun.

Tanner lowered the window, saying, "Goddamn, Eddie, you freaked me out walking up like that. It's damn good to see you. I was hoping you'd show up."

"Cut the engine," Eddie said. The gun was dangling loosely from his right hand.

"What?"

"Cut the engine, so we can talk."

Tanner shifted into park and turned the engine off. "Was that you in that little yellow car? You know they're looking for you, right? I mean, *everybody* is looking for you. It's friggin' crazy."

"Close the garage door," Eddie said.

Tanner could smell the body odor coming off Eddie like the stench of a wild animal.

"You okay?" Tanner said.

"I'll be better when you close the garage door."

Tanner punched the button and the overhead door groaned and creaked as it slowly closed. It was much darker in here now, without all that sunlight flooding in.

"Hand me the keys." Eddie said.

"I don't understand why you're—"

"Give me the damn keys, Tanner."

Tanner pulled the keys from the ignition and passed them to Eddie.

"Where were you going?" Eddie asked.

"Just now?"

"Yeah."

"Running up to the store for a few things," Tanner said.

Eddie stared at him for several seconds, then said, "What's in the bag?"

Oh, crap. The gym bag.

"Okay," Tanner said. "Truth is, I was hauling ass. The cops keep calling me and coming around, and I'm tired of that shit. I was heading out for New Orleans."

"Why did you lie just now?" Eddie asked. "There's no reason to lie to me. Why'd you say you were going to the store?"

Tanner stared straight ahead through the windshield now and shook his head. "I don't know, man. I'm just, like, it's second nature right now. Ever since the other night at the Beach Club, it's like I'm always having to think about what I'm saying, so I don't say the wrong thing. Know what I mean? It's hard keeping everything straight. That's why I'm avoiding the cops. I want you to know that I won't talk to them, Eddie. Not now and not ever. You don't have to worry about that. You got my word."

Tanner wasn't sure how to interpret the expression on Eddie's face. Almost a total blank, but there was something simmering under the surface. Anger. Impatience.

"Then why did you call Floyd Shaddy two days ago?" Eddie asked.

Tanner tried not to react, but he knew right then he was screwed. He swallowed hard. Tried to smile.

"He kept hassling me, trying to come by the house, so I was calling to tell him to fuck off for good," Tanner finally said. "I told him I wasn't gonna answer any more questions without my attorney present, and if he didn't like that, too damn bad."

For the first time, Eddie showed some emotion. He grinned. But it was an evil grin. A gotcha grin.

"I heard the voicemail you left him," he said.

Oh, God. Tanner realized he'd just made another colossal mistake. Probably the worst mistake of his life. Suddenly he really needed to take a leak.

"It was all a lie," Tanner said, desperate now, and knowing this was his final shot. "I told Shaddy I was ready to talk, but I was gonna say we saw someone else in the parking lot messing with Deke's car, and we didn't say anything about it because we didn't know for sure who it was. So what was the point in coming forward? That's all I was gonna say. I knew if we kept denying everything, he'd think we were lying, so I had to say something."

Eddie grinned again. "Wanna hear a secret?"

"What?"

"I didn't hear the voicemail. Just knew you was lying. Now get out of the car."

"Eddie, please."

"Get out."

Eddie opened the door from the outside.

"I'm your cousin," Tanner said.

"Come on out," Eddie said. "Don't worry, man, everything's gonna be fine."

Eddie backed up and Tanner got out of the Camaro, standing in the narrow space between the car and the wall.

"Close the door," Eddie said.

Tanner hesitated. He knew this was not going to end well—but how bad would it be?

Eddie raised the gun and pointed it at Tanner's head. "I have zero patience left. Close the damn door."

Tanner closed it. "It's not too late for us to—"

"Shut up. Go that way." Eddie gestured toward the front of the car.

Tanner walked past the front fender and in front of the car. His heart was racing. He felt nauseous. Should he turn and fight? Make a break for the door?

"Stop right there," Eddie said.

Tanner was in front of the car, near a pegboard full of tools mounted on the wall. He'd bought those tools when he'd inherited the house, knowing he might need to fix a dripping faucet or a faulty light switch. He'd never used any of them. It was always easier to call a repairman.

"Grab that hammer," Eddie said. He was standing by the Camaro's driver's door.

"What? Why?"

"Grab it."

"No. I don't understand why—"

"Grab it or I will shoot you right now. You understand that? But if you grab it, I won't shoot you."

"You're lying."

"Grab it."

"You want to make it look like self defense."

"Grab the damn hammer."

"I can't."

"Listen, you lying scumbag. This is the price you pay for being a traitor. You can either grab the hammer or get shot. One or the other."

Tanner was starting to cry.

Eddie said. "Three…two…one…"

Tanner grabbed the hammer off the pegboard.

"Now turn around," Eddie said.

"Don't shoot me."

"I won't. But turn around."

Tanner was openly sobbing now, chest heaving, tears rolling down his cheek. He slowly turned around with the hammer in his left hand.

"Raise it over your head," Eddie said. He was six feet away—out of striking distance. The barrel of the pistol looked like the mouth of a cave.

Tanner slowly raised the hammer, still in his left hand. If nothing else, maybe the cops would realize that he was right-handed, and that he'd never use his left to swing a hammer. Maybe, after he was dead, Eddie would pay for what he was about to do.

"Don't ever—ever—try to screw me around again. Understand? Don't lie to me. Don't think you're smarter than me. Because you won't get away with it."

Tanner nodded. Eddie noticed that a wet spot was spreading across Tanner's crotch.

Eddie laughed and said, "That's pretty damn pathetic, man."

Then he pulled the trigger.

35

Gavin McIntosh wasn't sure how it happened, but when he woke up in his cell on Friday morning, he realized without any doubt that his wife had never been replaced by a duplicate. There were no phonies or impostors. The only person who looked like Caroline—with that cute face, thick chestnut hair, and endearing laugh—was Caroline. The real Caroline. His wife.

"Good God," he muttered to himself as he sat up and placed his feet on the tiled floor.

He rubbed his face with both hands and sat there for a moment to ponder the past week. It had a dreamlike quality to it, but he knew it had all been real. Insane, but real.

Eddie Trask hadn't really been an ally. He had played Gavin like a pinball machine. Trask was a criminal, and a violent one at that. Gavin shuddered to consider what Trask might've done to Caroline if he'd been able to get away with it.

"Good God," Gavin said again.

He rose from the bed and paced inside his small cell.

He had never set foot in the Burnet County jail before late Wednesday—actually, it was early Thursday, to be accurate—and even though Caroline had described it to him on occasion, he'd been overwhelmed when he'd first arrived. This wasn't Otis and Andy in Mayberry. This was a massive 587-bed unit, which easily handled the county's needs, and excess space was leased out to other counties and some federal agencies, including the U.S. Marshals Service and ICE, who used it as a holding facility.

He had a cell to himself—in protective segregation—because he was the spouse of a prosecutor who had sent some of the inmates here. Things might not go well for Gavin if he were put in a cell with some of those people. He couldn't even go into the day room and use the phone when other inmates were in there. But using the phone was a waste of time anyway, because you could only make collect calls, and cell phones didn't accept collect calls, and who would he call? Until now, he hadn't even bothered trying to call a lawyer, because he was convinced the lawyer would be part of the network supporting the impostor.

Not anymore.

His cell door was made of steel, and it had a small window with holes drilled into it, but the window was covered from the outside with a small hinged hatch, which was currently closed. No way to see if any jailers were in the hallway.

Gavin realized that despite his circumstances—being in jail, with multiple charges pending, and a wife who might very well be planning a divorce by this point—his mood was good. Almost ecstatic. Because the grip had been released. He had woken up, or the spell had been snapped, or the trance had faded, or however you wanted to look at it. Bottom line, it was over and he was back to being himself.

He needed to get word to Caroline as soon as possible. She'd know what to do. Surely they wouldn't hold him accountable for the things he'd done under his mental condition.

Would they?

He pushed the wall-mounted buzzer that would summon a jailer. Then he looked at the camera mounted in one corner of the ceiling and gave it a friendly wave. A jailer would be watching him right now, just to see if he'd pressed the buzzer for anything urgent. Was he dying? Having a crisis? About to hang himself? Stripped naked? Smearing feces on the wall?

He sat back on the bed and waited, bouncing one foot impatiently.

Twenty minutes later, the hatch opened and there was the face of a jailer named Brad, who'd been around yesterday afternoon. Brad was about thirty, with sandy hair and a round face. Judging by the way he had to bend to look through the hatch, he was very tall. He seemed like a nice enough guy. Not into the power trip of being a jailer or anything like that. He said, "What's up?"

Gavin said, "Remember yesterday when I told you my wife had been replaced by an impostor?"

Gavin had told everybody about the impostor, including the

arresting deputies on Wednesday night and the judge yesterday morning. That same judge had denied him bail because he was a flight risk. Hard to argue otherwise, considering that Gavin had been on the run with a guy like Eddie Trask.

"That's kind of hard to forget," Brad said.

"Yeah, I bet. Even with all the stuff you hear around here. Well, here's the thing. I was delusional. I know that now. When I woke up just now, I realized how crazy I must've sounded for the past week."

Brad just looked at him for a long moment. Gavin was doing his best to appear calm and rational.

"You probably think I'm lying," Gavin said. "I understand that. But I promise, I'm not. Can you look up something called Capgras delusion?"

"What kind?"

"Capgras. It's a man's name." Gavin spelled it. "I looked it up at one point myself, because I knew it wasn't normal for me to have those thoughts about my wife—but the delusion was so strong, I was convinced I was perfectly rational. All of my behavior was because of that delusion. And now it's gone. Won't they turn me loose because of that?"

Now Gavin could only see pity in Brad's eyes. "I'm afraid it doesn't work that way," he said.

"Okay, then can you tell my wife? She'll know what to do."

"Sorry, I can't. I could get fired for communicating with an inmate's family. Best I can do is tell my supervisor and he can handle it."

"Handle it how?"

"He might pass it along to the sheriff's office."

"Or he might not?"

"Correct."

"Why wouldn't he?"

"He's a busy man, and he hears all kinds of stuff that isn't true."

"How about the DA's office? Can he tell them?"

Gavin suspected that if anyone at the DA's office heard that Gavin was thinking clearly again, word would eventually reach Caroline. Maybe.

"Like I said, best I can do is tell my supervisor," Brad said.

Time for the Hail Mary.

"I know I didn't make a lot of sense yesterday and I wasn't willing to answer any questions, but now I'm ready to tell somebody exactly what happened," Gavin said. "Eddie Trask planted cocaine in my wife's Tahoe, and he's the one who shot that guy outside his trailer. I saw both of those things happen."

Brad's expression changed. "Okay," he said. "Take it easy. I'll tell my supervisor."

"Is that man still alive?" Gavin asked. "The one in the Ranchero? How about Trask? Have they found him?"

Brad didn't say anything, but his expression was an answer in itself. No Trask yet.

"He probably took the Kia," Gavin said, knowing he was talking too fast, and that he probably appeared manic, but he couldn't help it. "I bought a Kia last week and we walked all the way to Marble Falls to get it on Wednesday. Then we parked it on the side of a county road behind my house that night. He probably took it when he ran away. Do the cops know any of this?"

Brad said, "Just hang tight," and he closed the little metal door that covered the window.

"They need to check his cousin's house on Lake LBJ!" Gavin called through the door. "Tanner Stockwell! Has anybody checked over there?"

Red strode down the long hallway toward the elevators, noticing that the hospital was a much more cheerful and less smelly place in the light of a sunny late-September afternoon, especially after it was clear your best friend was going to live.

Best friend.

Red didn't think about that kind of thing much—worrying about friends and such—but there was no denying that Billy Don was his best friend. Had been for quite a while. Red would be damn lonely if Billy Don wasn't around.

He reached the elevator bank and pressed the up arrow. The place was awfully quiet.

Billy Don had texted Red bright and early this morning, saying they were already moving him out of the ICU and into a regular room on the second floor. Red figured that was great news, and Mandy had agreed.

The elevator arrived empty and Red got on.

There was only one small thing bringing Red down at the moment, and he'd come to grips with the idea that he might not be able to do anything about it.

Eddie Trask was still on the run.

Mandy had been right last night when she said he could've been a thousand miles away, and now that distance was even greater. If he managed to get on a plane—or any moving vehicle shy of a horse—chances were good the cops wouldn't catch him for a good, long while.

The elevator opened on the second floor and Red got off. The little signs with room numbers told him to go to the right, so he did. Walked past the nurses station—nobody there at the moment—and found Billy Don's room, where the door was open about a foot. Red knocked and went in.

"Hey," Red said, and he could tell something was up, because Billy Don was sitting halfway up in bed and had a wide grin on his face. "What's going on? Was that cute nurse just in here?"

"No, something better."

"Better than a cute nurse? Those painkillers must be doing the trick."

"Just now figured it out, about half a minute ago."

"Figured what out?"

"I been watching the news about Eddie Trask, and following along on Facebook, and it looks like he got away."

Red sat down in the chair beside the bed. "Yeah, I know. Sucks big time, and all I can say is be patient. I'll catch him, or the both of us will, when you get out of here. We'll nail his ass sooner or later."

"I think it's gonna be sooner," Billy Don said, and the way he said it meant he had an idea of some sort.

Normally Red would've replied with a snide remark, but the poor bastard had been shot, and the least Red could do was show a little compassion. So he said, "When did you start thinking?"

Billy Don loved jokes like that, so he glared at Red and said, "Soon as I get out of this bed, I'm gonna kick your ass."

"You gonna tell me what you figured out or what?" Red asked.

Billy Don paused for a moment, being the drama queen that he was, and then he said, "I bet I know where Eddie Trask is gonna be tomorrow afternoon."

"Bullshit."

"No, really."

"Where?"

36

It was a beautiful afternoon for a demolition derby. Seventy-six degrees. Low humidity. Light breeze from the south. Partly cloudy. One of those gorgeous early-autumn afternoons in Texas that makes all the blistering one-hundred-degree days of summer worth it. Almost.

The crowd had set a new record for the derby—close to five thousand spectators so far. Out in the parking area, which consisted of grassy fields south and west of the arena, there was plenty of tailgating going on. People under canopies drinking cold beer and eating all kinds of great food. Country music blaring from truck stereos. Moms, dads, kids, groups of teenagers, and everything in between.

The rectangular dirt arena where the cars would do battle was completely surrounded by concrete barriers, except for one small gap in the northwest corner, where the vehicles could enter and exit.

The bleachers—neatly arranged around all four sides of the arena, but protected by the concrete barriers—were filling up fast. Compact cars were already lined up near the entrance corner, with drivers milling around in red shirts, pit crew members in neon green, and referees in black-and-white stripes. The compact division would go first in several heats for both men and women, followed by the full-size division, then the championship heat in each division.

All in all, the derby was shaping up to be one of the best ever.

But Red, who normally loved the winning combination of beer, brisket, and metal slamming into metal, was too focused on his mission to enjoy the day fully. Sure, he had a cold Keystone tallboy in one hand, but in the other, he held his binoculars, which he raised every so often to scan the crowd for Eddie Trask. Red was seated in the third row of the south bleachers.

If Billy Don was right—and Red tried to tone down his expectations by remembering that Billy Don was rarely right, and he'd been doped up—Trask wouldn't be able to resist attending the derby. He might be on the grounds right this minute, drinking a cold one or eating a taco or whatnot.

"He's a jealous sumbitch, and that's what started all this," Billy Don had said yesterday afternoon in the hospital. "He loosened the lug nuts on Deke Gilbert's car 'cause he couldn't stand the thought of him winning it again. He might notta wanted to kill Deke, but he wanted to ruin Deke's car, for sure. Now he's looking at serious jail time, 'specially after what he done to me. So I figure he's either pulled a Butch and Sundance and he's halfway to Bolivia, wherever that is, or he'll show up at the derby, just 'cause he can't resist it."

"That's crazy as hell," Red said.

"Yeah, but Trask *is* crazy as hell," Billy Don said. "Which is exactly why he'd go to the derby. Think about it. He's gotta know the cops are gonna catch him sooner or later, so he might as well sneak into the derby and have a little fun before he goes away to the gray-bar motel. Everything we learned about him, he loves that damn derby, and he wanted more than anything to win it. So he'll go this year, too, even if he can only watch. Mark my words, he'll go."

Red thought about it. It was a damn good guess, really. Made good sense. So he said, "I think it's pretty dumb, but if it'll make you feel better, I'll go to the derby and check it out."

They'd continued talking and agreed that if Trask did show, he'd have to change or conceal his appearance somehow, even if it was just a baseball hat and some sunglasses. Couldn't walk around looking like himself, could he?

"You gonna look through them binoculars all day?" Mandy asked, sitting two seats to Red's right.

"No kidding," Christie said, sitting between Red and Mandy. "You need to chill. Enjoy the day a little. If he shows, he shows, and if he doesn't, no big deal. They'll find him eventually."

Yep, Christie and Mandy had both come along. The more Red had pondered Billy Don's idea, the more he thought it might be right, and eventually Red hadn't been able to resist telling Mandy about it. He might've even accidentally presented the idea as his own.

Mandy had suggested that they should go ahead and tell Christie about it, too. After all, Christie was nearly eighteen—and she was more of an adult than most of the people they hung out with—so they should let her make up her own mind whether she wanted to go or not. So Red had told her too and she'd said she wanted to go.

"I think he's using those binoculars to scope out girls in skimpy tops," Mandy said.

"No need for that when my girlfriend is wearing…what do you call that?"

"It's a bustier top."

"Well, it's boosty, for sure. Very boosty."

"No complaints, then?"

"Complaints? Hell, I'm gonna buy you three more just like it."

"I'm gonna hold you to that," Mandy said.

"As long as there's some holding involved," Red said.

"I just vomited in my mouth a little," Christie said.

Mandy laughed. Red raised his binoculars and continued searching.

Eddie popped a cold one and started the Camaro's engine. Loved that deep, throaty rumble. He backed out of the driveway, where he'd parked the Camaro yesterday after moving the Kia into the garage. Better hiding spot.

All in all, it had been a quiet, uneventful night, but that's what Eddie had expected. Gavin had been wrong that the cops would be waiting for him to show up at the lake house, especially after he had last been seen several miles away, on foot. Eddie had taken a gamble that Gavin wouldn't tell the cops about the Kia, or where to look, and that had worked out just fine. Besides, they probably wouldn't have believed anything the crazy fucker said.

He dropped it into gear and proceeded slowly down the street.

It should be several more days before anyone could piece together what had happened here. Not that he needed that long.

"There's too many damn people here," Red said.

That included thousands of people in the bleachers and hundreds more outside the arena, some of them seated in lawn chairs on top of RVs. It was a wonder every year that one of those people didn't drink too much and fall off.

"Hey, why are those tractors over there?" Christie asked.

Red had forgotten that Christie had never been to a demolition derby before, because she hadn't been real close to her dad.

"Front end loaders," Red said. "They'll use them between heats to straighten out some of the cars."

"Good God," Christie said.

"Great, huh?"

"Uh, yeah. Sure."

"They've got acetylene torches over there. Sledge hammers. All kinds of stuff. You can make some repairs between heats."

"How does somebody actually win a heat?"

"Some of the cars stop running or break down, some get stuck in the mud, some get disqualified for a bad hit or for not making a hit every minute."

The public address system made a soft squealing sound and the announcer began to speak.

Ladies and gentlemen, I want to welcome you all to the 27th annual Spicewood Demolition Derby!

The crowd cheered and clapped and whistled.

Before we get started...As most of you know, we lost a good man and a talented driver recently. I'm talking, of course, about Deke Gilbert. He won an incredible six derbies in a row in the full-size division, and I don't know about you, but I suspect that's an accomplishment that will never be matched. So now, please join me in a moment of silence in memory of our good friend and derby legend, Deke Gilbert.

The crowd was respectful and everybody mostly shut up for a good twenty seconds. A lot of people removed their hats. Some even bowed their heads and mumbled a prayer. Others looked around, sort of wondering what they were supposed to do, and Red noticed quite a few people holding cans of beer high in the air in a silent toast to Deke. All in all, it was a nice tribute, and Red was glad Christie was there to see it. He also noticed that Mandy reached out to hold one of Christie's hands, and they stayed that way until the tribute was over.

Next, the announcer asked everybody to stand for the national anthem, and everybody did, because people around these parts knew the value of freedom, and Red figured anybody who didn't should be locked up.

Then, finally, the first heat of a dozen compact cars proceeded into the arena. Most of the vehicles were butt-ugly—on purpose. Many of them had been spray painted in a variety of colors and patterns, from flames to camo to graffiti, and many had a company name or web address sprayed on one of the fenders or across the hood. Several of the cars looked half-wrecked already.

The cars circled a few times, revving their high-pitched engines and slinging dirt, much to the delight of the screaming crowd. Red couldn't resist hooting and hollering a few times himself.

Then the cars all lined up neatly in two rows, door to door, the starter's horn sounded, and the derby officially began. The cars zipped this way and that, some in forward gear and some in reverse, as they jockeyed for position. Then one car managed to slam real hard into the rear passenger fender of another car.

"Whoa," Christie said, grinning. "That's pretty awesome."

"They go at it a little different with the compact cars," Red said. "Suspensions are lighter, so they go after the wheels a lot. With the bigger cars, they go after the radiator."

The announcer was really hyping it up.

Get out there and hit somebody!

Watch out, 59! He's coming for you! Oh, that was a close one!

Red found himself getting too interested in the action in the arena, so he had to remind himself why he was here. He raised his binoculars and began to methodically scan the bleachers to the west. One row at a time. One person at a time. Didn't need to bother with the kids. Didn't need to bother with the women, either, although he couldn't help lingering on a few of them, just as Mandy had suspected.

Look at that! He's got moves, doesn't he, folks!

Wow! I could feel that one all the way up in the cheap seats!

People were coming and going all the time, too, which made it harder for Red to be sure he'd checked everyone out. His arms would get tired from holding the binoculars up, so he had to take a break every few minutes. He studied the crowd during the first heat. And the next one. And the one after that. No luck spotting Eddie Trask.

"You're missing a hell of a show," Mandy said.

Red just grunted. He was too intent on his mission to say anything. He began to scope the north bleachers.

"Want another beer?" Mandy asked.

"Always," Red said.

"Be right back."

"Thanks, baby," Red said, patting her butt as she edged past him.

The action continued out in the arena, but Red did his best to ignore it.

Christie said, "I appreciate what you're doing, but you can give up if you want to. I don't think he's coming."

Red said, "Yeah, me neither. But I'm hardheaded."

"You? No way!"

Red laughed, and his binoculars stopped on a man in the second row of the north bleachers. Same frizzy hair as Eddie Trask's. Not wearing a hat, but he was wearing sunglasses. Then he turned to say something to the woman on his left and the profile wasn't right. His nose was way too big. Not Eddie Trask.

Red moved on.

37

Two minutes later, Red spotted another man who looked like Eddie Trask. Sitting in the third row, right next to a set of stairs. Drinking a beer. Hat and sunglasses. Blue T-shirt. Several days' worth of stubble on his cheeks.

Look at all that, y'all! His engine won't last much longer like that!

The man had no hair poking out from underneath his hat. None at all. He still looked like Eddie Trask, though, but without the hair. Had he shaved his head, or maybe trimmed it really short?

"Any luck?" Mandy asked as she returned, handing Red a Keystone tallboy as she eased past.

"Not sure," Red said. "I see a guy over there who looks like him, but I can't tell."

Red took a long drink of beer, put the can between his thighs, and raised the binoculars again.

The man in the blue T-shirt appeared to be alone, which made sense. Trask wouldn't be here with anyone. He'd simply want to blend in with the crowd, hoping to go unrecognized. He'd also want to come and go easily, which explained why he was sitting at the end of a row, beside the stairs. The more Red stared at the man, the more it looked like Trask, and Red was all but certain, just as—

We've got a fire, people! Look at those flames!

—everybody in the bleachers rose to their feet in excitement. They'd been waiting for the first fire of the derby, and Red couldn't help but stand to watch the spectacle himself. A couple of firefighters rushed out with extinguishers to smother the flames coming from the engine compartment of an old Buick. All of the other cars were required to come to a stop, and the driver of the Buick was able to hoist himself through the open window of the welded door and escape to safety.

When the fire was dead, the firefighters retreated and the derby resumed.

Red looked for the man in the blue T-shirt, but he couldn't find him. Red was having trouble finding the same spot in the bleachers all the way across the arena. Was he looking too far to the left? To the right? Was he looking at the right set of stairs?

These guys are putting on a show! Let's give it up for them, you hear?

The remaining cars in the heat continued to slam into each other, and the crowd was getting louder every second, but Red continued searching for the man in the blue T-shirt.

Now he was getting pissed. What if that had really been Trask? Red moved the binoculars in wider arcs, back and forth, scanning rapidly, and then he caught a glimpse of blue. He swung backward and found the blue again. Got him. Same man. Walking in the open space between the bleachers and the concrete safety barriers. He had his head down, like he didn't want anyone to notice him. Moving toward the concession area, to the east.

Drive it like you stole it, people!

"I've gotta go check this guy out," Red said, starting to rise.

Mandy said, "You think it's—"

"Probably not, but I gotta make sure. Be right back."

"We'll be here," Mandy said.

"Don't do anything stupid, okay?" Christie said.

"Can't make any promises," Red replied.

He squeezed himself past irritated spectators on his row and quickly reached the steps, then hurried to the bottom and turned right. As he walked, he looked across the arena for the man in the blue T-shirt, but he was gone again, already past the end of the east bleachers and out of sight.

Next up...the moment you've all been waiting for...the championship in the full-size division. So get ready for some more slam-bang hard-hitting action! We'll be back shortly.

Oh, great. Another break. That meant spectators were about to pour out of the bleachers. Red pulled the brim of his baseball cap low and walked faster, exiting the main arena and entering the concession area. He immediately spotted the man in the blue T-shirt, waiting in a beer line.

As spectators began to fill the area, Red edged closer to the man. He needed to get a good look without being spotted himself.

Red got in a short line for a taco booth next to the beer booth. Now he was less than twenty feet from the man who might be Eddie Trask, but the man was staring straight ahead and Red still couldn't get a good look. He did appear to have some hair, but it was cut very short. There were three people ahead of him in line.

Red was watching the man in the blue T-shirt—just waiting for him to look in this direction—when a different man at the front of the beer line left the counter with a Budweiser tallboy in each hand.

Red froze.

The man with the tallboys was Eddie Trask. No question about it.

"I've done quite a bit of research, and I talked to some colleagues, but I need you to understand that I really shouldn't be making a diagnosis without speaking to Gavin," Angela said by phone on Saturday afternoon. "In fact, it's not even a diagnosis. It's an educated guess, nothing more."

"I understand," Caroline said.

"And you shouldn't assume I'm right. I can't stress that enough."

"I won't," Caroline said.

"Okay. So I'm going to tell you what I'm thinking. You said something happened late last week—Gavin asked what you had done with Caroline, and he seemed to think you were an impostor."

"That's right," Caroline said. "It was very weird, but then he said he was joking. He said he was just playing around and it was part of a project he was working on."

"What kind of project?"

"He never said. He just dropped it. I didn't ask. I thought maybe it was like that old coffee campaign, where they replace the person's coffee with a different coffee and see if they notice. Who knows—maybe he was making some sort of creative analogy with impostor spouses."

"And maybe he was," Angela said. "Maybe I'm way off target here.

But there's something called Capgras delusion…ever heard of it?"

"No."

"It's an extremely rare disorder that involves a person becoming convinced that someone in his life—usually a family member or close friend—has been replaced by an identical impostor. I think I studied it briefly way back in school, but I've never encountered a case myself."

"But Gavin just made that remark one time, and then he let it go."

"Yes, but I've been wondering if he didn't want you to know what he was thinking. Maybe he wanted you to think he'd been fooled, even though he hadn't."

"So you think he was just playing along? That he still thought I was an impostor?"

"Like I said, it's a guess. I can't know for sure without talking to him. Nobody can."

"What causes this delusion?"

"The truth is, nobody knows for sure, but they do have some hypotheses, and I don't want you to panic when you hear them, okay?"

"Oh, great. I'll do my best."

"Well, it occurs most often in people with paranoid schizophrenia, but I would be surprised if that's happening with Gavin. I think you'd see quite a few other symptoms, and schizophrenia usually presents earlier, like in the late teens or early twenties."

"I agree—I think I'd know if he were schizophrenic."

Caroline could hear the shuffling of paper as Angela consulted some notes.

"Capgras also appears to be caused by various types of dementia or brain injury—trauma, stroke, neurodegenerative diseases."

"Oh, crap," Caroline said.

"I really don't want you to get worked up about this until Gavin is examined by a professional, and again, I think you'd probably see some other symptoms. But you didn't, right?"

"Not really, no. He seemed a little moody, and maybe a little…off. But not strange or irrational or anything like that. When we had lunch on Tuesday, everything seemed fine. In fact, he was so upbeat and cheerful, I thought maybe he was getting back to his old self. But then…"

"He stashed that phone in your Tahoe," Angela said.

"Right. Or we think he did. It didn't belong to any of the employees at the Quick Lube."

"You mentioned that he's tried quite a few different drugs for restless leg syndrome," Angela said.

"Right. Four or five."

"What is he on now?"

"I can't remember the specific name, but I remember that it's mainly used for Alzheimer's. They've found it can help people with RLS."

"Is it a dopamine agonist?"

"Yes, that's it."

"Okay, there seems to be a higher incidence of Capgras in people who have dementia and take one of those dopamine agonists."

"So it can be a side effect of the med?" Caroline asked.

"No, I wouldn't go that far. It's unclear what the connection is."

"Gavin has been wanting to stop taking it, because it doesn't seem to be helping and he's been having a lot of side effects."

"Like what?"

"He's cold all the time. He's put on a few pounds. Heart palpitations, dry skin, joint pain—stuff like that."

"You know what? That sounds like hypothyroidism," Angela said.

"Instead of side effects from the meds?"

"Well, here's the thing—dopamine agonists can cause thyroid issues, and there have been a very small number of cases where hypothyroidism has been linked to Capgras."

"So you're saying the meds might be causing hypothyroidism, and that in turn might be causing the delusion?"

"I can only say that it sounds like a logical conclusion."

"Does that mean if he stops taking the medicine, his condition would go away?"

"All I can say is, I think it's possible—assuming any of these guesses are accurate."

"He hasn't taken his pills for four days," Caroline said. "His prescription bottle is still sitting on the bathroom vanity."

Eddie Trask asked the lady behind the counter for two beers, because it was almost time for the main event. Needed to prep himself accordingly. Get the right attitude. These two, along with the beer he'd drunk on the way over here from Tanner's, should do the trick. Besides, these might be the last beers he could get his hands on for a long damn time. He knew that. He was okay with it. He hadn't planned for things to work out this way, but sometimes shit happens, and you just have to roll with it.

He paid the beer lady and casually walked away. That was half the trick to going unnoticed—acting like he didn't have a care in the world. The other half was the fact that he had slicked his hair back with some sort of gel he'd found in Tanner's bathroom. Hard to believe, but that simple little change completely transformed his appearance. No more frizzy hair. When he added sunglasses and a baseball cap, he was able to walk right past deputies without a second look. Dumb bastards.

There was one other big factor that played in Eddie's favor, which was that nobody in his right mind would've guessed Eddie would show up at the derby. Absolutely nobody.

38

Billy Don had guessed Eddie Trask would show up at the derby, but until this very moment, deep down in his bones, Red had been skeptical. Damned if Billy Don wasn't right. Red was so surprised, he almost let out an involuntary yelp or a shout. But he managed to keep quiet. Trask walked within ten feet of Red without noticing him. That gave Red an even better look at the man, and even though Trask had his frizzy hair slicked back and was wearing sunglasses, it was definitely him.

Red waited five seconds, then turned and followed.

The crowd out here was thick now, people moving in every possible direction as they made their way to various food booths and the porta-potties and out to their vehicles to drink beer or continue tailgating for the next fifteen minutes or so. The abundance of people made it easy for Red to follow Trask at a fairly close distance without being noticed.

Trask stopped beside a garbage can and tossed one of the empty tallboys into the trash. Damn. He'd guzzled it fast. Red wished he had a beer on hand to chug. Might help steady his nerves a bit. His heart was pumping hard. He took a deep breath. He was in control. He had the upper hand and the element of surprise. Just take some time and think it through.

But now Trask did something unexpected and headed toward the parking lot. Was he leaving? Red kept his distance as Trask veered left and began to walk through several rows of cars. Red branched right and headed toward his truck, but he was able to keep Trask in sight.

Five minutes, y'all! The full-size championship final is coming up!

As Trask got closer to a slick-looking red Camaro, he raised a key fob and unlocked it. Where the hell had he gotten that car?

Red's old truck had no key fob, so he inserted the key into the lock and opened the door. He climbed inside and was lucky to have a clear view of the Camaro about eighty feet away. Trask was sitting inside it now, and Red started his truck, ready to follow the Camaro at a discreet distance. If Trask spotted him, the Camaro could leave Red in the dust in a matter of seconds.

But Trask didn't leave. The Camaro sat for three minutes. Trask tossed his second empty beer can out the car window.

Better buckle up, buttercup, because things are about to get wild!

Trask started the Camaro's engine. Even from this distance, Red could hear the deep, throaty rumble.

Red couldn't believe Trask was leaving before the final. Maybe he'd lost his nerve and was afraid of getting spotted. Maybe he couldn't bear to watch someone else win the derby yet again.

Red heard the starter's horn as the championship heat began.

Trask eased the Camaro backward, out of its spot, then proceeded north between two rows of cars. Up ahead, he would turn right on the main caliche road that led out of the parking area.

Except he turned left.

Red was still waiting in his truck. Still watching.

What a hit! He'll feel that one tomorrow morning!

After Trask made the left turn, he moved west slowly along the outside of the arena, behind the south bleachers where Mandy and Christie were seated. Maybe he couldn't resist one last cruise around the arena before he left, because the chances were good he wouldn't be able to attend the derby for many years to come. That thought made Red grin.

Trask continued west, then reached the corner of the arena and began to curve north and out of view. Red didn't think Trask would be able to leave that way. He'd have to circle back this way to go out the one exit.

Problem was, Red could no longer see the Camaro, so he backed out of his spot, drove south to the end of the row, and took a right. Then he turned right on the next row over. Now he could see the Camaro again, and...

Trask had driven in a wide arc, so that he was now facing the northwest corner of the arena. That was where the derby vehicles entered and exited the arena. There were a couple of officials standing nearby, but they were facing the opposite direction, watching the championship heat.

Right then, Red knew exactly what was about to happen. He felt it in his bones, and he couldn't believe he hadn't figured it out sooner.

Just as Red gave his truck some gas, the Camaro's rear tires began to spin and sling dirt, and when they finally found traction, the car raced forward, blowing right past the derby officials and into the arena.

Eddie idled at the northwest corner for a moment.

He knew his time was limited. This wouldn't last longer than a few minutes, so he wanted to enjoy every second of it. He wouldn't be driving the way he'd normally drive in a derby. Screw that. This was the time for total kamikaze driving. No reason to protect the car. No reason to hold back or pace himself.

He lowered the side windows to stop shattered glass from flying into the passenger compartment. Couldn't do much about the front and back glass.

Then he floored the gas, the tires spun briefly, and the Camaro shot like a rocket into the arena.

Looks like we, uh, have a late entrant, folks...

Without wasting any time, while he still had momentum, Eddie took aim for the nearest car—a Mercury Montego painted a bright orange. He drove at it head-on. The driver of the Montego saw him coming and tried to swerve, but the Camaro was moving too fast. Their front ends slammed together with a satisfying intensity. Good thing Eddie had planned ahead and unplugged the airbag module under the console.

The driver inside the Montego looked confused and angry, wondering what the Camaro—obviously not a derby car—was doing in the arena. Eddie knew the driver from last year's derby, but he didn't remember the guy's name. Eddie laughed and shot the rod at him.

Folks, this might be a staged act, but if it is, nobody told me about it.

Eddie backed up to go looking for his next victim, but getting traction from a dead stop was difficult. This derby allowed street tires only, so every vehicle slipped and spun quite a bit—which kept speeds down. But the Camaro's fat tires were even worse than the skinnier tires most competitors chose.

I'm being told this is not part of the program. Drivers, please remain in your vehicles and do not move.

Red arrived at the northwest corner just in time to see Trask slamming into a bright-orange Mercury Montego.

It was obvious what Trask had planned. He wanted to do as much damage as he could—and turn the derby into a chaotic mess—before anyone could stop him. Go out in a blaze of glory.

Red wasn't sure what to do. By now he could see several deputies standing on the safe side of the concrete barriers, but they might hop over and attempt to put a stop to Trask's nonsense. Then again, it would be pretty stupid to enter the arena on foot. The announcer was now asking the drivers to remain in their cars.

For now, Red eased his truck forward to block the gap in the concrete barriers. Trask wouldn't be able to leave without going through Red first.

Trask was backing the Camaro up, sliding quite a bit on fat tires, but none of the other vehicles were moving. The drivers were doing as they'd been instructed, which must've taken a hell of a lot of restraint.

The audience, meanwhile, was going crazy—on their feet and shouting and loving every minute of it. What could be more fun than watching a rogue driver smash up a sixty-thousand-dollar car? Despite what the announcer had said, some of them probably thought it was some kind of publicity stunt. Some of the deputies might have thought the same.

"Oh, Jesus," Mandy said from her seat in the bleachers, right after a gorgeous red Camaro suddenly dashed into the arena and slammed head-on into an orange car.

"Is that Eddie Trask?" Christie asked, raising her voice above the sudden shouts from the crowd. At this point, everybody was on their feet, confused, but enthusiastic. The announcer also didn't seem to know what was going on.

"I figure it's gotta be," Mandy said. "Or some other lunatic is on the loose."

"Where's Red?"

"I don't know. He's probably—oh, crap. There he is."

"Where?"

Mandy pointed toward the same corner where the Camaro had made its entrance. Red was pulling his truck forward to block the gap in the concrete barriers.

The announcer was telling drivers to stay in their cars and not move.

The red Camaro backed away from the orange car, then began to make a loop around the arena. A few of the drivers used the opportunity to jump out of their cars and hop the concrete barricades.

"I told him not to do anything stupid," Christie said. "But that's not going to help, is it?"

"No, honey, but at least you tried."

Red watched as Trask dropped it into forward gear and began to make a loop around the arena, honking the horn and intentionally fishtailing this way and that. Putting on a show.

Spectators, please remain in your seats.

Once Trask had some traction and was moving along at a decent speed, he straightened the Camaro out and headed toward a Chevy Caprice station wagon—broadside this time. He aimed for the driver's side door, which had a bright yellow X painted across it. Eddie was about to commit the ultimate infraction in a derby.

He slammed hard into the Caprice and shoved it backwards by several yards. Instantly, the crowd began to boo and scream. People hurled beer cans and other items at the Camaro, most falling short, but some finding their mark. The Caprice driver appeared to be okay, moving from the driver's seat to the passenger side, just in case another hit was coming.

Please do not approach the concrete barriers.

At that point, probably because Trask had put the Caprice driver in such danger, two deputies hopped the barricades and began to approach the Camaro, using unmoving vehicles for cover. But what could they do? It would be foolish to fire a gun in this environment, considering that the arena was surrounded by people on all four sides. A ricochet could kill a spectator.

Trask reversed the Camaro and began to slip and slide across the arena again.

Now Red wondered if Trask was still armed. If he was, he probably wouldn't hesitate to fire at the deputies. He had an advantage in that he didn't have to worry if he hit someone else.

Mandy and Christie.

A bullet could hit one of them. Unlikely, but possible.

Red decided it was time for him to do more than watch.

39

The meeting was to take place in an interview room inside the massive jail complex. The fact that an assistant district attorney would meet with Gavin on a Saturday afternoon told him they were taking his claims seriously. They were ready to listen, and hopefully ready to deal.

It had been a long night, and Gavin had fidgeted for hours. He'd slept some, but not much. Maybe two hours. More like dozing, really—that state where you're somewhat aware of sleeping, but also somewhat aware of nearly being awake. Like you aren't aware that you aren't fully asleep until you wake up, and then, in hindsight, you know you were not in a deep sleep. Did everyone experience that? Gavin wasn't sure.

Thirty minutes prior to the meeting, a jailer told Gavin he had a visitor. Who would that be? Gavin was escorted to the visitation room, where a well-dressed woman in her forties was waiting on the other side of the Plexiglas.

Gavin took a seat. He felt certain he'd never seen this woman before. They both had to pick up telephone handsets to have a conversation, and it felt like a cliché out of a movie.

The woman spoke first. "Mr. McIntosh, my name is Anita Haught. I'm a criminal defense attorney. Your wife hired me to represent you. How are you doing?"

He recognized the name. Caroline had mentioned Anita Haught as one of the shrewdest and most knowledgeable attorneys she'd ever faced in court.

Gavin could recall only a handful of moments in his life when he'd experienced pure and total elation. One was the moment his father had received some positive news after a life-threatening health scare.

Another was the time he'd been recognized by a leading advertising journal as one of the top illustrators in the nation. And, of course, there was the moment Caroline had agreed to marry him. That ranked number one.

And now this.

The fact that Caroline had hired this woman changed everything. She hadn't abandoned him. Just the opposite. She wanted him out. She wanted him back home.

Gavin could hardly speak. "I'm doing okay. Much better now. How is Caroline?"

"She's doing fine, but we don't have much time before your meeting with the ADA starts, so I need to get right to it. We need to talk about your mental state. Caroline consulted with a psychiatrist and...have you ever heard of a condition called Capgras delusion?"

Gavin smiled, and then he laughed, and then, without seeing it coming, he began to get emotional.

"Yeah," he said. "I've heard of it."

Red knew, just as Eddie Trask had known, that once he entered the arena, it would be hard to gain traction and build up speed. The mud was too thick and deep.

So Red backed up about fifty feet, shifted back into forward gear, and waited. The timing would be critical. Trask was still out there in the middle of the arena, spinning and sliding, no doubt loving the fact that nobody could stop him. Beer cans and other items continued to rain down on the Camaro from the bleachers. Several more drivers had bailed out of their vehicles and vaulted the concrete barrier.

We ask that you stop throwing items into the arena.

Yeah, good luck with that.

Red put on his seat belt.

Then he waited.

"Oh, my Lord," Mandy said.

"What?"

"Look at Red."

He was backing his truck away from the gap in the concrete barrier.

"What's he doing? Leaving?"

"No, darlin', he's waiting for a clean shot. He wants to build up a good head of steam."

"Oh, man, this is crazy," Christie said. "Why doesn't he let the deputies handle it?"

"How can they?"

Christie didn't have an answer. "Maybe they should just get out of there, then."

"Probably so," Mandy said. "Just let the idiot drive in circles until he runs out of gas."

"But that won't happen, will it?"

Mandy laughed. "That's not how we do things around here."

The two deputies were hunkered behind an empty Buick Electra. Maybe they were hoping to use pepper spray or a Taser on Trask. That could shut him down. But how could they get close enough to use either of those weapons? Red didn't think they could. They were more likely to get hit by the Camaro.

Red waited.

Trask managed to gain some traction and hit the Caprice again, this time on the passenger side, pushing it halfway across the arena as the Camaro's engine screamed and whined.

Somebody hurled an unopened beer can with amazing accuracy. It struck the Camaro's rear glass dead center and shattered it into thousands of tiny pieces. The crowd roared with enthusiasm. When Trask backed up again, the front bumper of the Camaro tore loose and fell onto the mud. The hood had a pronounced crease across the center.

Red waited.

The deputies scampered from the Electra to a Dodge Diplomat near the center of the arena. Several other deputies had set up around the perimeter of the arena, ready to hop the barriers at a moment's notice and rush the Camaro if an opportunity presented itself.

Red waited.

The shower of cans, bottles, and other garbage from the crowd was constant now. The announcer had gone silent, apparently realizing that the audience was not going to listen to any instructions or warnings.

Trask decided it would be fun to do some donuts, and he completed several before his rear passenger fender smashed against a Lincoln Mark IV and came to a stop.

Then it happened.

He gave the Camaro some gas, but the car didn't move. It appeared he had finally gotten stuck in the mud. The audience jeered and taunted him. He tried reverse, then forward gear, then reverse again, but he couldn't get enough traction to get out of the rut. The Camaro rocked and bucked, but it wouldn't move more than a few inches in either direction.

The deputies behind the Diplomat began to come around from behind the car—slowly, tentatively—both with Tasers in their hands.

Trask continued to try to free the Camaro. Now the crowd was openly laughing and shouting all kinds of insults, although Red couldn't hear them well at this distance, inside his truck.

The two deputies walked closer, Tasers raised, and were within fifteen feet of the Camaro when Trask managed to get it out of the rut.

Trask floored it and the rear of the Camaro swung around wildly, flinging a rooster tail of mud in its wake. The deputies scrambled out of the way, but the mud was too deep for them to run. One of the deputies fell down. He tried to stand, but he appeared to have twisted an ankle. The other deputy returned to help him along, but now the Camaro was heading in their direction.

Red knew he couldn't wait any longer. He gave the engine enough gas to get the truck moving, and then he stomped the pedal all the way to the floor. His old truck responded like a champ. By the time he roared through the gap in the concrete barrier, he was moving faster than he had even hoped.

He eased right to go around the Mark IV, then left to miss the Dodge Diplomat. He lost a little speed, but his tires were finding more traction than he'd expected.

When he passed the Caprice, the driver raised a fist and cheered him on.

Now the Camaro was dead ahead, broadside, but moving forward, as the deputy with the bad leg lurched and staggered toward the Dodge Diplomat, while the other deputy tried to help him.

Red didn't think he was going to make it in time. Trask was going to run the deputies over with the Camaro.

Trask was just forty feet away, but Red's truck was going slower with every yard.

Then the Camaro hit a soft spot and lost some traction.

Thirty feet away.

Then Red hit some solid ground. He could actually feel the difference under the tires. Traction. He covered the last twenty feet quickly, picking up speed, and the truck's big steel grill guard hit the Camaro square in the driver's door and lifted the left side of the car off the soil for a brief moment. When it thudded back to earth, Trask was staring at him, wide-eyed and angry, but he appeared unhurt.

The deputies were now behind the Diplomat again.

Red rolled forward and made contact with the Camaro again, pushing, pushing, and pushing until he had it pinned against a concrete barrier, with ecstatic spectators just ten feet away. The audience erupted into the loudest cheer yet.

Trask appeared to be looking for something on the passenger seat, or possibly in the glove compartment.

Red's tires were spinning now, so he backed up fifteen feet, then made another run at the Camaro, making contact just as Trask seemed to be coming up with an object in his hand. The impact made him drop it.

Red backed up again, further and further, into the center of the arena, but before he could drop it into forward gear, Trask got the Camaro moving again, heading into the northeast corner, then turning left and coming in Red's direction.

Okay, then. It would be a game of chicken. Red had no problem with that.

He gave it some gas, felt the tires slip, and then gain traction.

The Camaro was already coming fast.
The two vehicles raced toward each other—faster, faster—
Red said, "Holy sh—"
And he was thrown forward violently as the vehicles collided with amazing force.

40

When Gavin and Anita Haught entered the interview room, Gavin immediately spotted Roger Langston, an assistant district attorney. Gavin had met him on several occasions. They'd had a brief conversation at a party last year about the Texas Longhorns baseball team. Nice guy. No more than 35 years old. Single. Originally from San Antonio.

"Hello, Anita," Roger said.

"Roger," Anita Haught said and shook his hand.

"Gavin," Roger said.

"Hi, Roger," Gavin said. He was cuffed and couldn't shake hands.

Standing beside Roger was a man in his forties, with weathered skin and a walrus mustache.

"Hello, Glen," Anita said. To Gavin, she said, "This is Glen Tuggle, an investigator with the Burnet County Sheriff's Office."

"Good to meet you, Glen," Gavin said.

Glen nodded.

Everybody sat down.

Anita Haught exuded confidence and competence, and Gavin was glad his future was in her hands. She got right to it.

"Gentleman, we're here because my client has some information to share about the drugs that were found in his wife's car, and about the shooting of William Donald Craddock. He was an eyewitness to both of those incidents, and, of course, he played a role in the incident involving Detective Shaddy. Before we get to that, I need to let you know that in the week or so leading up to those events, and during those events themselves, he was suffering from a condition called Capgras delusion. Are you familiar with it?"

"I am not," Langston said.

Glen Tuggle said nothing.

"It causes the sufferer to think a loved one—in this case, his spouse—has been replaced by an exact duplicate. An impostor. Imagine the confusion that results from something like that. The panic and the fear. He thought his wife had been replaced by a lookalike—but where was the real Caroline? He thought she had been abducted and was in danger, so he went on a quest to find her and rescue her. Along the way, he encountered Edward Trask, who recognized that Mr. McIntosh was in the throes of a mental illness, and he exploited that fact. He preyed upon my client by using a series of lies to manipulate him."

"What causes this delusion?" Langston asked. He didn't sound convinced, but he didn't sound skeptical, either.

"In this case, we think it might've been caused indirectly by a prescription medication Mr. McIntosh was taking, but the truth is, we might never know exactly why it happened. All we know is that it happened. Simply put, he wasn't in his right mind. The good news is, the delusion is gone now and he is ready to make a statement about what he saw. All he asks is leniency for his failure to report those crimes after they took place, and for participating in the incident with Detective Shaddy. He is willing to be interviewed by an independent psychiatrist of your choosing to confirm the condition. If we reach an agreement, I can assure you that Mr. McIntosh can provide information that will tie your cases up into a neat bow."

"What kind of deal are you looking for?" Langston asked.

"Time served, plus a period of probation," Haught said.

"How long?"

"I think five years is fair."

"That's a tough sell," Langston said. "He was there when a man was shot. He was there when Detective Shaddy was held at gunpoint, stripped of his weapon, and left bound on the floor. That's kidnapping."

"I understand that," Haught said. "At that point, understand, he was convinced that Detective Shaddy was part of an evil network that had abducted his wife. I believe Detective Shaddy can corroborate that himself, based on the things Mr. McIntosh said to him. He could even wind up as one of our most powerful witnesses."

"He has to serve some time," Langston said. "There's just no way around it."

Haught had explained to Gavin that the DA's office might insist he serve some time. Otherwise, how might it look if the husband of an ADA received what many people would view as a sweet deal?

"What did you have in mind?" Haught asked.

"One year," Langston said. "That's non-negotiable."

"I could see six months, but—"

"Has to be one year, and that's a great offer," Langston said.

One year. But it wouldn't be a full year. Probably more like six months. He'd behave well and qualify for parole. Afterward, he'd seek out media interviews and tell his story, so his friends and family members and even strangers would know why he'd acted the way he had.

Six months and he'd be back home with Caroline. Back to the career he loved.

Besides, what choice did he have? Go to trial? Plead insanity? Risk losing? All in all, the situation really sucked. He'd had no control over his thoughts or actions. He couldn't have known that—

Oh, Lord. Hang on a minute. An idea. He'd just had an amazing idea.

He could take this horrible experience and do something positive with it. He'd write about it. He'd just experienced an extremely rare mental disorder, and if that wasn't amazing fodder, what was it? Instead of writing a novel as he'd always planned, he'd write a memoir instead. His story of this nightmare. Six months would be the perfect length of time to get it done.

Gavin realized that in his excitement he'd gotten lost in thought for a moment.

Anita Haught was saying, "—and get back to you in the next few days."

"No," Gavin said. "We can answer now."

Haught looked at him, surprised. "Pardon?"

"I want to take the deal," Gavin said. "I understand what I did and I think this is fair. Let's do it."

Red's ears were ringing. His vision was blurry.

The truck was not moving. The engine had died.

Red could feel something warm flowing from his forehead. He realized that despite the shoulder harness, his head had whipped forward and struck the steering wheel.

The Camaro, also unmoving, was steaming from under the hood. Not just steam, smoke too. So much steam and smoke that Red couldn't see Eddie Trask inside the Camaro.

Red wiped his forehead and could feel a large horizontal gash right below his hairline. He opened the door and staggered from the truck.

The Camaro's engine was racing at a high RPM, but holding steady. The vehicles were crammed nose to nose, so Red slogged through the mud around the back of his truck, moved along the passenger side, and by the time he reached the front fender of the Camaro, the smoke had thickened, and now flames were beginning to show from the edges of the hood.

The next five seconds seemed to last an hour.

Red moved through the smoke, past the flames, and when he reached the driver's door, it appeared Trask was just getting his bearings again. He was in worse shape than Red was, with a broken nose and a bottom lip split so severely, both sides flapped downward, exposing teeth and gum.

Red began to cough, and his eyes were burning.

Trask was looking at Red through the open window with wild eyes, and he said something, but it came out as garbled nonsense.

Then he raised a handgun. Semi-automatic. Smith & Wesson .40, from the looks of it. Four feet from Red's chest.

Red leaned to the right just as Trask pulled the trigger. And nothing happened. Empty chamber.

As Trask tried to rack the slide, Red leaned in close to the window and threw a big right cross as hard as he could, connecting with the side of Trask's face. Trask grunted, but continued to fumble with the gun.

Red threw a second punch, pain shooting through his hand, and then another punch, and another, and the gun dropped into Trask's lap, and his chin fell to his chest, and Red kept punching, and suddenly he was wrapped up and hustled away from the Camaro by someone big.

When the person finally let Red go, forty feet from the car, Red saw that it was one of the firefighters, who simply grinned at Red and shook his head. "You nailed that son of a bitch," he said, and then he was gone.

Red stumbled backward, then fell into the mud, and by now, deputies had swarmed the Camaro, trying to extract Trask as the engine bay continued to burn. Two firefighters with extinguishers were trying to put the fire out, but it wasn't working.

Now some spectators were beginning to spill into the arena. There weren't enough deputies to stop them.

The Camaro's driver's door wouldn't open, so two firefighters reached inside and pulled Trask out through the window. He was unconscious, his head lolling, his face a bloody mess. They placed him on a stretcher and quickly hauled him away.

Red struggled to his feet and took a few steps toward the Camaro.

Now everybody pulled back from the Camaro, knowing it was a total loss. It would burn completely, and there was no reason to save it. Red could only hope his truck wouldn't catch fire, too.

"Listen," Red said, but nobody was paying attention.

He heard something over the noise of the crowd. A thumping sound.

"Listen," Red repeated, but it was useless.

The scene was total chaos. Now most of the arena was filled with derby spectators, except for a big empty circle around the Camaro. People were laughing, drinking beer, shooting selfies with the burning car in the background.

Deputies had formed a loose circle to keep the spectators away from the car. One deputy had a megaphone.

Move back! Exit the arena immediately!

Red heard another thump. Was he crazy? Did he have a concussion? He knew he was still juiced with adrenaline. His right hand was swelling quickly.

"You hear that?" Red said to nobody in particular.

"You okay?" a young female EMT asked, suddenly at Red's side.

"Yeah. You hear that?"

"You're gonna need stitches for your forehead," she said. "Come over here with me."

"I will," he said, but he started wandering closer toward the Camaro.

"Hey," she said. "Where are you going?"

Was he as crazy as that dude in that short story, hearing something that wasn't really there?

Red ran as best as he could through the mud, between two deputies, and went straight toward the Camaro, where a thick plume of black smoke was reaching for the sky. He could feel the heat as he got closer. The engine compartment was totally engulfed, but the passenger compartment hadn't caught yet. A horrible acrid odor filled the air.

Red reached the rear of the Camaro just as a deputy grabbed his shoulder from behind.

"You need to come back—"

"Hear that?" Red shouted.

Now Red heard several thumps in a row, and he could tell from the deputy's wide eyes that he'd heard it, too.

"Somebody's in the trunk!" Red shouted.

The deputy ran to the trunk and tried to lift it. "Need a crowbar!" he shouted to several other deputies who had approached the car. One thumbed his microphone and informed somebody that they needed a crowbar.

No time for that. There was another solution

Red took a deep breath and held his arms up to shield his face. Then he approached the driver's door. Smoke was billowing out from the open window, but Red leaned in anyway and began to look for a trunk latch. He couldn't see. He was already hungry for oxygen, but he didn't want to breathe the black smoke.

He had to lean further into the window, climbing halfway into the Camaro, feet dangling, to feel around for the trunk latch. He had his eyes closed and still wasn't breathing, but he couldn't hold out for much longer.

Where was the goddamn thing? He was running his hands along the floor between the door and the driver's seat, but he wasn't finding anything. The heat on the left side of his body was growing intense. Almost time to give up. He opened his eyes, but that was a big mistake.

Somebody wrapped their hands around his ankles, and just as they began to pull him out of the car against his will, his hand found a button low on the door. He pushed it.

Then he was out of the car, falling onto his knees and elbows in the dirt, his eyes burning, tears and smoke blurring his vision. The same hands lifted him up and steered him away from the car, running with him, one hand on his back. Ten seconds later, they came to a stop. Red could tell from the voices surrounding them that they were surrounded by people again.

"Did they get him out?" he asked.

Red had his hands on his knees, and he was gasping for oxygen. He couldn't see anything. He'd been pepper-sprayed once on a dare, and this was twice as bad.

"Yeah, they got him. I don't know who it was, but they got him."

"Christie?" Red said. "Is that you?"

"Yeah, I'm here," she said, grabbing him by the forearm.

"You're the one who pulled me out?" he said.

"Yeah," she said. "That might've been the dumbest thing I've ever seen. Probably the bravest, though. I thought I told you not to do anything stupid."

41

"She said it's the bravest thing she's ever seen," Red said seven days later.

"Yep, I know," Billy Don said. "You've done told me a hundred times."

It was a Saturday afternoon, and they were seated on the back porch. Two ice-cold Keystone Light tallboys were resting on the railing. The pellet gun was cradled across Red's lap, ready to go, but the squirrel was staying just out of reach yet again. Smart little bastard.

"The bravest," Red said. "Ever."

"She said 'probably,'" Billy Don reminded him. "And she also said it was dumb."

"The emphasis was on brave," Red said. "Besides, sometimes you gotta be kinda dumb to be brave, don't you?"

"And you're living proof," Billy Don said.

"Proof of being the bravest sumbitch around," Red said.

Billy Don said, "Funny thing is, all you had to do was pull the keys out of the ignition and open the trunk with the remote. Didn't have to fumble around for the button on the door, turning it into some big drama."

"Yeah, but I didn't *know* that at the time," Red said.

The swelling in his hand had gone down considerably. He wasn't sure if he'd broken a bone in there or not, because he'd refused to go to the doctor. Didn't want to pay for a bunch of tests he didn't need. He knew he'd made the right choice when Billy Don saw how much he owed the hospital when he checked out yesterday. Some third-world countries spent less on defense.

"Plus there was another button under the license plate," Billy Don said. "If one of those deputies or firemen had found that button and—"

"But they didn't, and that's the point," Red said. "I think you're just jealous that I was out there being a hero while you was laid up in the hospital."

The man who'd been in the trunk of the Camaro was named Tanner Stockwell, Eddie Trask's cousin. Apparently, Stockwell had helped Trask remove the lug nuts from Deke Gilbert's car that night at the Beach Club, and he'd survived that wild ride in the trunk of the Camaro with remarkably few injuries. The day after, he'd hired a lawyer and told the prosecutors everything they wanted to know about Eddie Trask. Rumor had it that on the day before the derby, Trask aimed a gun at Stockwell and pulled the trigger, but there hadn't been a bullet in the chamber. Trask did it just to be mean. Sick son of a bitch. Then he'd taped Stockwell up—same as he'd done with that sheriff's investigator—and made him stay that way all night, before putting him in the trunk of the Camaro.

Turned out the other guy who had been with Trask when Billy Don had gotten shot was the husband of a prosecutor in Burnet County, and he was cooperating, too. Red didn't know what that guy's story was, but he'd heard the man had been suffering from some kind of mental disorder. It was called Cap Gun Syndrome or something like that. But it was gone now. Weird.

Then there was the bartender, Teresa. Apparently she'd seen Eddie Trask and Tanner Stockwell messing around with Deke Gilbert's car that night outside the Beach Club, but she'd been too scared of Eddie to say anything—just as Red had suspected all along. But once the other witnesses had come forward, she did, too.

On top of all those witnesses, the cops had been able to pull a DNA profile off one of the lug nuts, and it was a perfect match for Eddie Trask. The bastard was doomed. Going away for a good, long time.

"Sorry I didn't get the chance to kill him for you," Red said.

"Can't count on you for nothin'," Billy Don said. "At least you knocked a few of his teeth out."

"Four. That's more than a few. And don't forget the broken cheekbone."

"That might've been from when you hit him head-on," Billy Don said.

If you didn't know he'd been shot, you wouldn't be able to tell without seeing the scars from the surgery.

"No, I felt it give when I hit him," Red said. "Don't sell me short."

He could hear a vehicle approaching on the county road. A minute later, he could hear the vehicle turning onto his driveway and slowly making its way up the hill to the trailer. That would be Mandy and Christie, returning from town. They'd decided they needed to throw a little celebration to mark Billy Don's return home, so they'd gone to Ronnie's Barbecue in Johnson City to get a bunch of brisket and sausage, along with all the sides. Red could hear them parking out front, the truck doors closing, then both of them walking around inside the trailer.

"Hard to believe that little girl pulled you out of that car," Billy Don said.

"You're telling me," Red said.

"Wish I'd seen it."

"Felt like a full-grown man had me by the ankles."

"You owe her one," Billy Don said. "You mighta been just about to pass out from all the fumes."

"Maybe so," Red said.

A few minutes later, the back door opened and Mandy stuck her head out. "Billy Don, I'll bring you a plate. Red, if you wanna eat, better get in here and get some."

Before Red could object, the door closed.

"She's a keeper," Billy Don said, grinning.

Gavin was taken into the visitation room again on Saturday, and Caroline was waiting on the other side of the glass. This was her second visit. She'd also come on Thursday, two days earlier, because Thursdays and Saturdays were the only days inmates in segregation were allowed visitors.

They both picked up their telephones.

"Hey, it's me," she said, smiling.

"Yeah, I know," he said.

"The real me," she said.

He couldn't blame her for joking about that. If they couldn't joke about it, the whole thing would fester and eventually drive them apart.

He'd done more reading about Capgras delusion, and he was confident that's what had been afflicting him. But he'd had no relapses, and, of course, he hadn't taken any more of his prescription medication. He'd been sleeping poorly, but that was nothing new. He would explore other avenues of treatment when he got out.

He'd also had an MRI to rule out brain injury or a tumor, and that had come back negative, thank goodness.

"You still going back to work on Monday?" he asked.

"Absolutely," she said. "Looking forward to it."

"I'm glad. I almost wrecked your life, honey, and I'm so sorry that I—"

"Stop," she said. "You didn't know what you were doing. You don't have to apologize."

He nodded and looked down. He didn't deserve this woman.

"I did something I need to tell you about," she said.

"What?"

"I wrote a long Facebook post and described Capgras delusion in detail. I wanted everyone to know what you'd gone through and why it all happened. I figured some people wouldn't accept it, or they'd think it was nonsense, and you know what? Screw them. We don't need them. But it's turning out just the opposite. I haven't received one unsupportive comment yet. Not one. And that's after nearly five hundred comments. I'm saving all of it for you, but I thought you'd want to know. Everybody—and I mean everybody—is behind you. It's amazing."

"Thank you," he said. "Thank you."

He reached up and placed his palm flat on the glass. She did the same.

She agreed that if he behaved himself—and of course he would—he would serve about half his time.

"Six months," he said.

"Six months," she repeated.

After they'd eaten, Red started another campfire from cedar

stumps, and all four of them gathered around it. There was no wind, so the smoke rose straight into the air.

Billy Don stifled a belch. "That was so much better than hospital food," he said. "Thank you. It's good to be home."

"Ah, honey, it's good to see you up and around," Mandy said.

Red had noticed that Christie had been awfully quiet all day, but now she spoke up.

"I really appreciate both of y'all. I hope you know that," she said. "Everything you did as far as figuring out what happened to my dad."

Red nodded slightly. Billy Don mumbled something.

Christie smiled. "I have to admit, I was a little apprehensive about living with a couple of, uh…"

"Rednecks?" Mandy said.

"Well, yeah," Christie said. "But it's been great. It really has."

Billy Don had been staring at the fire, but now he raised his head. "Sounds like you're going somewhere or something," he said. "You're not, are you?"

Christie looked at Mandy, who said, "You should tell 'em. They'll be all right."

"Okay," Christie said. "You remember me talking about my friend Sara? Her dad works at the sheriff's office? Well, she talked to her parents yesterday—I didn't know anything about it—and now they've asked me to come live with them until the end of the school year."

"Oh," Billy Don said.

Red kept looking at the fire.

"I think it's probably a good idea," Christie said. "I like the school down here okay, but if I live with Sara, I could go back to my old school. I'd be able to see all my other friends, too. They even have an extra car I can use. And that way you don't have to deal with having a teenage girl in your house."

Red didn't say anything. He could feel Mandy's eyes on him.

A long moment passed.

"I hope you're not mad," Christie said.

"No, of course not," Red said. "Not mad. I could never get mad at you. I'll just—"

Just that quick, he had to stop talking. He couldn't talk.

Mandy rose from her chair and came up behind him, placing her hands on his shoulders. She leaned and whispered in his ear. "It'll be okay. I promise."

He waited half a minute. Then he said. "I'll just miss you, is all."

Now he could hear Billy Don sniffling.

"I'll come visit," Christie said. "I mean, if you want me to."

"You'd better," Red said. "We'll keep your room clear. Won't we, Billy Don?"

Billy Don grunted and rubbed his nose with the back of his hand.

"I believe I'll go get myself another beer," Red said, and he got up out of his chair.

He was halfway to the trailer when he heard the footsteps behind him. He turned, and there was Christie, and she gave him a hug. He hugged her back, this sweet girl, and he didn't want to let her go.

Want to know when Ben Rehder's
next novel will be released?

Subscribe to his email list at www.benrehder.com.

Turn the page for an excerpt from

THE DRIVING LESSON
By Ben Rehder

THE DRIVING LESSON

1

If, during the last week of my freshman year, you'd asked me what I was planning to do that summer, I can guarantee you that becoming a fugitive would not have made the list. Not even a really long list. Especially if you'd told me that I wouldn't be alone, that it would be me and my grandfather—seriously, my Opa—together, on the run, the subject of a nationwide manhunt. *Yeah, right*, I would've said. *Are you friggin' nuts?*

But, as we know now, that's exactly what happened. Events sort of conspired, as Mr. Gardner, my English teacher, would say. And before the entire fiasco was over, we'd become an international phenomenon. The chaos would grow to include...

Cops across Texas asking the public for help in tracking us down.

Newspapers from Los Angeles to New York plastering our photos all over the front page, me with my baby face and blondish-white hair.

John Walsh talking about us on *America's Most Wanted*, stressing that we were most likely unarmed. Most likely?

People tweeting about us, talking about us on Facebook, posting videos on YouTube that supposedly showed us eating breakfast at an Iowa truck stop or camping out at Big Bend National Park.

My parents, Glen and Sarah Dunbar, appearing on CNN, Mom pleading for God to deliver "her baby Charlie" home safely, while Dad sits there looking uncomfortable and the smoking hot newsbabe nods with sympathy.

So, yeah, you can kind of understand why I didn't see any of this coming. Silly me, I thought the highlight of my summer would be getting my learner's permit.

~

The last Saturday in May plays an important role in this story, because that's when Matt, my best friend, talked me into doing something really dumb. Actually, two dumb things in a row, the second one worse than the first.

It was about thirty minutes before dark and we were walking to the bowling alley. Yeah, it sounds lame. Who bowls, right? But it's something Matt has done since he was about five, and I've known Matt since third grade, so I usually tag along, and sometimes I bowl, too. My high score is 114. Matt's is 223. So you can tell which one of us applies himself.

Anyway, we were walking past a home under construction on the edge of the neighborhood where we both live. There aren't many empty lots left in our subdivision, but every so often, one of the remaining lots sells and a new home gets slapped up in a matter of a few months. We're not talking high-dollar mansions, just tract homes that look like all the rest in the area. This particular home was nearly complete, and there was already a for-sale sign stuck in the freshly sodded yard. *I'm gorgeous inside!* the sign proclaimed. (My dad joked that that sounded like the title for a book designed to build self-esteem in teenage girls.)

That's when Matt stopped walking and said, "Charlie, check it out." He was looking at the house.

"What?"

"The front door is open."

And it was. Wide open. Like somebody forgot to lock it and the wind had given it a shove. The construction workers were gone for the day. The place was quiet and still.

I stopped, too. So what if the door was open? Nothing good could come from going inside a home under construction, especially since we'd gotten into trouble less than a month ago for skipping an assembly at school. Under those circumstances, only an idiot would go inside this house.

Matt said, "Let's go inside."

"Forget it."

"Just for a minute."

"Why?"

"Why not?"

"It's stupid."

"I just want to look around."

"Be my guest."

"Come with me."

"Nope."

"It'll be fun."

"It'll be trespassing."

"Don't be a pussy."

And there it was. Matt's trump card. Whenever he wanted to push my buttons, he'd call me a pussy. I *hated* it and he knew it. But, of course, my only option was to act like I didn't care, or he'd still be calling me that name when we were living in a retirement home. So I said, "Whatever, dude."

"Pussy."

"Real mature."

"Pussy."

"Jeez, Matt, grow the hell up."

"Pussy."

"You might want to broaden your vocabulary."

"Pussy."

I knew from experience that it wouldn't do any good to keep arguing with him. He can be a persistent little jerk. So, even though I wish I could go back and do that night over—use some common sense—instead, well, you can probably see where this is going.

~

We closed the front door behind us and stood there for a few seconds in the tiled entry hallway, which would be called a foyer in a larger home. I have to admit, my heart was pumping pretty good. We weren't supposed to be in here, but we were, and it was exciting. Exhilarating, even.

"Come on," Matt said, and he stepped slowly into the living room, onto the carpet, which was clean and perfect. The entire house was spotless. I could smell fresh paint.

But something was strange. Sort of familiar. Then I figured it out. I whispered, "You know what? This place has the exact same floor plan as my house."

And it did. Dining room over there. Three bedrooms down that hallway. Fireplace with a window on either side. Weird. It made me wonder how many other homes in the neighborhood were just like mine—except maybe with a different coat of paint on the outside, or bricks instead of plywood siding.

Matt didn't say anything. He was just looking around with this odd little grin on his face. Enjoying the rush. The light was fading as the sun was beginning to set, but I noticed that his sneakers were leaving smudges on the carpet.

"Let's go, Matt," I said.

"Not yet."

"There's nothing to see in here. The place is empty."

No response.

"Matt!"

He moved toward a swinging door on the other side of the living room. I knew that was the way to the kitchen, just like in my house. Matt went through the door, but I stayed behind, near one of the windows, so I could keep an eye on the street.

I was starting to get nervous. What if someone had seen us come in? It wasn't like we were real sly about it, walking right up to the front door. Anyone watching would've known we didn't belong in here. Which could mean the police might be on their way right this very minute.

"Matt!"

If we got caught...I didn't even want to think how my mom would respond.

Suddenly Matt, still in the kitchen, said, "Sweet!" And here he came through the door again, holding something. "Dude, look what I found."

It was a cordless drill. My dad had one like it, but a different brand. Yellow instead of blue. I was with him at Home Depot when he bought it. Nearly two hundred bucks, which is a lot of money.

"Put it back," I said.

"Somebody must've forgot it."

"Quit screwing around."

He pulled the trigger on the drill and it made a powerful whirring sound. It seemed awfully loud in the quiet house.

"Man, I could *use* this!" Matt said.

"For what?"

"Stuff."

"Don't even think about it."

But he had that grin on his face again. Sometimes I hate that grin.

At this point, I should mention that I outweigh Matt by about thirty pounds. I'm nearly six feet tall, one of the biggest kids in the freshman class, and sometimes my size has its advantages. Like making nose guard on the football team. Or like right now. If I had to, I could wrestle the drill away from Matt and put it back in the kitchen. Then we'd leave. Sure, Matt would be pissed, but he'd get over it. Later, he'd realize how dumb it would've been to steal the drill. He'd realize that I'd actually done him a favor. So that was the plan, to try to talk him out of it, and if that didn't work, to use my superior physical attributes to impose my will.

And that's when we heard the car door out front.

~

Here's what would happen if I got caught.

I'd get grounded, for sure—probably for at least a month, and maybe for the entire summer. No cell phone, no computer, no video games, no TV, no iPod. No hanging out at the mall, no riding my bike, no going to the movies, no having friends over to share in my misery. Guess what I'd be expected to do instead?

Read the Bible.

Seriously. My mom would insist on it. Didn't matter that I'd already read it several times, cover to cover, in my nearly fifteen years. When I was younger, parts of it sort of freaked me out, especially in the Old Testament. I mean, come on—people think *Mortal Kombat* is gruesome? The Bible has this big long list of reasons to stone people to death. It's got plagues, brought on by God, that wipe out entire cities, plus human and animal sacrifices, fathers having sex with their daughters, and a bunch of other bizarre events. Kind of disturbing when you're a kid. Now that I'm older, frankly, it just bores me. But Sarah Dunbar—that's my mother—is a firm believer that reading the Bible can cure all ills. The King James version, of course.

Any time I got in trouble, even for something relatively minor, like being tardy to class, she'd say something like, "I didn't raise you to be a juvenile delinquent," and then she'd pronounce my punishment. Could be a few verses, a couple of chapters, or even a full book. If she was really angry, I'd have to write a report about what I'd learned, assuming I'd had any luck deciphering what I'd read.

So maybe you can understand just how badly I didn't want to get caught in that house.

~

Matt's eyes got really big. I'm sure mine did, too.

I peeked out the window and saw a green Ford Explorer parked at the curb. A woman was coming around the front of the SUV, walking slowly, because she was in the middle of a conversation on her cell phone. She was about my parents' age, dressed nicely in a skirt and high heels. Everything about her said real estate agent. She was in charge of selling this house. She probably had some clients coming to look at the place right now.

"Oh, crap," I said, because I'm such a master of the English language. Now my heart was really pounding.

"Who is it?" Matt hissed. He hadn't moved.

"Some lady. Maybe a realtor."

"Is she coming in?"

"She...she..."

"She what?"

"She's stopping at the for-sale sign. It has one of those little boxes for flyers. She's checking to see if there are any flyers left."

Matt came up behind me and peeked over my shoulder. I was beginning to feel sick. "This is your fault," I said.

"Maybe that's all she came for, to check the flyers. Maybe she'll drive away."

The real-estate lady, still talking on her phone, let the metal lid slap shut on the rectangular box. Then she started up the driveway toward the house.

I turned quickly. "Follow me," I said.

He did, too. Amazing how, all of a sudden, Matt was willing to listen to a pussy like me. He was too frozen with fear to realize that all we had to do was go out the back door, which we did, closing that door just as we heard the front door opening.

It wasn't until we'd ducked through a gate in the privacy fence and started jogging down the street that I noticed Matt was still carrying the cordless drill.

~

I got home around nine-thirty, and I halfway expected my parents to be waiting for me, looking stern, ready to tear me a new one, because I just knew the cops had already solved the crime and had come to the house looking for me.

I'm a wimp that way, a total bundle of nerves when it comes to the possibility of getting in trouble—so much so that my mom can usually tell just from looking at my face that I've been up to something.

But that didn't turn out to be a problem tonight, because my parents were nowhere to be seen when I came through the front door. Normally, one or both of them would be hanging out in the living room, watching TV or reading. Or mom would be busy in the kitchen while dad was in the study working or just goofing around on the computer.

Then I heard them, just a low murmuring from their bedroom. The lights were on in the hallway. I decided I'd just duck into their doorway, say a quick good night, and go to bed before my own behavior gave me away. Then I began to wonder if going to bed so quickly would be a giveaway in itself. Maybe it would be better to talk to them for longer than a few seconds. Sheesh.

I started down the hallway. *Just act normal. Be yourself. Don't be an idiot.*

I was literally two steps from their bedroom door—and they still didn't know I'd come home—when I heard my mother say, "Here? Honey, you know that won't work. He'll have to end up in hospice."

Now she saw me in the doorway, and I saw them sitting on the edge of the bed, holding hands.

"Charlie," she said. That, and nothing else. It was strange, the way she said my name, and the odd expression on her face. Like she was surprised to see me. No, that's not exactly right. She looked like I'd caught her doing something she shouldn't be doing, or maybe saying something she didn't want me to hear.

"I'm home," I announced. Well, duh.

My dad looked up and caught my eye, but only for a second. He was acting weird, too. Angry about something? Sad? Were his eyes red?

"How was bowling?" Mom asked.

"Okay." Not really. I'd scored an 82, with three gutter balls. My mind had been on other things, like the fact that I'd taken part in a burglary.

Dad got up and went into the bathroom. Mom looked at me and gave a weak smile. "How is Matt?"

"Fine." *Despite being a felon in training.*

"Are you hungry? There's some pizza left in the fridge."

She's always trying to feed me—I'm a big guy and I burn a lot of calories—but I got the distinct impression she was making small talk to sort of gloss over the odd vibe in the air.

Had my parents been arguing about something? Or about somebody? And what in the heck was a hospice? I knew it had something to do with nurses or hospitals. Which meant there could only be one person they were talking about.

2

My phone chimed at 8:37 the next morning. A text message from Matt.

Any prblms?

I'd been awake for nearly an hour, but I was still in bed, just thinking about things. About last night. Not so much about the stolen drill, but about "hospice care." I'd looked it up on the Internet and was not happy with what I'd learned.

Yeah, there are problems, I thought.

That was made even more obvious by the fact that church started at nine and it appeared we weren't going. Mom hadn't even knocked on my door to get me up for breakfast. I didn't smell bacon frying or coffee brewing. In fact, I didn't hear any movement or talking at all in the house.

I lay there for several minutes, just feeling crummy. To be honest, I was kind of enjoying leaving Matt hanging. He was always doing stupid stuff and somehow getting me involved. Like this thing with the drill. So I texted him back.

Cops came this morning

His reply came within fifteen seconds:

Srius?

I could picture the panic he was feeling. Pretty funny.

I denied evrythng

Not funny

Not a joke

I put my phone on silent mode because I knew what he'd do next, and sure enough, it rang. I let it go to voicemail. Thirty seconds passed. Then he sent a text:

Where r u

Cant talk now

Im freaking out whats happening

Cops r chcking the nborhood door 2 door

U r lying

Wish i was

OMG 4 a stupid drill?
Doesnt mttr its stil theft
The door was open
Rmembr whn ur bike was stolen?

Now there was a long pause and I realized I had a huge smile on my face. I was getting him good. Last year, somebody had taken Matt's mountain bike when he'd left it in front of a convenience store. His dad had been really pissed that he'd left it unlocked and wouldn't buy him a new one. That's why we walked everywhere now—Matt had no bike.

Finally he said: *Shld we put it back?*

That caught me by surprise. Put the drill back? I thought about it, then said: *Door wont be unlocked now*

Cld leave it on back porch
Might get caught
We'd b careful
Not we, u
U wont go?
No
Plz go w me
U stole it u return it
I need a lookout
Good luck
Y r u being such a jerk

Was I? Maybe I was. Regardless, I was tired of stringing him along. And he deserved to know what was really going on, since he was my best friend. So I said:

Think my g'father is dying

~

Later, I found Mom in the living room, folding sheets and watching Pat Robertson, and she acted as if everything was fine. When I asked why we hadn't gone to church, she said Dad hadn't been feeling well when he woke up, so she let him sleep late. Then she asked if I was hungry, and before I could even answer, she said, "Of course you are," and went into the kitchen to make me some breakfast.

She seemed awfully cheerful. Maybe I was wrong about Opa. That's what we called him, because of his mother's German ancestry.

Maybe I'd misheard what Mom had said last night, or maybe they'd been talking about someone else.

I was even more convinced of that when, a couple hours later, Dad finally emerged from his bedroom—fully dressed, apparently feeling much better—and said, "Grab the keys, Charlie!"

"Huh?"

"Time for another driving lesson!"

~

"Parallel parking," Dad said very seriously, "is the most important part of the test."

He was bending down to look at me through the passenger window. It was a long way down for him, because he's six foot four. I get my size from his side of the family.

Dad continued, saying, "When I was your age, it counted for a full thirty points. So if you screwed it up, the best you could get was a seventy, which meant you were just one point—one measly point—from a failing grade." His voice was rising with mock outrage. He was kidding around because he has a weird sense of humor. I think he got it from Opa, who is even more of a goofball. Dad went on. "It didn't matter if you drove with the precision of Richard Petty and the skill of Dale Earnhardt, if you couldn't parallel park like you'd been doing it all your life, you didn't get your license. Personally, I don't think that's very reasonable, but that's the way it was. What're you gonna do? Bunch of bureaucrats."

I couldn't help grinning at him. "That's what happened to you, huh, Dad?"

"Is it that obvious? Yeah, well, my instructor was a hard-ass."

He used words like that sometimes when Mom wasn't around. It was understood that this was a guy thing, only between us.

"Okay, you ready to give it a try?" he asked.

We were in the huge parking lot of the exposition center on the east side of town. This is where they held the rodeo, dog shows, tractor pulls, and various concerts, but no events were taking place today, so it was a ghost town.

The parking lot was basically a wide-open expanse of pavement, with the occasional curbed island of concrete here and there to divide the big lot into smaller sections. We'd come here for previous lessons, and Dad had taught me the basics—shifting gears smoothly, braking hard without locking up the tires, backing up for a long distance—all the things that would be on the driving test.

Today, Dad had placed a pair of orange traffic cones exactly twenty-five feet apart, with each cone about six feet out from a long, straight section of curb. It was my job to parallel park our Toyota between those two cones.

I didn't know why he was making such a big deal out of it. It looked simple enough. He had already demonstrated for me a couple of times. As you back up, he said, you whip the wheel this way, then, at just the right moment, you whip it the other way, and presto, you slide right into the slot. Take it slow. Keep an eye on the cones.

Piece of cake, I thought. *No problem. It's not trigonometry.*

On my first try, I totally crushed the cone in front.

Dad was ready with some sound effects. He screamed like I'd just run over a pedestrian. "Aaah! Oh, my god, help me! My leg! You crushed my leg!"

Yeah, okay, I'll admit I laughed. Then I pulled out, he stood the cone up again, and I gave it another shot. I whipped it too late and rolled over the rear cone. Another pedestrian. It was like I was playing *Grand Theft Auto.*

Dad said, "For the love of God, somebody stop this maniac! An ambulance! I need an ambulance!"

Right about then, I was grateful there wasn't another soul within a mile of us. It was embarrassing.

The third time, with some verbal coaching from Dad, I did a little better. Didn't hit a cone, but wound up parked about three feet from the curb. You're supposed to be eighteen inches or closer.

But I got better with each try. After about a dozen attempts, I finally nailed it.

"There you go! Now you've got it!"

Three more times in a row, I managed to park without sending any imaginary pedestrians to the hospital or the morgue. It felt good.

Dad climbed into the passenger seat and closed the door. "You know what? I'm thinking you should drive us home today."

"Really?" That would be cool. I hadn't driven on any real streets yet, just this parking lot.

"Yeah, we'll take the back streets. No highways. Think you can handle that?"

"I think so, yeah."

"I do, too. You're getting the hang of it. I'm proud of you. But first, why don't you cut the engine for minute. We need to talk about something."

I knew immediately what was coming.

~

The word "grandpa" might bring to mind a certain image for some people: a little white-haired guy with arthritis and poor hearing. My grandfather wasn't like that at all. Not even close.

Yeah, he was sixty-three years old—getting up there—but he was very active, always running around doing something. Like he was a big-time swimmer. Went to a public pool in his neighborhood four or five mornings a week. He played the guitar and wrote his own songs. He attended political rallies and book signings and all kinds of fundraisers.

He dated a lot, too. He and my grandmother had gotten a divorce before I was even born, and Opa had never remarried. Instead, he had what my mother called "lady friends."

He traveled with some of these friends to other states and even other countries. Just last summer, he went to Ireland with a redheaded woman named Linda. A couple years before that, he went to Africa with a woman whose name I can't remember. For a while after that trip, he wore a shirt called a *dashiki*. It had all these wild colors, and I thought it looked pretty cool, but my mom always said he looked like some old nut. Other times, when she was being nicer, she used the word "eccentric."

My point is, he wasn't some decrepit geezer ready for a nursing home. Heck, he had more energy than me and most of my friends. Or he used to.

~

"You know that Opa hasn't been feeling good."

I nodded.

Dad said, "He...well, for a while, nobody could say what was wrong with him. The doctors didn't know. He just didn't feel right, so they ran various tests, and everything looked okay. They said he was probably fine, just getting old, and he shouldn't worry too much about it. We told you about that. Remember right after Christmas?"

My face was starting to feel very warm. I nodded again. I did remember. First they told me Opa might be sick, then they said maybe he wasn't, then, just before spring break, they said it was a "wait and see" type of thing. We hadn't really talked much about it since then.

"In early April," Dad said, "he went to a special hospital in Houston. It's one of the best in the country. They ran even more tests, different tests, and this time they were able to figure out what the problem is." He paused for a second. "Unfortunately, it wasn't good news. He has a type of bone cancer that is very aggressive. It's already in the advanced stages."

Does it make me a pussy to admit my eyes were starting to fill with tears? A real tough guy, right? Big football player. Macho and all that. But cancer is scary. Everybody knows that.

I was looking down at my lap. My dad had his arm on the driver's headrest behind me. Now he placed his hand on my neck, rubbing it, trying to make me feel better, but I was this close to bawling like a baby. Some snot dripped from my nose and landed on my jeans.

Dad said, "It gets a little more complicated, because Opa has some wild ideas about what he should do next. He isn't thinking straight. Maybe it's his age, or maybe he's just scared, but he's decided that he doesn't want to undergo the treatment plan the doctors are recommending."

Now I looked up. "Why not?"

"Well, it can be pretty rough on the patient. And the chances that it would be successful are pretty slim. It comes down to what they call 'quality of life.'"

I knew the answer, but I asked the question anyway. "Is he going to die?"

I don't know whether my dad had decided hours ago to be completely honest with me, or if he made the decision right then and there. But when I think back on this moment, as painful as it was, I'm glad he didn't sugarcoat it or give me any false hope.

He simply said, "Yeah, he is."

Now the tears really began to flow.

He said, "I'm sorry, Charlie. I'm really sorry. Even with the treatment, he...that would only delay it, or maybe it wouldn't even do that."

Now he was getting emotional, too, and I couldn't bring myself to look at him. I looked down at my lap again, and we just sat there for another minute or two, neither of us saying anything.

Then, when I thought I could talk without blubbering, I said, "How soon?"

~ ~ ~

ABOUT THE AUTHOR

Ben Rehder lives with his wife near Austin, Texas, where he was born and raised. His novels have made best-of-the-year lists in *Publishers Weekly, Library Journal, Kirkus Reviews*, and *Field & Stream. Buck Fever* was a finalist for the Edgar Award, and *Get Busy Dying* was a finalist for the Shamus Award. For more information, visit www.benrehder.com.

OTHER NOVELS BY BEN REHDER

Buck Fever
Bone Dry
Flat Crazy
Guilt Trip
Gun Shy
Holy Moly
The Chicken Hanger
The Driving Lesson
Gone The Next
Hog Heaven
Get Busy Dying
Stag Party
Bum Steer
If I Had A Nickel
Point Taken
Now You See Him
Last Laugh
A Tooth For A Tooth

Made in the USA
Middletown, DE
13 July 2020